VERTIGO

THE UPGRADE SERIES #2

WESLEY CROSS

PUBLISHER INFORMATION

This is a work of fiction. Names, characters, businesses, places, events, and incidents are either the product of the author's imagination or used in a fictitious manner. Any resemblance to actual persons, living or dead, or actual events is purely coincidental.

Published by
Cerberus Prints
PO BOX 90399
Brooklyn, NY 11209

1

____

July 2007
Westchester County, New York

The roof was hot. Jill Cooper could feel blisters forming on her unprotected elbows as she lay prone under the scorching sun, watching the semicircular driveway in front of the formal boxwood garden. The massive slate and stone English manor was nestled on top of a gently sloped hillside surrounded by two acres of sweeping lawns and stately trees. As she looked down at the narrow brook, to the right of the house, gurgling down the hill and disappearing into the woods, Cooper thought she would've even enjoyed her stakeout if not for the unforgiving July sun.

It was worth it. *Everyone has a weakness,* she thought, as Cooper listened to the growing rumbling sound of a powerful engine drawing closer. A minute later, a bright-red Ferrari F430 Spider with an open roof burst out of the cover of the trees, made a screeching turn and came to an abrupt stop in front of the house. The man she'd been tracking for the last six weeks killed the engine and pulled out a Blackberry.

"Hey, baby," he said, the words drifting through the hot, humid air like half-deflated helium balloons. Neither capable of running toward the cloudless sky nor ready to come back to Earth. "I have to work this weekend again."

Cooper watched him pause as he exited the car and stretched without bothering to listen to the person on the other end.

"I know, I know," he brought the phone to his face again, "but the merger is getting close, and it'd be big for us. It's a miracle it's even happening considering what's going on with the markets. I'll make it up to you, I promise. Kiss the girls for me, okay?"

The front door on top of the marble steps squeaked, and he held up a cautionary finger as a woman in a pink silk negligee appeared on the porch.

"I love you too," he finally said and hung up the phone.

"I love you too," the woman on the porch parroted. "You said you were going to tell her."

"Sydney—" the man started saying, but the woman cut him off with a wave of her hand. Before he could protest, she turned around and went back to the house, slamming the heavy oak door behind her. The man rolled his eyes and loosened his tie, his broad clean-shaven face turning a shade brighter than the Ferrari.

Cooper felt like rolling her eyes as well, but instead, she lowered her head, making sure she was well out of the man's sight, beads of perspiration rolling down her face as she held her cheek close to the hot surface of the roof. The door opened, then closed, and after a few seconds, the sounds of a muted quarrel were coming from inside of the house. She waited for another minute, and when the argument moved from the foyer deeper into the house, Cooper lowered herself off the side of the roof, steadied her breath, and let go. She softened the twenty-foot drop with a roll and then sprang to her feet, ready to flee if discovered. The house remained quiet save for what now sounded like passionate lovemaking.

Cooper sprinted to the porch, climbed the set of marble steps and pulled on the front door. She winced as it squeaked, but the moaning coming from the bedroom only grew louder, and Cooper crept through the hallway, her footsteps swallowed by the soft beige runner with geometrical designs.

A bright pink silk tie was hanging on the bedroom door handle, and Cooper picked it up. The tempo of the sounds coming from inside the room was getting quicker, and she risked a quick peek through the narrow opening. She took mental stock of the objects in the room, trying her best to ignore the heaving bodies on top of the light-blue linen-clad bed. Satisfied with what she saw, Cooper headed for the bathroom and hid in the linen closet, wedged between a towel drier rack and some fluffy bathrobes that cost more than some people's entire wardrobe.

After a few minutes, as Cooper peered through the slightly opened closet doors, the sounds reached a crescendo and then stopped. There was some giggling and shouting, and finally, Cooper could hear the footsteps leading to the bathroom.

"You better be ready when I come back," the woman shouted as she entered the bathroom.

As Cooper stayed quiet, she watched as the woman filled the tub with hot water, stepped into it and lay down, her head resting on the side of the Roman tub. Without making any noise, Cooper opened the closet door and walked to the bathtub in two quick strides.

The movement must have caught the woman's attention as she lifted her head and turned to see what was happening behind her. Cooper could see as fear flashed in lovely brown eyes and the woman's mouth opened as if for a shout that was not meant to be. Cooper hooked the silk tie around the woman's neck as a garrote and bore down with all her might.

The neck snapped with a sickening crunch. Cooper left the tie on the victim's neck and stood up. There was no reason to hide anymore. She pulled out a 9-millimeter Glock 19 and walked back to the bedroom.

"That was fast—" the man started saying, but his words caught as he saw Cooper with the gun in her hand.

"Stay still," she commanded, coming closer.

"Who are you? What do you want?" he demanded.

Cooper ignored him, walking around the bed and toward a

wooden Yukon coffee table by the window.

"I have money," the man said. "I can—"

"Shut up. That's why I'm here," she said, beckoning him with the gun. "Follow my instructions, and I'll be out of your hair before you know it."

The man stood up and took a few steps toward the table. He hadn't made an effort to cover his nakedness.

"Sit down," Cooper commanded and pushed an ottoman closer to the table. "All I need you to do is to write a few lines to your wife, confessing the affair."

"Why would I do that?"

"Because, otherwise I'll kill you." Cooper produced a humorless smile. "Do as I say, and once I have the note, you'll pay me fifty grand. Cash. I'll keep the note as my insurance so you can never come after me."

"I'll pay you the money, no problem," he said, "but what's gonna stop you from demanding more money later?"

"Nothing," her smile was genuine now, "but that's not how I do business, so you'll have to trust me on this. Sydney's fine, by the way. I'm glad you're concerned."

The man cast a nervous glance at the door and sat down. He drew a deep breath and then moved a legal pad in front of him and picked up an old Bic pen from the pile of bills, magazines, and shopping receipts.

"Write *I'm sorry, Rebecca. I shouldn't have done it.*"

The man tensed at the sound of his wife's name. Cooper watched his knuckles whiten as he squeezed the pen. She pressed the Glock into his right temple. The man stayed immobile, and for a moment she thought he might try to attack her. But, finally, his shoulders slumped, and his hand started to move. Elegant cursive covered the top of the page, each letter almost the same exact height. He put down the pen.

"Impressive penmanship. A dying art," Cooper said and pulled the trigger.

The sound was deafening. The man's head jerked away from the gun as if it'd been hit by a battering ram; red splatter, with bits of something dark, covered the white rug and the light-blue bed sheets. His body turned and slowly slid off the ottoman, hung on the edge for a moment and then hit the floor head first. Inertia carried it forward until the body flipped over and came to rest on its back. A dark circle started to spread on the rug around the man's head.

Cooper watched the ruined face. The bullet must have hit the thicker part of the bone as it exited through the man's jaw, taking a part of his face with it. She placed the Glock into his hand and pressed his fingers into the gun, then stood and looked around. She replayed the man's trajectory in her mind, concentrating on the movement of his right hand. Finally, she placed the gun on the rug about a foot away from the body. It looked as if it had fallen out of his hand as he had slid from the ottoman.

She spent another hour at the villa, painstakingly removing every shred of evidence that there was ever somebody else in the house but the two lovers. Then Cooper returned to her car, an unremarkable Toyota Camry, parked in a forest clearing, a few miles from the property. Once by the car, she took out a simple flip phone and sent a text to a memorized number.

I bought two steaks for dinner, like you asked.

The reply was almost instantaneous.

Nice! I got a bottle of merlot for you, so we're all set.

A few moments later, Cooper's phone beeped, alerting her of a million-dollar incoming transfer.

She looked at the confirmation with relief. It was always a big gamble taking on new clients, regardless of how much time she'd spent vetting them. But the payout was quadruple her going rate, and it seemed now that the client was solid. So far, the gamble seemed to be paying off.

She took the battery out of the phone and then broke the phone in half and shoved the pieces under the roots of an old tree. Then, she got in the car, put it in reverse, and backed out onto a gravel road. Fifteen minutes later, Cooper merged onto I-87 South and set for New York City.

There were few people in the world who could make a double hit look like a suicide and Jill Cooper was the best in the business.

2

____

July 2007
Arlington, Virginia

$\mathcal{T}$he thermometer on the wooden panel, below the sliding bulletproof divider, read 88°F, but Rovinsky thought it was well over one hundred. The open parking lot outside of the Ronald Reagan Washington National Airport offered no protection from the blazing sun baking the black town car and its passengers.

"Could you crank up the AC?" he called out to his driver.

"It's already on full blast, sir. I'm sorry."

They'd been sitting in the back of the limousine for over an hour, and by now his suit was drenched in sweat. Yet, the heat was only partially to blame. It was the second time in his decades-long intelligence career that Rovinsky felt as if he were out of his depth. The first time came when two weeks into his first job at the agency he was assigned as a junior analyst to a case of an operative who'd gone rogue.

A team of FBI agents searched a hotel room in Honolulu, acting on an anonymous tip. There, inside of a suitcase, they found a small, plastic travel pack with a calendar and an address book. Both belonged to a former CIA officer, Jonathan Lee, and contained handwritten notes with classified information, meeting places, and the true names and phone numbers of CIA sources in China.

The find triggered a two-week-long hunt for the rogue agent to prevent him from transferring the data to the Chinese, which would've led to a dozen CIA agents in China killed or imprisoned. During those two long weeks when Rovinsky slept in the office at least on four occasions, too tired to drive home, he questioned the wisdom of joining the CIA and his mental capacity for the job. But the breach was prevented, and Rovinsky received a promotion, making him one of the youngest senior analysts at the agency. Today, he reflected, the stakes were higher by orders of magnitude.

"It looks like Mr. Hunt's car," the driver said, pointing to a white Maybach sedan pulling up next to them.

A tall blond man in a seersucker tailored suit stepped out of the vehicle as soon as it stopped and then dived into the limo. The privacy glass smoothly rose into place.

"Nice to see you, Andy," Rovinsky said, shaking his friend's hand.

"Hey, Jim, long time, no see." The man smiled, his eyes studying Rovinsky. "Sorry for being late. Got stuck at JFK."

"How's Audrey?"

"She's well." Hunt stretched his legs and shifted in his seat, making himself comfortable. "Should be back from Kenya next week. They are about to open a new school there. But I know you're on a tight schedule. What have you got for me?"

"Well, I'm not sure." Rovinsky opened up a leather dossier and took out a few pages of what looked like financial reports printouts. "Maybe you could help me make heads and tails of this. Are you familiar with Bill Clinton's repeal of the Glass-Steagall Act?"

"Not in depth, but sure." Hunt scratched his chin, collecting his thoughts. "He didn't repeal it, per se. In 1999, if memory serves me right, Clinton signed the new law that repealed *some* of the provisions of the original act of 1933."

"You're gonna have to do better than that," Rovinsky said, chuckling. "You might as well be speaking Chinese."

"Well, let's see. Congress passed the original act after the Great Depression and prohibited commercial banks from engaging in the investment business. But the new law allowed the commercial banks to buy investment companies again. I'm sorry, what exactly are you looking for?"

"I stumbled upon something I wasn't specifically looking for. I'd been going down a completely different rabbit hole," Rovinsky said, flipping through the pages, "when I came across some interesting political contributions that led me to the co-sponsors of the new bill. Nothing criminal, just questionable."

"Ah," said Hunt, sarcasm in his voice, "what a shocker in this town."

"I know," Rovinsky smiled back, "and yet it set off some bells in my head."

"You think somebody pushed the bill through for some greater agenda?"

"I don't know, Andrew; you tell me. You're the expert here."

"I'll have to look into this." Hunt shook his head. "As far as I remember, the bill passed the House and the Senate with enough votes to make it impossible for the president to veto it. There was clearly enough support for it on both sides of the aisle."

"That might be true," Rovinsky persisted, "but what if the seeds simply fell on fertile ground? I'd like you to think of it in global terms. What could be done by our adversaries using this bill?"

"Adversaries? Like who? The Russians? The Chinese? You're scaring me, man. The resources to influence something like this would have to be enormous. It sounds impossible. You're not going full paranoid on me, are you?"

"It's way too late to worry about my paranoia," Rovinsky said, smiling, "but look into it for me as soon as you can."

"Sure."

"Also," Rovinsky looked his friend in the eye, "there's another reason I wanted to talk to you in person."

"Thank God," the other man said. "I almost thought you dragged me down to DC just to check on my legislative history skills."

Rovinsky reclined in the hot leather seat, gripping the folder in his hands, his fingers tracing the rugged surface of the old leather. He'd come here prepared to do this, but now, sitting across from his old friend, he couldn't bring himself to say the words.

"Jim?"

"All right," he said, straightening. "A few heads came together at the agency, and I decided that we need a new organization. I call it *the Unit*. There are some new forces at play, man; I'm sure of it. It's a new threat, and it's unlike anything we've ever faced. What I've found and what I'm asking you to look at is just the tip of the iceberg. I can't quite articulate it, but I've been seeing a lot of loose threads hanging in all the wrong places. The problem is—I can see it, but I don't understand it. What I do understand, and I can tell you this with as much certainty as I've ever had during my years in this town, is that if we don't act now, by the time we figure things out, it'll be too late."

"Wait a sec. What kind of forces?"

"Global forces, Andy." He made a circling gesture with his hand. "I think some international bigwigs have formed a cabal and they are ruthless, Andy. They are bribing, extorting, and killing, and will do anything to get their way. This is a power grab on a massive scale that transcends international borders. I don't understand how far this goes and it scares me. And you should know by now that not a lot of things scare me, Andy. That's why we need a global reach. No congressional oversight, no bullshit. For now, pick the guys from Delta and the teams. Later, establish our own shop. A training camp and the whole nine yards."

"And POTUS is on board with this?"

Rovinsky didn't answer and stared at his friend.

"Shit, Jim. That's crazy. I don't know if I want in, man. Frankly, I'm not even sure I want to hear about it at all. I don't like the idea of spending the rest of my life in Gitmo or some other dark hole with no visitation rights. Besides, what would I even do at a place like that?"

"You'd take the helm," Rovinsky said. "You can—"

"Stop. Jim, this is madness." Hunt interrupted him. He turned around and grabbed the door handle. "I'm an analyst. That's all I've ever done for the agency."

"Wait—"

"No way, Jim. No fucking way. I'm going. In fact, I'm leaving the agency. Period. This conversation never happened."

He reached out and grabbed Hunt's shoulder and turned him around, locking his eyes with his old friend.

"You're not just an analyst, Andy. Don't fucking play coy with me. But yes, to a degree, you're still an outsider. But I *need* an outsider," he said forcefully, "an outsider who understands the rules. I can't let one of the locals make decisions like these. I don't know who to trust and they're too deep in this; they can't see the big picture. Don't give me the answer now. Take a week. Look at the docs, use that big head of yours and let me know."

"I'll look at them, but the answer is still no."

Rovinsky watched as the man disappeared inside the enormous Maybach. A moment later, the white beast effortlessly accelerated away, the understated roar of its powerful engine echoing throughout the parking lot. Rovinsky flipped the switch, taking the privacy screen down, and rolled down the windows.

"Going back, sir?"

"Yes," he said, relaxing. The draft from the windows was hot, but it was better than the stale heat of the car.

He'd made the right choice. Andrew Hunt might have said no for now, but he hadn't seen the documents yet. The trail of crumbs he'd found was leading somewhere so dark, it made his skin crawl. And if he could sense it, there was no way one of the smartest minds in the country would miss it.

What he was proposing was dangerous. And if things were to go off the rails, spending the rest of their lives in jail could be a real possibility. He closed his eyes and took a deep breath. If there were other solutions, he failed to see them. For better or for worse, there was no other way.

3

July 2007
Kenya

"This is unfair," the boy whispered.

"I know," she whispered back, without moving.

"I'm scared, Miss Audrey," he said, and leaned his head on her shoulder. "They are very bad people."

"It's okay to be scared, Dalmar," she said, "but we have to keep calm. I promise you, we'll figure something out. We need to stick together."

The place still smelled of wood and fresh paint. Two dozen tablet-armchair desks with gray tops and bright-blue seats filled the classroom in neat rows. A few days ago, she had watched them being brought in, assembled, and put in the classrooms with quiet joy. She made this possible. Because of her and the tireless help of a few local administrators, there was going to be a brand-new school in a place where kids knew nothing but war for the longest time.

Four years ago, when Audrey Hunt first visited the town, the place now occupied by the new school was an abandoned pharmacy with a faded sign quoting the Bible: *"Jesus is the way, the truth and the life. John 14:6."* A few rusted satellite dishes were perched on top of the sign, as if trying to receive a message from God himself. Now, the new school, she hoped, was going to be a launching pad for success for countless bright minds who hadn't stood a chance before.

The pain abruptly ended the trip down memory lane. Her bound feet and wrists were starting to feel numb. Her shoulder, where the butt of the AK-47 landed, was hot and sore. But she was still alive.

She had been standing in front of the building with the director, his nephew Dalmar, the school administrator Canab, and a security guard when a rusty Toyota Hilux with a mounted machine gun pulled up. Her memories were hazy after that. She remembered the guard being shot, his body collapsing onto the dusty road. She remembered the director trying to shield them as one of the guerrillas slammed the butt of his rifle into the old man's face. She pulled the boy into her arms as the men forced them back into the building. She tried to protest, and that was when one of the soldiers hit her in the back.

The three of them were tied up and then thrown into one of the classrooms on the third floor. After one hour, two men came in and dragged a sobbing Canab out. A few seconds later, Audrey could hear the woman's screams from the room next door, and that's when she made Dalmar hum a song. A few minutes later, a lone shot rang out, and the screaming stopped. She listened to the angry men's voices outside, and for a few long minutes, she sat on the hard floor, heart in her throat, preparing for the worst. But the voices sounded farther and farther away and then there was silence.

"You need to do something for me, Dalmar, okay?"

"Yes, Miss Audrey." His voice cracked with emotion, and he corrected himself at once. "I will, Miss Audrey."

"We need to maneuver, so our backs are against each other," she said. "Do it slowly, so you don't fall. Lean on me the entire time. I need you to find my fingers with yours, okay?"

They wiggled on the cement floor, trying to keep contact with each other. Her shoulder burned with pain, but she persevered until her numb fingers touched the boy's.

"We did it," he whispered happily.

"Good job." Despite the predicament, she found herself smiling. "Now keep still. I'll try to untie you."

That was much easier said than done. She fumbled with the knots for what seemed like an eternity, but finally, the rope yielded, and she felt Dalmar's hands wriggling themselves free.

"It really hurts," he said. The boy was shaking his hands and grimacing in pain.

"That's okay," she said. "That is just the sensation coming back to your hands, that's all. It'll pass. But I need you to untie my hands now. Can you do that for me, Dalmar?"

It took the boy even longer, but after a while, she welcomed the pins and needles on her skin as the blood started to flow back to her hands. After she removed the remaining bonds, Audrey slowly stood up, trying not to make any noise.

"We have to get out of here," she said to the boy, "but we have to be quiet, okay?"

She walked to the window and peeked outside. The pickup truck was still parked in front of the school, the flared nozzle of its machine gun pointing at the darkening sky. Two guerrillas were leaning on the vehicle, listening to an older stocky Caucasian man dressed in military fatigues. She could see his gray beard move as he spoke. The director's body wasn't visible, but she didn't let hope rise in her chest —chances were the bastards finished him off.

She looked around the empty classroom for a makeshift weapon. There was a broom in the closet, but the handle was too long to be useful, and she couldn't risk breaking it without making too much noise. After some consideration, she unscrewed the handle and took it anyway, the heft of the polished wood in her hands giving her some sense of security.

"C'mon," she said, taking the boy's hand. "Let's find a way outta here."

She put her ear to the door and listened. As far as she could tell, there was no one outside of the classroom but there was only one way to find out. She motioned to Dalmar to stand away from the door and slowly turned the handle. Sweat trickled down her back as the lock softly clicked, and she pulled the door open. There was nobody on the other side, and as she peeked through the narrow gap, there was no one in the long, dark hallway either.

She waved to Dalmar, and together they crept to the staircase at the west wing of the building. They started making their way down when she heard the voices again.

Peeking over the banisters, Audrey could see two men smoking at the bottom of the stairs. There was no way for them to get out of the building unnoticed, but hopefully it didn't mean the game was already over. She squatted and pulled the boy close, whispering in his ear.

"We need to go down to the second floor, but we have to be quiet as a mouse, okay? Stay by the wall and take one step at a time, real slow."

The boy nodded, his face serious, and took her hand in his. Unlike the hallway, the stairwell was brightly lit, making her feel vulnerable as they made their way down clasping each other's hands. She regretted taking the broom handle now. The long stick swayed back and forth as they walked, making her nervous that she would bang it on something and give them away.

Finally, they made it to the second floor. Audrey peeked into the hallway first, making sure there was no one around and then, as silently as they could, they ran to the administrative office. Once they were in, she barricaded the door with the broom handle and went to the desk.

The desk was empty, save for a few loose papers with handwritten notes on them and a large, beige, old-fashioned rotary phone shining in all its cheap plastic glory. She couldn't remember ever being so happy to see a phone before. She grabbed the handset and dialed the State Department number she'd memorized a long time ago. After what seemed like an eternity, the line beeped.

"Alpha, hotel, niner, niner, zero, seven," she blurted into the mouthpiece.

"Please hold the line," the female voice responded almost immediately.

"Mrs. Hunt, this is Senior Chief Rower," a deep baritone cut in. "What's your emergency?"

"The school's under attack," she said, trying to keep her voice low.

"At least five people, possibly more. There's a truck with a machine gun parked in front of the building. I'm with a kid; they tied us up but we managed to get away. We are on the second floor right now, in the admin's office."

"Anyone hurt?"

"We are fine, but…" she cast a guilty glance at Dalmar, "but the administrator and the director, they, I don't think—"

"I got it." He cut her off. "We have assets in the area, but it will take a couple of hours before they get there. Are you safe at your location?"

"I don't know," she said, pondering the question. "If they don't check on us, then maybe."

"Can you get to the roof?"

She thought about it for a moment. The locks hadn't been installed yet in most of the building, so chances were they could make it to the roof. But if she was wrong, and while they were out there looking for a way to climb to the roof their captors decided to check on them, then their current hiding place would become impossible to get back to. And then she would have no way to communicate their position to the rescuing party.

Audrey Hunt had a decision to make.

4

July 2007
New York

ndrew Hunt had been coming to the Sunshine Diner well
before he could rub two nickels together. The coffee was
mediocre at best, the place smelled of burnt toast and bleach, but their
Eggs Benedict was phenomenal, and the booths were just small
enough and tall enough to grant some privacy.

This was the place where one warm April evening he saw Audrey
for the first time. She came with a posse of students, dressed in a pair
of jeans, a peach-colored top, and a pair of rather worn-out sensible
shoes, but Andrew felt momentarily blinded, as if he looked directly at
the sun. Her golden hair was cut in a simple angled bob that exposed a
long delicate neck and framed the cheekbones that most fashion
magazines would pay top dollar for a chance to feature them on their
cover page.

He hadn't dared to approach her that night, stealing glances in her
direction, convinced that she was so far out of his league that he
didn't stand a chance. He then spent two agonizing weeks beating

himself up for being a coward and seriously depleting his meager savings by spending each and every night at the diner. He got lucky—after two weeks she came back, and this time he didn't squander his chance.

Today, as he sat in his usual spot by the window, he found himself more distracted than ever. He watched pedestrians going about their business as his thoughts wandered back to the time when Audrey was pregnant with their son, Jason. Hunt had just branched out on his own, and they were crammed into a tiny studio apartment on what he thought was the smelliest block in Hell's Kitchen. They came to the brink of bankruptcy twice that year, but somehow survived, using loans to pay credit cards and paying credit cards from Audrey's infrequent tutoring gigs.

It was the best of times, it was the worst of times, he thought. The time of sneaking into movie theaters and ramen noodles for dinner.

The waitress came by, asking if he wanted more coffee, and unceremoniously plucked him from his daydream. He sighed and picked up the worn-out leather dossier from the table. The papers were now neatly stacked and arranged alphabetically.

Rovinsky had been modest about his investigating abilities. He clearly had seen more in the documents than he let on during their brief conversation down in DC, and he'd assembled a compelling case. It wasn't just a collection of random articles—there was a brief narrative describing how the conspiracy, which Rovinsky christened in the papers as *the cabal*, had come to life, and how, through the progression of covert and overt actions, it had grown in influence and reach. Andrew could see it now, too. The slithering tentacles of a great beast feeling its way into the places of power. Political contributions, corporate takeovers, reshuffling of senior personnel at the top of some of the most powerful corporations in the world. Abrupt resignations of people who hadn't shared the right vision. A series of convenient accidents.

Things like that happened before, of course. And the fact that despite the circumstantial evidence he had presented, Rovinsky didn't show him a single viable suspect didn't make it easier to accept it was something bigger than a wild conspiracy theory. But Andrew couldn't deny that there seemed to be a greater purpose in those ostensibly unconnected events: a concerted push, moving things in a specific direction. It was easy to dismiss something like that before diving into the deep end as a conspiracy, but he didn't think that Rovinsky was wrong. There was a movement out there in the great shadows cast by titans, and there was no power that could balance the growing menace. The question was—was he the right man for the job?

This wasn't the first time he was in this predicament, of course. His thoughts went back to the first meeting with Rovinsky, when the then-intelligence officer had tried to recruit him to the CIA. Hunt said no and left the meeting, flattered and pissed off at the same time. Flattered, because the famed agency thought he was capable of helping. Upset, because he instantly understood that to be determined capable, he must have been watched and analyzed for a long time.

The requirement to keep anyone and everyone in the dark didn't sit well with him either, as it meant he had to lie not only to his friends and colleagues but also to his wife and the mother of his child. Yet, after a few days of arguing with himself, he called Rovinsky back and took the job and accepted the responsibility.

It wasn't nearly as glorious as he'd thought it would be. There was no sneaking into secret rooms with guns drawn, no car chases or dead drops with coded messages. The vast majority of his work was spent behind his desk, analyzing financial statements of entities suspected of terrorism and money laundering. But despite never quite feeling like James Bond, the job gave him a sense of purpose and the sense of pursuing something bigger than himself.

He felt as if his path had completed a full circle, but this time the stakes would be even higher. For that reason alone, he was probably not going to accept Jim's offer, he thought. It was too great of a responsibility, especially considering the lack of approval from the appropriate governmental channels.

It was tempting, of course. To have the power to shape the world for the better. To be the tip of the spear in the fight against the darkest and ugliest manifestations of human nature.

But that was the poetic part of it. How would they even get the funding? It was one thing to oversee clandestine operations when you operated outside of public scrutiny, but received full support and funding from the United States government. It was a completely different story when you had to hide your actions from the public eye and from the president himself. There was also a not-so-small issue of making life-and-death decisions on a daily basis.

Hunt took a deep breath, fished out his phone, and scrolled through his contacts, looking for Rovinsky's number. Jim Rovinsky, he decided, was going to have to tap somebody else to play his spy games. Before Hunt was able to dial his old friend, the phone vibrated in his hand, startling him.

"Jim? Were your ears burning?" he asked in surprise. "I was just looking for your number."

"There's something you need to know—"

"I read the dossier," Hunt interrupted him, "and I want you to know that I seriously considered it. You've done a hell of a job putting it all together. But the answer is—"

"Audrey's in trouble," Rovinsky said, cutting him off in turn. "The school's been ambushed by some guerrilla fighters, presumably Al-Shabaab, and they took her hostage, along with one of the kids. It sounds like she managed to escape the room where they were being held, but she's still in the building."

"Is there something you can do?" Hunt was standing now, without any recollection of how that happened.

"Yes. We have some assets in the area, but it might take some time before they get there. An hour, maybe two."

"Shit."

"She's a resourceful girl. She'll pull through. I gotta go, pal. I'll update you as soon as I hear anything at all."

"I need to get there."

"There's a plane leaving in three hours for Camp Simba from Virginia. If you can make it to the airport before that, I'll put you on that plane. That is the best I can do on such short notice."

"I'll be there," he inhaled sharply. "Thank you, Jim. I owe you one."

Hunt threw some cash on the table and went outside. He stood on the sidewalk for a few seconds looking at his phone, considering if he should call his son, but decided against it. Jason wouldn't be able to help in any way and considering that his son didn't know about his involvement with the agency, it would create more questions than Hunt was ready to answer now. He scrolled through his contacts and dialed his assistant.

"I need Clive to be ready to take off in forty-five minutes. And have somebody pick me up from the heliport on West Thirtieth in fifteen."

He hung up the phone and waved a taxi down. Even through the haze of overwhelming worry, the irony of the timing of this development wasn't lost on him. He couldn't turn down Rovinsky's offer after all. To turn away the chance to wield such great power and be able to use it against the scum like those terrorists who had kidnapped his wife. He might regret it later, he decided—probably sooner than later —but there was no way on Earth he was going to say no.

Hunt squinted against the sun as he dived into the cool belly of the taxi. His fingers ran across the soft leather of the dossier, feeling the creases and scratches of the surface. It occurred to him that many things of great importance started with an ordinary object like this dossier, chock-full of information that most people wouldn't understand.

He took a deep breath. It might have been a rash decision, if he was going to be honest with himself. But those people who had kidnapped his wife and others like them deserved to burn in hell, and he was personally going to put them there and then make sure that the coals never grew cold.

5

July 2007
New York

Mary Chen stepped out of the car before the driver had a chance to walk around and open the door. She hated when he did it. It made her feel like a spoiled brat, unable to fend to herself.

It was a rough day. The board was pushing for the merger with Guardian, and she'd found herself on the defensive. Long-term, it wasn't making any sense. Rapid Science had been on the rise, and in another five or six years, Mary could see it being able to actually compete with the giants like Guardian Manufacturing.

Sure, if Guardian acquired them now, the large shareholders—Chen included—would get a nice fat check, instantly multiplying their wealth. But then the company she'd spent years building from the ground up would be dissolved in the massive belly of Simon Engel's behemoth. And just like that, their vision—*her vision*—for the future of Rapid's research would become irrelevant.

Not on her watch. She may have been employee number seven

when the company only had seven employees, but six short months later, when venture capital had dried up, and everybody was jumping ship, including the founder and then-CEO, she stayed on. Her persistence paid off, and now, a decade later, she was at the helm of one of the fastest-growing biotechnology companies in the world.

She had to be realistic, however. Rapid Science's success and meteoric rise was both its blessing and its curse. Its greater visibility made it easier to attract new capital, but it also attracted vultures like Guardian. It wasn't going to be able to fend off attacks from the likes of Simon Engel for much longer unless they got bigger. Much bigger. There was going to be a merger, just not the one the board was hoping for.

A few weeks ago, Chen had hired Peter Shultz, of Peter Shultz and Associates, a mergers and acquisitions firm. She disliked the man on a personal level, who seemed to be always standing a tad too close and touching her back or a shoulder as they went through the papers, too often to be appropriate. But the man knew how to deliver business. In the short span of two weeks, he introduced her and carried her through a few rounds of intense negotiations with Lightning Labs, a startup from San Francisco, looking to gain a foothold on the East Coast.

Under different circumstances, she'd stay the course, slowly but surely growing the business. But this merger was going to be the next best thing. It would be a marriage of equals, where as long as the parties compromised, her vision would be preserved.

The elevator chimed as it opened into the hallway of her apartment. She kicked off her Louboutins without turning on the lights, marched to the massive refrigerator, opened a bottle of white, and poured herself a generous amount. Then she positioned herself on a couch, set the glass on a small round coffee table and prepared to let the view of Central Park, framed by the curved glass of her thirty-sixth-floor windows, calm her nerves.

The greenery down below was dyed by the deep orange tinge of the setting sun. At this hour, the darkening skies washed out the buildings at the northern tip of the park and it looked like the green patch of trees continued on forever, separating the opposing armies of high-rise buildings on either side.

"You really can't beat the view," the voice said behind her, making her jump.

Only now she noticed a petite woman who was standing in the dark corner of her living room, pointing a small glistening object at her.

"Who are you? How did you get here?" Mary demanded as her heart raced. She lowered her feet to the floor, considering her options.

"Don't make any moves," the woman said, ignoring the question. A sound of a cocking gun sounded like thunder in the quiet apartment.

"What do you want?"

"What does everybody want?" the woman said, an irony in her voice. "Money."

"I can pay you," Chen said.

"Oh, of course you will," the woman replied, "but I need some insurance first. Take off your clothes."

"What? No," Chen said forcefully. "You won't get away with it. This building is full of high-resolution cameras. Leave now, and I promise I won't call the police."

"I'd suggest you start undressing, unless you want me to shoot you through your knees, and after I'm done here, visit your sister out in Queens," the woman said, steel in her voice. "All of it, now."

She obeyed this time, her trembling fingers fumbling with buttons and hooks. Finally, she was standing there, cowering in anger and shame. Yet she refused to cry.

"That won't work," the woman snapped. "Lie back on the couch and sell it to me. Either that or first your knees, then your sis."

Defeated, Mary robotically followed the woman's directions, moving this way and that, taking positions as a small camera clicked away.

Satisfied, the intruder put the camera on a table.

"Now drink up."

"Why?"

"Wasn't it what you wanted in the first place?" The woman chuckled. "Besides, I can't allow you to run after me the moment I leave your place."

"What kind of a person are you? Who does things like that?"

"Wouldn't you want to know?" the petite woman snapped. "Now drink. I need you to finish this bottle right now, or there'll be violence."

Mary forced herself to down a glass and poured herself another. She considered throwing the bottle at the woman, but she was too far away and would dodge it with ease. Besides, Chen had no desire to find out whether the woman would fulfill her threat of shooting her knees.

"So, how's it going to work?" She could feel herself getting woozy. "Do I write you a check or something?"

"No. Tomorrow you will withdraw one hundred thousand in twenty-dollar bills and put them in a gym bag. You'll be carrying this bag with you at all times. Then, sometime next week, I will call you with instructions on where to deliver it, and you will have thirty minutes to bring it to the place of my choosing. If you're late, even by a minute, I'll post these pics everywhere. You'll be ruined."

"What if I don't care? Everybody's got their pictures online now, so what?"

"Well, in that case, I hope you'll remember that I know where your sister lives." The woman waved her gun in a circular motion. "You wouldn't want anything to happen to your adorable younger sister Helen, would you?"

Mary finished another glass and stared at the bottle. She hadn't eaten since lunch, and three glasses of wine were making her stomach feel funny. She was sure that if she finished the bottle, she was going to be sick.

"I don't have all day," the woman in the corner said.

Hesitantly, she emptied the bottle into the glass and forced it down in one long swig. Neither of them said anything for a few minutes. Her head was getting heavy, and she leaned back on the couch. She could tell she was about to pass out.

Strong hands unceremoniously grabbed her and brought her to her feet.

"Whatchadoingtome," she managed, her tongue two sizes too large for her mouth.

"You're drunk," the voice said in her ear. "You need some fresh air."

She felt as the hands half-guided, half-carried her across the living room, around the coffee table and chairs toward the floor-to-ceiling window.

"Imgonnabesick," she spat, the waves of nausea sweeping her body, moving from her stomach upward.

"That's why you need to get some air," the voice insisted, pushing her forward.

The pressure in her stomach finally reached the boiling point, and she doubled over, spraying the white Persian rug with foamy yellow liquid. She was sweating profusely now, her knees buckling under her weight. Strong hands guided her onward and the other woman pressed something heavy into her hand. It pinched, and the pain briefly penetrated the drunken fog. Mary tried to pull back, but her strength abandoned her.

"Stop," she managed, as dark panic swept her whole body.

The woman swung her hand, sending the heavy object crashing into the window. It cracked, and the woman hit the window again, breaking it this time, pieces of glass raining to the streets more than three hundred feet below. Mary tried to turn, but before she could do that, she felt a hard push. There was weightlessness for a brief moment, the rush of air enveloping her naked body like a cool blanket.

Then there was nothing.

6

July 2007
Kenya

Mike Connelly threw his deployment bag out and away from the helicopter and swung his legs to the outside of the Black Hawk. The roar was deafening, as the machine hovered above a patch of sandy ground wedged between the rocks, its blades chopping hot, dry air.

"Go."

Connelly let the training take over, guiding his body in a series of precise movements. He pushed himself off the skid and dropped into the void below, the rope swooshing through his guide hand, as he accelerated toward the ground. He landed on the balls of his feet, keeping his knees bent, and let go of the rope. He then stepped aside and brought his submachine gun to his chest level, ready to cover his teammates.

They'd landed two miles north from the school, just outside of the town. He would have preferred finding a more secluded spot and then trekking toward their destination under cover of darkness. But in reality—right now their best ally was speed, even more so than stealth.

This was not an American-friendly neighborhood by most standards. Located less than five miles from the porous Somalian border, the town quite often served as a pit stop to a host of different terror groups roaming free back and forth between the two countries. The population of the small town had lived in constant fear of drug dealers and warlords who came and went, taking whatever they wanted along the way. Most of the shops and stalls had to account for a part of their profits to be used for payoffs just to be left alone. That was the only way to survive.

It hadn't always been this way, but the steady rise of terrorism since the infamous Nairobi bombing brought groups like Al-Shabaab and fringe factions of al-Qaeda to the area. They were careful at first —coming in the middle of the night and slipping out before the daybreak. But as the years passed, they'd grown more brazen as the local government, plagued by corruption and the chronic lack of resources, didn't, or couldn't, do anything to bring them to heel.

The Black Hawk banked hard and sped away, quickly gaining altitude from the drop site, the noise of its rotors disappearing into the night. Connelly's group consisted of six soldiers, two snipers, and the breach team, which included Connelly himself. Under normal circumstances, the two snipers would do the initial recon around the target, clover leafing around until they found the best vantage point onto the site where the hostages were located. But this was a fluid situation and they were going to have to improvise.

The team was between the missions when the orders came down the chain. Last night, they came back from a large raid that they executed alongside their SAS counterparts against a pirate base in Somalia. The raid was a success and Connelly was looking forward to taking it easy for the next two days when he and his team were called into the captain's quarters. They were up in the air in less than an hour after that.

On their way to the drop-off site, they pored over satellite images and settled on two locations that would give the sniper team a commanding view of the school building. One was a rusty sixty-foot-tall radio tower, located near a small mosque. It was roughly four hundred yards away from the school and provided an unobstructed 360-degree view of the town. The other was a patchy hilltop covered with copper-colored boulders. It looked down the dirt road leading to the T-junction where the school was located while also letting the sniper keep an eye on the main road. If any additional trouble was headed this way into the town, the sniper would have enough time to alert his teammates.

The two snipers left first, the long silhouettes of their SR-25s pointing to the sky. The remaining four soldiers split up, with Connelly and his bearded partner, Smith, heading to the western part of the school building while the other two moved to the eastern wing. They were halfway to the school, squatting next to a dirt hut with a broken slate roof, when the speaker in Connelly's ear came to life.

"One is in position," the voice said.

"Two is in position," another one added a few seconds later.

Connelly clicked his mic twice in response, acknowledging the snipers. As he turned to cross the dusty road, he looked at the two large words scribbled in white paint on the side of the hut.

LOVE LIFE

"No shit," he mouthed to himself and shuffled over to the next building in a combat crouch.

The school was a broad four-story brick building straddling the T-junction. Its bright-white façade with green and brown stripes, large clean windows, and freshly painted signs looked decidedly out of place flanked on both sides by the rows of rust-colored shacks.

"Why do you think they took it?" Smith whispered to him as they came to a halt next to a grocery store a block away from the building, his face glistening from sweat. "It ain't worth much."

"Who cares," he whispered back, scanning the area in front of the school. "Maybe they want to change careers. Let's go."

He flipped the safety off on his Heckler & Koch MP5 submachine gun and gestured to his partner.

"The ditch?" Smith said, his teeth gleaming on his dark face like a row of white pearls. "It looks like a good spot to me."

"Yeah, it should do it. Watch the Ma Deuce."

As they crawled over the intersection, Connelly kept his eyes glued to the beat-up Toyota pickup truck on the other side. Whatever went down tonight, they had to make sure none of the assholes got to use the fifty-caliber M2 machine gun mounted on top of the vehicle. That bad boy could quickly spoil any party. Connelly rolled over the ridge of the drain and slid down into the foul-smelling cavern.

"Three is in position," he said quietly into his mouthpiece.

"Four is in position," responded a voice in his ear.

Connelly planted his elbows in the dirt, moving his MP5 in a short arc, covering the front of the building. Now all they had to do was to wait for the sniper team to give them a signal and after that, there'd be a blur of fire and blood.

Hopefully their fire and only the other guys' blood, he thought. He wiped perspiration off his forehead with the back of his hand. By now, Connelly'd been on more missions than he could count, but the wait before things kicked into high gear never got easier.

"This is One. We have two tangos at the entrance, one by the truck and another at the west end of the building," came the voice of one of the snipers. "Two, take the guy on the truck. Three and Four, on my mark."

Connelly tensed like a coiled spring. He planted his right foot on the slope of the trench, gripped the MP5 tighter with his gloved hands, and readied himself to scramble over the edge of the ditch and toward the school.

"Wait up, wait up, wait up," another voice sounded in his ear, its urgency unmistakable. "We have a truck heading your way. Looks like it has army markings. Possibly more tangos."

"Could it be one of ours?" Connelly heard Smith whisper into the microphone.

"Negative."

Connelly could hear it now too—a whiney sound of a large vehicle growing louder by the second. A minute later, a pair of brilliant headlights flooded the schoolyard, and a beat-up AM General diesel truck still bearing the markings of the US Army pulled up into the school front yard.

"You gotta be shitting me," he heard Smith say under his breath.

As Connelly watched two dozen heavily armed men spill out of the truck, his adrenaline surged. Their rescue mission just got a whole lot more difficult.

7

July 2007
New York

*H*elen Chen cringed as "Umbrella" by Rihanna started playing for the fifth time in a row. She liked the song when it first came out, but by now, she must have heard it a thousand times, and this café seemed to have it on a loop. She took a sip of her iced coffee and watched the traffic going down Seventh Avenue, first past the Chase bank on the corner and then the esteemed Carnegie Hall across the street.

Her phone rang with a blocked caller ID, and she declined the call without bothering to see who it was and returned her attention to the laptop sitting on top of the scratched wooden table. The page it was opened on had an official communique issued by the Department of Defense on June 22.

"The Pentagon is exposed to perhaps hundreds of attacks a day, and the department has backup systems in place. A variety of precautionary measures are being taken. No classified information was compromised, and we expect the non-vital computer equipment that was temporarily taken offline to be operational again soon."

Two weeks ago, the same person who wrote that statement told her, and a few other contractors gathered in a dimly lit windowless room who were brought in to investigate the breach, that it was "the biggest fuck-up I've seen in a long time."

On June 21, a successful spear phishing attempt cracked open fifteen hundred computers storing some of the most sensitive information from a project code-named Nyctalope. After the theft, the machines were wiped clean.

None of the contractors were told about the contents of the compromised files, and soon Chen had learned that even the name of the project was removed from further communications with people who joined the task force a day later. With a limited number of people involved and disappearing evidence, the whole thing smelled like a cover-up.

She'd never heard of the word Nyctalope before, but after a quick Google search, Chen found a Wikipedia page dedicated to a pulp fiction hero with the same name. It was created at the beginning of the twentieth century by French writer Jean de La Hire. The hero may have been the first cyborg in literature and was seen by some as a significant precursor to the superhero genre. The character possessed an artificial heart and special powers, such as excellent night vision, which explained the source of inspiration for his name. The idea that the US Army was working on a project related to cyborgs made Chen's skin crawl.

"C'mon, come with us. It'll be fun."

"Um, I'd love to, but I need to work." She looked up at the man as if seeing him for the first time and then nodded at her laptop. "I can't. Please go."

"There'll be booze and good music." The man leaned in and lowered his voice to a whisper, "God forbid, you might actually enjoy yourself."

He had approached her at the café when she was having lunch and persisted in trying to convince her to go out despite her polite, but firm objections. He left her for a few minutes to reconvene with a few of his buddies at the bar, but now he was back again and she was starting to lose patience.

"Listen, Brian."

"It's Dylan."

"Whatever. I told you I have a boyfriend, right?" She feigned a sigh. "I can't. You seem charming and all, and if I were single, I'd consider it. Now, please leave me alone before I start breaking your shit."

The man backed off, a startled expression on his face, then got up and walked away from her table, mumbling something under his breath. Chen watched him leave and switched windows on her laptop. She'd been swimming in the muddy waters of the internet's chat rooms for the past two weeks looking for a person going by the handle Delgado, who had claimed to have some information on the attack. So far, she was only convinced of two things—one, that Delgado was a man, and two, that he was probably telling the truth. When she logged in to one of the IRC chat rooms where she went by the Witch, there was a new message waiting for her from Delgado.

Supermen are real. Look for them in Keeper's Workshop.

She read the note again and looked at the gray dot next to the user's name. He was offline. Chen pondered the message for some time. Delgado wrote Supermen as in plural, so that was the reference to the cyborg project; that much was obvious. But the rest of it wasn't clear. The message was a riddle designed only for her, which meant she was supposed to be able to decipher it. It was customary when dealing with people who operated in the gray area of the law to speak in code and use it as a security blanket of plausible deniability. But it didn't make it any less frustrating.

Keeper's Workshop? Who's the Keeper and was there any significance to the words being capitalized? And what about the workshop? Was it something that she was supposed to be familiar with? Something obvious? Or was it a hint to something more obscure that Chen needed to make a connection with?

Her phone buzzed again with a blocked caller ID. Annoyed, she put it on mute.

Chen pulled up an Excel spreadsheet with the list of people and organizations one way or another connected to the project. Individuals were listed by initials while organizations were listed by acronyms only. What made things worse—the list was a mix that contained people with top-secret security clearances and those who didn't have any clearance whatsoever. A mix of those who might have been in the know and those who delivered supplies, mopped the floors, and copied papers. Over fourteen hundred people and almost a hundred companies.

When she requested the actual names, first someone told her that it was on a need-to-know basis only and then five minutes later, she got an email directing her to delete the file altogether and prohibiting her from making copies under penalty of law. Chen didn't risk copying the files from the server, fearing that it might create a log of such action on the system and instead took pictures of her monitor to recreate it on her laptop later.

She sighed in frustration. This was like fighting a professional boxer with one hand tied behind your back.

Keeper's Workshop. What could it be? She ran a Google search, but nothing she could see was making any sense.

Gorilla keepers. Zoo workshops. Wisdom Keepers. Animal Keepers: Ten million results that she couldn't parse. Chen closed the tab and considered her options. Checking out companies was the first logical step. There were a few of them, and she could figure out most of them by using the list of acronyms. Could Keeper's Workshop be a company? She scanned the list, but there were no companies with an acronym KW. That wasn't particularly surprising, though—Delgado didn't use the word *cyborgs* either; he used a code—Supermen.

Maybe, she thought, she could look up some synonyms for those words. She opened a new tab and typed *www.thesaurus.com* and then searched for synonyms for the word *Keeper.* She was grasping for straws, Chen realized, but she was running out of ideas.

The page turned up a few columns of highlighted words.

Attendant, caretaker, curator, custodian…

She wrinkled her nose—none of the words were jumping out of the page. *Archivist, conservator, guard, jailer.* Her eyes wandered around the page and then she saw another highlighted word she hadn't noticed first, right under the word *Keeper:*

noun **guardian**

Guardian, she mused. That was a strong word, and somehow it fit. Guardian's Workshop? Perhaps watching the *Robocop* movies when she was younger was to blame, but now she couldn't shake off the image of the government building a cyborg police force and calling them *Guardians*.

Her phone silently flashed a Blocked ID sign again.

"Wow," she said out loud, looking at it in disbelief. "What a persistent asshole.

"Yes," she said angrily, answering the call. "Who the hell is this?"

"Is this Ms. Helen Chen?" said a man's voice.

Something in the tone of it made her sit straighter and forget her annoyance with the caller.

"This is. Who am I talking to?"

"This is Detective Sanchez with the Midtown North Precinct. Do you have a minute?"

"Yes." She felt goose bumps forming on her neck and running down her spine. "What can I do for you, Detective?"

"Do you mind me asking where you are right now?"

"I'm in Midtown Manhattan," she replied, the sense of dread covering her like a cold, wet blanket. "Why?"

"I'd like you to come down to the precinct as soon as possible." He gave her the directions. "I'm afraid I have some bad news concerning your sister."

8

July 2007
New York

Chen left the precinct as if in a haze. She took the stairs from the detective's office, walked through the hallway covered in WANTED signs, and went outside. She pushed her way past a group of uniformed officers, lost her footing going down the three concrete steps on the side of the building, and would have fallen head first if one of the cops didn't catch her by the arm.

"Are you okay, miss?" he asked. There was a genuine concern creasing his cleanly shaven, weather-beaten face, which, for a moment, made her feel better.

"I'm fine, thank you." She wiggled herself free, walked around a cruiser parked on the curb, and crossed the street. Her feet continued to carry her past the dry cleaners and then by the group of young men smoking in front of Uncle Vanya Café.

"You're pretty. Come drink with us," one of them shouted, rolling his *R*s.

Chen flipped him the bird without stopping and carried on.

"C'mon," the man persisted. "We don't bite."

She ignored him and picked up the pace. She grabbed a taxi at the corner of Ninth Avenue and gave the driver her sister's address. Normally she would have walked the few blocks, but right now she didn't trust her legs to continue to move. Now, alone in the darkness of the backseat, she closed her eyes and tried to process what she'd learned from the detective.

She and Mary had always been close. Not as close in the past few years as they used to be, as Mary's success came with an ever-increasing responsibility and ever-decreasing free time.

The last time she spoke to her sister was a month ago at their mutual friend's bridal shower. It wasn't really a place and time to catch up on each other's lives, but they did have a brief conversation, and Helen could not remember her sister looking depressed. Stressed and overworked, yes. Suicidal? She didn't think so.

The police seemed to be treating this as an open-and-shut case. Too much wine and suicide. The fact that Mary saw a psychologist also weighed on their decision, but Helen knew it was something wealthy folks like her sis did to unwind and refocus. It wasn't her cup of tea but to each their own. When she told that to the detective, he was sympathetic, but he didn't seem to share her suspicions.

"Look," he said, giving her his card, "there's nothing that indicates foul play as far as we can tell. We're finished with the scene so you can go in and look around if you'd like. You've said that you've stayed there on a few occasions. Do you still have a key?"

"Yes, I do," she said, pulling her keychain from the purse. "I have a copy."

"Great," he said, standing up. "Once again, my condolences. And please, if you see something unusual or suspicious, feel free to give me a call."

The taxi pulled up to the building, and Chen climbed out, squinting against the bright light. She nodded to the doorman and took the elevator to the top floor, steeling herself as it stopped at the penthouse.

It was hot inside, the split system whining above her head, going on full blast, unable to keep up with the scorching draft coming from the boarded-up window. Chen stepped over the threshold and stood in the hallway, taking it all in. The place that Helen once called a "neat freak's paradise" was a mess. The wind was strong up here, and before the broken window was covered with sturdy four-by-fours, it managed to wreak some havoc inside the apartment.

The glass bookcase that used to stand next to the window was shattered to pieces, and the floor was now peppered with loose papers, books, and shards of glass. An ugly yellow stain defaced the expensive white rug in the middle of the room.

Chen stepped into the living room, noting the pair of stylish shoes with bright-red soles under the coffee table and a pile of her sister's clothes next to the couch. An empty wine bottle was standing at the edge of the table next to the pieces of the broken wine glass.

This doesn't make any sense, she thought, looking around in bewilderment. The last time she saw her sister drunk was when Chen'd turned eighteen, and they snuck out to the roof of their parents' house in Queens. They brought two sleeping bags with them and stayed there all night—drinking, watching the city lights, and making plans of conquering the world until they both passed out. Luckily for them, it was their father who discovered them the next morning. They were mortified, but he only shook his head and quietly sent them to clean up. Thus, they were spared being grounded for the rest of their lives, which would undoubtedly have happened if their mother had found them first.

Chen put her bag on the floor in the hallway and set out to clean. First, she put away the glass shards and other debris and vacuumed the place and then methodically combed through the papers and books. By the time she was done, she was drenched in sweat, but the papers were stacked in a neat pile on Mary's desk, the books were lined up against the wall in alphabetical order, and the apartment no longer resembled a war zone.

She rummaged through the fridge and settled at her sister's desk with a bottle of cold water to look through the documents. After a few minutes, she caught herself spacing out—the documents weren't the most exciting read. Accounting statements, corporate bylaws, minutes from board meetings. Chen rubbed her face, trying to stay focused.

One paper caught her attention—an engagement letter of Peter Shultz and Associates, a mergers and acquisitions firm. She skipped the legalese at the beginning of the letter and traced the relevant part with her index finger.

To provide financial advisory and investment banking services in connection with a financial restructuring or reorganization of and/or one or more merger and/or acquisition.

This was new. Chen didn't know that her sister was considering a merger, but then again, she didn't know most of what her sister did at her job. She tried to stay in the loop when Mary had first started, but as the company continued to grow, she'd lost interest. But this could be something, she decided, and put the engagement letter aside.

It seemed that Rapid Science was pretty far along in negotiations with Lightning Labs, a company out of the West Coast, operating in the same space.

Was she not happy with her business? Chen thought. Her sister was one of the most driven people she knew and fiercely proud of her company. Chen decided that she'd have to look into why Rapid Science was pursuing a merger in the first place. If her sister's company was falling apart, Chen had to concede, it could be a real reason for Mary's alleged depression. But a suicide still sounded like a stretch—her sister wasn't a stranger to failure and to take an easy way out would have been out of her character.

She finished going through the rest of the papers, separating documents related to the merger and putting them aside. It was getting late now, and she decided to take the docs home and continue from a place that had working air conditioning. Chen packed her bag, finished the water from her bottle and threw it in the wastebasket next to the desk. Then she turned off the lights and headed for the elevator when something stopped her in her tracks.

She returned to the desk and picked up a crumpled piece of paper from the wastebasket she hadn't noticed before. It was a printout of an email.

The body of the message had only one line of text—*tomorrow at noon*—and the address line was empty, but as Chen looked at the subject line, printed in all caps, her pulse quickened.

RE: GUARDIAN MANUFACTURING

"I'll be damned," she heard herself say.

9

July 2007
Kenya

 p close, it was obvious that the AM General was no longer in the care of the United States Army. The dark-green camouflage paint was peeling along the side of the truck and the exposed metal was showing signs of rust. The front grille bore deep scrapes, as if the truck had plowed through some gates, and the front bumper was gone.

With growing alarm, Connelly watched as a group of young bearded men started to disembark the vehicle, most carrying AK-47s, but some with American-made M16s slung across their shoulders. Despite their youth, the fighters didn't look like greenhorns—they went about their business with a purpose and efficiency of experienced soldiers.

"We gotta hit them now before they spread out through the building," Connelly furiously whispered into the microphone.

He peeked out of the ditch. The solution couldn't be any more obvious to him—if they allowed the reinforcements into the school, the mission was royally screwed. They'd be outnumbered five to one and still would have to go room by room.

Connelly didn't like those odds one bit. Here, in the open, with two snipers crisscrossing the yard with bullets and the element of surprise on their side, they still had an excellent chance. As long as the assholes didn't get their hands on the Ma Deuce. The 50-caliber machine gun was the wild card in the deadly game they were about to play. It was like a flag in an RPG match, the penalty shot during extra time of the scoreless soccer game. Sudden death.

For now, the nose of its business end was pointing to the sky, but the moment it started spitting lead, it'd be game over.

"Hang on, Three," said the voice in his earpiece. "There are two more coming out of the school. Go, go, go."

Connelly shot out of the ditch like a lethal jack-in-a-box from hell. He pushed hard as he sprinted toward the truck, his boots making scraping sounds as they dug into the sandy ground with every step. As he accelerated, he heard the almost simultaneous whistles of two subsonic bullets punctuated by wet plops as they found their targets. The two guerrillas in front of the building collapsed, causing a momentary confusion among the newcomers.

Connelly cut down two more fighters by the side of the AM General with a short burst from his MP5 and sprinted toward the Hilux with Smith breathing down his neck and laying suppressive fire. One of the fighters dashed toward them and jumped on top of the pickup truck, reaching for the machine gun only to find himself at the wrong end of Smith's submachine gun.

"Cover me," Connelly shouted to Smith and without stopping, catapulted himself onto the truck. He slung the MP5 to his back, swung the platform around to aim at the AM General, pulled the charging handle back in one fluid motion and let go. A bullet nicked his helmet as his thumbs found the trigger shaped like an upside-down V and squeezed.

The night exploded in fire.

The roar of the 50-caliber machine gun ripped the silence of the night as if the god of war himself descended from the dark skies above and unleashed his wrath upon the puny humans. Half-inch-wide bullets capable of ripping a man's arm with a shockwave while passing the person within five feet bit into the truck, punching fist-sized holes.

As Connelly moved the barrel in a long, sweeping semicircle, his body shook from the mighty recoil of the machine gun. He watched the truck disintegrate as if in slow-motion. The tires blew out, and the driver's door flew open, swaying and bending as if made from silk rather than metal. Then the gas tank caught, and the fire blossomed through the sides of the truck, showering Connelly with glass shards and knocking him off his feet and over the side of the Toyota Hilux.

The automatic fire thundered from one of the school's windows, hitting the pickup truck and biting into the dust next to Mike's feet. He scrambled to take cover behind the Hilux truck and Smith joined him a second later.

"That was some crazy shit, dude." Smith exhaled, his face stretched into a wild grin.

"I know." Connelly found himself grinning back, bumping fists with his partner.

"It ain't over yet." Smith nodded at the school.

The shooting stopped now, but the moment they'd stuck their heads out, it would resume.

"One, can you get the fucker in the window? Second floor, right above the entrance," Connelly said into the microphone. "We're sitting ducks here."

"I can't see him, but I'll cover you guys until you're inside."

"Four? Are you good?" Mike called out to the two-person team flanking the school from the east.

"Ready when you are."

Connelly nodded to Smith and swapped the MP5 for the tactical H&K Mark 23 pistol with a suppressor.

"Let's do it."

The glass windows above the entrance exploded as the sniper team laid suppressive fire and Connelly, Smith in tow, dashed toward the front door.

Garcia and Jenkins, from Team Three, were already by the entrance, their rifles trained on the second-floor window, ready to push back on the insurgents. The windows remained empty, and Garcia threw a flashbang into the dark of the school's hallway and a split second later, Connelly rushed in, the reassuring heft of the Mark 23 in his gloved hands.

His eyes caught a movement, and he spun around in time to see two fighters wielding AK-47s coming down the stairs. Connelly's pistol barked twice, and one insurgent collapsed, head first, as two red spots appeared on his dirty shirt. Garcia cut down another guerilla with a short burst of his MP5.

They cleared the ground floor first, not meeting any resistance, and then Connelly signaled the rest of the crew to take the stairs. They ascended in a line, their weapons covering all angles until they spilled out onto the second floor. The hallway was empty. In the middle of it, above the entrance into the school, the window was broken. Pieces of glass covered the windowsill and the floor. The walls and the window frame were pockmarked with bullet holes, but the shooter had seemed to have escaped the assault as he was nowhere to be seen.

"Connelly, come here," Garcia whispered, pointing at one of the rooms.

Something in the tone of his voice made Connelly tense. He walked over to Garcia and looked through the opened door. Connelly had been an operator for a long time, but the sight of two dead bodies in the corner of the room made him recoil. The older man's head was bashed in with something blunt. The woman's heavily bruised body was naked, and her dark hair was slick with blood from what appeared to be an execution-style headshot.

"Filthy bastards," Smith muttered under his breath and pointed at the bloody tracks leading to the room. "Fucking savages dragged the bodies from somewhere else."

"It's not her. We still have to find the woman and the boy. Let's go," Connelly said, regaining his composure.

The team searched the rest of the second floor and continued to move on. They found the rooms where the hostages had been held captive and where the administrator was executed in the eastern wing of the third floor, but there were still no signs of the American woman and the boy. As the team prepared to ascend the stairs to the last, fourth floor, the speaker in Connelly's ear cracked with the voice of one of the snipers.

"This is One. Guys, we might have a problem."

"What's up?" Connelly felt as his grip on the MK23 tightened.

"There are two tangos on the roof, and it looks like they have a hostage."

10

July 2007
New York

The windows of the apartment that she rented on the second floor of a two-family house looked toward the East River. From her kitchen, that most days doubled as her office, Chen could see the Robert F. Kennedy Bridge, better known as the Triborough Bridge, as it gracefully stretched over Astoria Park. Late in the year, when the trees shed their leaves, she could see the water and make out the edge of Randall's Island on the other side. Now, with the park still covered in green, she could only glimpse the bright spots of the bridge's lights reflected on the dark water of the East River, blinking in and out of existence as the night's breeze swayed the leaves.

Nowhere as swanky as her late sister's apartment, the place was not without charm, and she'd been calling it home for almost five years now.

When she first moved back to New York after college, she'd moved around for some time, crisscrossing the town while resisting her parents' suggestions to stay at the family home.

At first, she stayed in Downtown Brooklyn, where she shared a three-bedroom apartment with an ever-rotating crew of roommates. Then she briefly ventured to the city, renting a shoe-sized studio in Battery Park City that consumed more than half of her monthly income, and finally settled down in Astoria. Later, when her mother passed away, and then two months later, her father, she considered moving back, but couldn't bear the idea of staying in the same place that once housed them all.

Neither of the sisters had it in them to sell or rent out the family house either, and it had been sitting vacant ever since, and Chen occasionally stopped by to wipe the dust off the furniture covers, mop the floor, and browse the library.

She turned on the light in the kitchen and put on a kettle. One part of her wanted to frantically start digging for whatever information she could find on Guardian Manufacturing, to try to understand how it fit into her sister's death or the hack of the Department of Defense. But she knew better—she had to be in the right state of mind and look at things from a ten-thousand-foot view to create a logical explanation for what lay ahead and not invent some wild conspiracy theories that would lead her nowhere. Going down that rabbit hole would be a waste of time, and she had no intention of doing it.

The kettle started to whistle, and Helen went about the routine of making gunpowder green tea that her father had taught her when she was only eight. She remembered being confused by the name at first. Gunpowder tea wasn't made from real gunpowder, of course, her father told her. Its English name came from the resemblance of its leaves, rolled into a small round pellet, to grains of gunpowder.

Her father, always a man of particular tastes, only drank a rare variant grown in Sri Lanka, at altitudes over six thousand feet, its tiny pellets still rolled by hand rather than by modern machines. Helen wasn't as picky, but the routine was her special link to her father; something that went far beyond the simple making of a drink. She suspected for all his ramblings about how special the tea was, and how the impossibly small pellets signified the highest quality, he cared for the drink much less than for the fact he made it with his youngest girl.

Finally, she set an off-white teapot on her desk next to the laptop, poured herself a steaming cup of fragrant tea, and opened a Google page.

"Let's start with the basics," she said out loud and typed *Peter Shultz and Associates* into the search bar and hit Enter.

On the top of the results page was a LinkedIn profile of a man with a broad, clean-shaven face and spiky red hair. There was also a link to the company website and Chen spent a few minutes browsing the pages filled with stock images of people in business attire, windmills, and wide-angle shots of New York's skyline. The page with a corporate client list read like a Who's Who in the business—Peter Shultz seemed to be doing well for himself.

She returned to the Google results and scrolled down the list. There was a different Peter Shultz, a physician, a White Pages link that claimed to have 75 people named Peter Shultz in its database, and a newspaper article with a story of a murder-suicide in Westchester County. Chen inhaled sharply as she read the first few lines of the article.

Peter Shultz, of Peter Shultz and Associates, death an apparent murder-suicide—note left; housekeeper found...

She clicked on the link, her calm concentration out the window, scanning the article and trying to control her rapid breathing.

...Housekeeping staff found Mr. Shultz, a successful mergers and acquisitions guru, inside his Westchester County residence.

Law enforcement officials told the news channel that it appeared that Mr. Shultz strangled his mistress and then proceeded with shooting himself in the head with a black-market Glock pistol. As per detectives, evidence, including the condition of the estate and the presence of a note, pointed to a murder-suicide out of guilt. Mr. Shultz is survived by his wife and two daughters.

Chen stopped reading and rummaged through her purse for the business card she got at the precinct. The phone only rang twice before it connected.

"Detective Sanchez." He sounded crisp and alert despite the late hour.

"Hi, sorry to bother you so late," she said timidly, but then collected herself. "This is Helen Chen, Mary Chen's sister."

"No bother at all. What can I do for you, Ms. Chen?"

"You told me to get back to you if I find something suspicious. I think I've got something."

"What'd you find?"

"I've looked through my sister's things today. Were you aware that my sister hired a mergers and acquisitions firm?"

"No, ma'am. Do you think it's of any significance?"

"I don't know. Perhaps. I've found the engagement letter hiring Mr. Peter Shultz of Peter Shultz and Associates."

"Okay," he replied. Chen could hear a pen clicking and then a rustling of paper as if he was taking notes. "Have you reached out to them?"

"He's dead," she said. "Apparent murder-suicide in his house up in Westchester. A few days before my sister's death. There's an article in a local paper, but I'm sure you can get more information from the local police department."

There was a silence on the other side of the call, long enough to prompt her to take a look at her cell phone to make sure the call didn't drop. "Are you there?"

"Yes," he replied, the tenor of his voice changing from polite to business-like. "This is new information for us. I'll reach out to the Westchester PD to see if there's anything that can allow us to connect some dots."

"Thank you—"

"I have to warn you, though," he said, interrupting her, "I understand how something like that could look suspicious on the surface, but it could very well be a coincidence. I don't want you to have your hopes up."

"I understand," she said, unsure what else to add.

"Was there anything else you found? You knew your sister better than anyone else. Was there anything unusual?"

Chen mulled the question over. Her impulse was to tell him about the email she found in the trash bin, the words *GUARDIAN MANU-FACTURING* pulsating in her mind's eye like a huge neon sign. But the question was—how was she able to share that information?

The email itself turned out to be a draft that had only one sentence: "Tomorrow at noon." There was no recipient. And she couldn't impress the significance of the find upon the detective without telling him how such significance occurred to her in the first place. The DOD hack and all the information about it was far above the detective's pay grade and sharing it with him was going to land her in a whole lot of trouble rather than helping her to find the truth.

"There was nothing else, Detective," she said out loud. "But I'll keep digging, and if I find it, you'll be the first to know."

1 1

July 2007
Kenya

*A*udrey Hunt hung up the phone and looked at the boy.

"Are you okay, Dalmar?"

"Yes, ma'am," he said, with courage in his voice that she suspected he didn't feel.

She went down to the boy's level. "Some really brave people are coming here to help us," she said, looking him in the eye, "but we need to make sure we do our part to help them."

The boy nodded, his somber eyes searching for answers in her face.

After some consideration, Audrey decided to leave the broom handle behind and hid it in the closet. She looked around the office for anything that could be useful, hoping for a pair of scissors or a knife, but there was no such luck.

She was ready to give up when she noticed a single-blade disposable razor next to a window that someone must have used to clean excess paint off the window glass. She picked it up and taped one side of the razor with some Scotch tape, glued the improvised weapon to her bare back with a Band-Aid, and covered it by her blouse.

"What is that for?" asked the boy, curious despite the fear.

"Hopefully nothing," she said, trying to sound reassuring. "Let's go. We gotta make it to the roof."

She carefully opened the door and peeked outside. The hallway was empty, but she could hear the muted sounds of the soldiers talking on the first floor. They made their way to the staircase again and started their ascent when she heard an unmistakable sound of the boots coming up the stairs.

"Quickly," she whispered to the boy as they tiptoed their way as fast as they could without making any noise.

As they reached the top floor, the muted sounds from below turned into angry shouts. By now their captors must have discovered the empty room where they were held before. There was no time to look for the roof exit anymore. Audrey looked around, trying to get her bearings, and ran to the window. She unlocked the sash locks, opened it, and looked outside. A ledge, jutting over a foot wide, ran around the building.

"Come," she said to Dalmar, putting her foot on the windowsill.

"No, no, no, no, no," he said, pulling away and sitting down on the floor. "I can't, Miss Audrey. I'm sorry. Please don't make me."

She stepped back and squatted next to the boy. She could hear crashing sounds from downstairs as the guerrillas were going room by room, looking for them.

"I know this is scary," she said, offering him her hand, "but we have to do this. You know these people are bad. We have to hide until the good guys come. Please. Trust me."

For a moment, she thought the boy wouldn't comply, but then he nodded, took her hand and she pulled him to his feet.

"Atta boy."

Audrey climbed out into the hot evening and pulled the boy up, helping him get on top of the windowsill. She closed the window behind them, and they slowly moved away from it just in time as the guerillas spilled out onto the floor, their shouts reverberating through the hot air.

"Do not look down," she whispered to the boy, holding his hand tight as they clung to the wall. "Keep looking at the wall, and follow me."

They shuffled their way toward the edge of the building, pausing before windows to make sure nobody was looking.

"Miss Audrey." Dalmar gently tugged on her hand, when they stopped again. "I don't think I can do this anymore."

She looked back at the boy, and his wide-open eyes told her everything she needed to know—he was barely controlling his panic.

"All right," she said, making a decision. "We need to sit down, okay? They can't see us from below, so we are safe for the moment. But we cannot go back in just yet. We need to wait them out until they stop searching. I'll sit down first and then will help you. Make sure not to make any sudden moves."

Audrey steeled herself and slowly turned away from the building. The height was dizzying. With great care, she lowered herself to the ledge and let her feet dangle in the void below. She let out a slow breath, trying to remain calm.

"All right, do not let go of my hand and slowly turn and then sit down."

She maneuvered the boy and helped him turn around and then lower himself to the ledge as well. The sky, bathed in amber and purple of the setting sun, was getting darker by the second. A few birds, their wings burning in the last rays of the day, were circling in the sky above the group of trees so dark they looked like one-dimensional cut-outs.

"This is beautiful," the boy whispered, looking far in the distance, "but my grandma will kill me if she ever finds out."

"This will be our little secret, I promise," she said, not being able to contain a smile.

After a while, the sounds of the search died down, and Audrey decided to risk going back into the building and looking for the roof exit. Trying to get up on the ledge turned out to be much more difficult than sitting down, but finally, she managed to stand up and move to the window. She peeked around the frame into the hallway for a few seconds, but there seemed to be no movement, and she dug her nails under the top of the window frame and pulled. Her fingers, slick with sweat, slipped, almost making her lose grip.

"Mother—" she started under her breath but caught herself. She wiped her hands on her blouse as best as she could and tried again. This time, the window gave. Audrey let Dalmar climb through first and then followed him as well. They came to the narrow ladder leading to the roof, and Audrey checked the lock. It was opened. Overwhelmed with emotion, she pulled the boy into a fierce hug.

"We're okay. We're okay."

The roof, covered in hot, sticky tar, was almost bare, save for the few air-conditioning units and a large electrical access box. A pair of red emergency Exit signs drowned the area in the ominous blood-colored glow. Audrey took a few steps to look around, her feet almost getting glued to the surface with each move. Now, when they finally were on the roof, she regretted leaving the broom handle back in the administrative office. Without it, there was nothing to barricade the door with.

There was a sound of a truck driving up to the school, and then the hail of automatic fire ripped the silence without warning, making them both jump. A few seconds later, an explosion shook the building, briefly illuminating the dark skies.

"There." Dalmar pointed at the electrical access box. "We should hide behind it."

They sprinted toward the box, and as they made their way around it and squatted out of the line of sight, the roof door flew open with a bang. Hidden behind the box, Audrey watched as two men climbed out to the roof and frantically looked around as they backed away from the hatch. They were not pursuing them, she decided; they were fleeing. But her hiding place was going to be compromised any second now.

"Listen to me." She turned to the boy. "No matter what, stay out of sight, and don't make a peep. Do you understand?"

She made him lie down so he would be less visible, and then

stepped out from behind the box and made a few strides toward the two men.

"All right," she said, startling them and almost causing them to unload their rifles at her, "you got me. But by the sounds of it, you're going to need me alive."

12

July 2007
Kenya

There was some shouting on the roof as Mike Connelly stuck a miniature video camera on a flexible cable over the edge of the roof door. The grainy image showed a woman held by a burly man with a pistol to her head, keeping her in front of him as a live shield while another man trained his automatic rifle in the trap-door's direction. There was no sign of a boy.

Connelly slowly opened the hatch and rose above the threshold, leading with his gun. "Easy there, big fella."

"Let us go, or we kill her," the burly man shouted in accented English as Connelly cleared the edge, keeping him in the sights of his MK23.

"That is not how it works, asshole," Connelly replied, moving to the side and letting his teammates climb out as well. "If you kill her, you've got no bargaining power, and I promise, you will wish you were dead before it's over."

"I'll kill her, I swear," the man shouted again, pressing the pistol into the woman's temple. "Go back."

"No," Connelly said, "you're not listening. She's the only reason why I haven't shot you yet. Keep her intact, and you'll get to see another day."

The boy's absence was complicating things—there was a chance that the woman managed to hide him before they took her hostage, but without knowing it for sure, taking action could jeopardize the kid's life. Mike strained his eyes, trying to read the faces of the two men in the dim light of the emergency signs.

The broad-shouldered fighter didn't strike him as a religious zealot and Connelly suspected he could reason with the man. But the other combatant, short and thin, with a pale face and a long scraggly beard, seemed to be on the verge of panic, his fingers straining on the trigger of the AK-47. He planted his left foot on the low barrier that separated the roof from the void below, and his muscles seemed tight like a coiled spring.

The way Connelly saw it, the man was ready to rain lead on infidels and jump to his death, to make sure they weren't going to be able to take him alive. And the way the short man looked back and forth between his comrade and Connelly as they talked, Connelly suspected the man didn't understand what was being said. That wasn't going to help to ease the situation.

"Let us go, right now," the big man repeated. His hands kept moving the woman, so she was squarely between him and the weapons of Connelly's team.

"Listen," Connelly said, "I think your buddy doesn't understand what's happening and it'd be better if everybody was on the same page. Tell him to put down the weapon, then do it yourself, and then we can have a conversation."

"He won't do it," the burly man said and threw a glance at the other fighter. "He'd rather die in the name of Allah than let the infidels capture him."

There was some desperation in the tone of the man's voice. If not for his partner, he could be reasoned with, but with the other man ready to die a martyr, the list of options was rapidly shrinking.

"You should try," Connelly encouraged the man.

"I can't." The man's breathing became faster. "I'm sorry, I really can't."

A quick movement caught Connelly's eye and before he had time to process what he was seeing, a small shadow dashed from behind an electric box and crashed into the short insurgent, knocking him off the roof. The rifle barked as the man instinctively squeezed the trigger, sending a few bullets over Connelly's head.

Startled, the burly fighter loosened his grip and then cried out in pain as the woman pushed his arm away. A trickle of blood ran down his elbow and then dripped to the ground, and a second later, the pistol fell out of the man's hand.

"Bitch," he shouted, trying to hit the woman with his good hand, but she pushed him hard, and this time Connelly had a clean shot.

The first bullet hit the man in the shoulder. He stumbled, taking a step back, and Connelly added two more to the man's chest.

"Dalmar," the woman cried out and ran to the boy, who was now sitting next to the edge of the roof, scooping him into her arms. "I got you. I got you."

"I killed him," the boy said in a half-whisper, his entire body trembling, as Mike approached them. "I killed that man."

Connelly squatted next to the two of them and patted the boy on his back without saying anything.

"I pushed him off the roof," the boy said.

"You did well, little man. C'mon, buddy," he said finally and stood up. "Let's get you guys out of here. I don't think staying here for too long is a wise idea."

"Where will you take him?" the woman asked, standing up next to him. "He has some family in the village, but I don't know if he's going to be safe there."

Connelly looked at the woman. Her face was pale and smeared with dirt; her clothes were in disarray but she looked cool and collected, and he couldn't help but admire her. Over the past few hours, she'd been through what most people never had to experience in their entire lives. She witnessed a murder, then was kidnapped and bound. Then she had to listen to another captive being tortured and killed while she and the boy were left for what seemed to be an inevitable death as well.

And yet, she found the courage and wits not only to save herself but also to protect a kid who happened to be in the wrong place at the wrong time. Even now, the first question out of her mouth wasn't about her own safety but the boy's.

"There are no survivors here," he finally said. "Dalmar will be okay if we return him home."

"Are you sure?"

"Yes," he looked at the boy, "but you have to promise me, Dalmar, that you will never, and I mean, ever, tell anyone what's happened here. You were not here, do you understand?"

The boy looked up at him, his face serious as if studying Connelly's face for clues.

"I did a bad thing," he finally said. "He was a bad man, but killing is worse. But I didn't know what else to do. I had to protect Miss Audrey."

"You didn't kill him," Connelly said and put his hand on the boy's shoulder. "You tried, and that's okay because you were trying to protect Mrs. Hunt. But before you pushed him, my sniper shot him straight through his heart. Look at the radio tower over there. I'm going to ask my sniper to send me a signal, okay?"

"Okay."

They looked, and a second later, a faint light blinked twice on top of the dark silhouette of the tower.

"Did you see it, Dalmar?"

"Yes," the boy said.

"I told you. It's not on you."

The boy looked back at Connelly, a mix of fear and desperate hope swirling on his face.

"You want to see the signal again?"

"Yes, please."

The faint star blinked twice again and then three more times in rapid succession.

"He shot his rifle, before he fell, remember?" Connelly pressed. "He did it instinctively after a bullet hit him. You were trying to help, but you only pushed a dead man. It's not on you. But you must never tell anyone that you were at school today, then you'll never be in danger again. Are we good?"

"Yes," the boy said seriously and stretched his hand out. "We're good."

Connelly shook the boy's hand and turned toward the roof's door, gesturing to his teammates to follow. They had to make it to the rendezvous point in less than two hours, and they still had to make a detour to deliver the boy to his relatives in the village. There was no time to spare.

As they walked out of the school and headed west, Smith and Garcia taking turns to entertain the kid, Audrey Hunt caught up to Connelly and squeezed his arm.

"He fits right in," he said, pointing at the boy, who was now marching between his two teammates. "I might end up taking him with us."

"Thank you," she said in a half-whisper, "for what you told him. And for what all of you did, of course."

Connelly looked at her as they walked by the hut with the two large words LOVE LIFE written on it in the bold white paint.

"Just doing my job, ma'am," he said, a smile coming to his lips. "Just doing my job."

13

July 2007
New York

Chen hung up the phone and crossed the last name off her list. Her father was a first-generation immigrant who'd originally moved to California from mainland China, where he married an Irish girl before they both moved to New York for business. Most of their friends and distant family, from her mother's side, still lived in the San Francisco area. She called everybody early in the morning New York time, ignoring the three-hour time difference, half-hoping to get voicemails rather than having some prolonged and painful conversations.

The strategy mostly worked, but preparations for the funeral still took Chen almost until noon. While they grew up in a family of a non-practicing Buddhist and a self-proclaimed "lazy Catholic," neither of the sisters were religious, and she figured Mary wouldn't care for a religious ceremony.

The funeral home she called suggested a closed-casket burial but she only shuddered, remembering the grisly photos of her sister's remains—having them in a casket, even a closed one, seemed wrong. She opted for a cremation instead, and after looking at an obscenely large selection of urns of all shapes, colors, and sizes on the funeral home's website, she picked a simple, silver-coated urn. Now, having taken care of the dead, she was itching to take care of the living. Unlike the detective, she was convinced that Mary hadn't taken her own life and that Peter Shultz didn't go out willingly either.

She switched between windows and logged into the IRC chat room. To her delight, there was a small green dot next to Delgado's name, indicating that the user was online. Her fingers flew over the keyboard, typing a message to him.

I have new information. We need to meet.

We just did, came an almost immediate reply. **Talk.**

Not like this. Meet me in the RW. Somewhere public.

No.

It's bigger than you think. I need to know that I can trust you.

You have 30 seconds to tell me what you came here to tell me. Here, not in the RW.

Please, she pleaded. *It's not just the hack. They killed my sister. Other people too.*

There was no reply for a while and for a painful moment Chen thought Delgado disconnected from the chat.

Meet me by Peter Cooper's statue in exactly one hour, the message said. **Third Ave and East Seventh. If you're late or not alone, you will not hear from me ever again.**

The green light next to Delgado's name blinked and changed into gray, indicating that the user was no longer online.

Chen looked at the clock on her laptop—12:47 p.m. She considered her options. She could walk to Ditmars Station, which would take her less than fifteen minutes, and grab the W or the N train to the city, but that would be tight. At this time of the day, the notoriously unreliable trains weren't running as frequently as during the rush hour. Taking a taxi was a risky bet as well, but she figured she had enough cushion to get to the meeting on time even if she hit traffic. She called the local car service, grabbed her keys and the laptop and rushed outside. A few minutes later, a livery cab pulled up next to her house, and she jumped in.

"Should we take the FDR?" the driver asked after she gave him the address.

"No," she said, "take Twenty-First Street to the Midtown Tunnel. It'll be faster."

They got lucky—the traffic was light, and except for a few blocks when they got out of the tunnel, they almost didn't slow down. Chen got off on the corner of Second Avenue and the famed St. Mark's Place with almost thirty minutes to spare. She walked west to Third Avenue and then turned south until she hit a small park, Cooper Triangle, named after Peter Cooper. The statue of the bearded American industrialist sitting in a throne-looking chair and gazing into the distance dominated the northern corner of the tiny park.

She took a seat on the bench facing the monument and looked around. It was a fascinating part of town—an eclectic mix of grandiose past of the Cooper Union Foundation building, sleek lines of the ultra-modern twenty-one-story tower of the Standard Hotel, and the hulking boat-like silhouette of the Cooper Union Academic Building designed by the celebrated Thom Mayne.

"Hello, Witch," a voice said behind her, and a moment later, a petite woman of Japanese descent sat next to her on the bench. She was wearing a transparent tank top with a black bra underneath and a pair of distressed jeans. But that was the only ordinary thing about the woman.

Her jet-black hair was cut into a blunt, chic bob framing a delicate, heavily made-up face with high cheekbones and eyes so dark they almost bordered on black. A magnificent red and green dragon tattoo was slithering up her right arm, around her shoulder and neck, and finally resting its head with half-closed eyes on the left side of the woman's chest.

"Hello, Delgado," Chen replied. "I thought you were a man."

"Delgado isn't here. I'm just the messenger," the woman said in lightly-accented English and moved her hair back to one side. Only now Chen noticed a small black microphone in the woman's ear.

"That's not what we've agreed on," Chen said.

"Look, don't shoot the messenger. I'm trying to help. Delgado never meets anyone in person like this. This is as much as you get—take it or leave it."

Chen studied the woman's face for a few seconds. Behind the impenetrable façade of a doll face, there was an unmistakable wit, and a no-nonsense attitude.

"Will he answer my questions?" she pressed.

"We're here, aren't we?" the woman responded, avoiding using a definitive pronoun.

"My name is Helen Chen, and I'm a freelance contractor for the DOD," she began.

"You also work for the CIA," the woman interrupted her.

"Yes, sometimes I contract for them as well, but it's not important. My sister, Mary Chen, died in what the police ruled a suicide by jumping from her apartment window. Before her death, Mary hired a mergers and acquisitions company led by Peter Shultz to facilitate the merger between my sister's company and an outfit out of San Francisco. Said Peter Shultz died of an apparent suicide a few days before my sister's death."

The woman tipped her head to one side as if listening to the microphone in her ear.

"Why do you think it's connected to the hack?"

"I found a draft of an email. It appeared to be an invitation to a meeting, and it was supposed to be about Guardian Manufacturing. Isn't that what you meant by the Keeper's Workshop—Guardian Manufacturing? I don't think she ever sent it and I don't know who was the intended recipient. But I suspect that Guardian didn't want the merger to go through, so they killed Shultz, and then Mary."

The woman nodded as if agreement and closed her eyes for a few moments, listening to what was being said into her earpiece. Then she pulled out a piece of paper from her back pocket and a ballpoint pen, wrote down a few lines of text, and gave the paper to Chen.

"These are the instructions on how to get into an email server," she said, getting up. "The name of the person you're looking for is Simon Engel. Now you have to go."

"Thank you," Chen said, getting up as well. "I appreciate it."

She turned around and started walking away.

"Helen," the Japanese woman called out after her.

"Yes?"

"You don't strike me as a person who takes other people's advice. But if you did, I'd say this—walk away."

14

July 2007
Camp Lemonnier, Djibouti

Audrey Hunt watched her husband pace the sparsely furnished room. An old air conditioner was rattling under the window, hopelessly fighting the harsh afternoon sun, but the room was stiflingly hot and smelled of stale sweat, sand, and gun oil. After a while, Andrew Hunt grabbed a chair and sat down, looking out the dusty window.

"Did you know that they originally built this camp to accommodate the French Foreign Legion?" he finally said, still not meeting her eyes.

She smiled, watching his handsome face. When Andrew got nervous, he always became professorial, drawing courage from the vast set of cold, hard facts stored in that big head of his. She remembered when he approached her for the first time in a diner, he kept talking about the history of Hell's Kitchen. He started with an anecdote about the late 1800s when the *New York Times'* reporter, who was investigating a series of murders, ventured into a building at West

Thirty-Ninth Street with a particularly seedy reputation. According to that tale, the reporter referred to the tenement as Hell's Kitchen and the name stuck and later expanded to the surrounding streets.

She learned more during that evening about the gang wars that used to rage in the neighborhood, speakeasies with secret tunnels, and mysterious murders than most people who spend their entire lives between Thirty-Fourth and Fifty-Ninth Streets in the west side of Manhattan.

"No, I didn't," she said softly, "but I did know that you've been working for the CIA."

He looked at her, a mixture of shame and relief on his face.

"Not from the beginning," she continued, "but I've known for a long time."

"I must be a terrible spy," he finally said. He got up, walked across the room, and sat next to her on a stiff bed, taking her hands in his. "I'm so sorry."

"Look," she squeezed his hands, searching for words, "I would be lying if I said it didn't bother me in the beginning. But then I realized it wasn't your secret to share. What were you going to do—turn on the shower to make sure no one can eavesdrop and whisper state secrets in my ear like they do in the movies? C'mon."

"It did cross my mind," he said, not being able to contain the smile. "I wanted to."

"I'm sure you did. But I thought that sooner or later the opportunity would present itself, and you'd be able to tell me the truth without breaking any rules. Obviously, I had no idea it would be under such dramatic circumstances, but it is what it is."

Audrey leaned in and planted a soft kiss on his cheek, then stood up and stretched. They arrived at the camp at four in the morning but even after a hot shower and a meal, she found herself too wound up to be able to fall asleep. But after a series of briefings, they were finally left to their own devices and now she was crashing, exhaustion seeping into her bones.

"There's something else," Andrew said quietly. Something in the way he said it made her adrenaline surge, bringing her back to full attention.

"No more secrets," he said, looking at her. "No more lying. I can't make a decision like this on my own."

"Okay." She sat down next to him again. "Whatever it is, I'll help you through it."

They sat in silence for a few moments, as she watched her husband's internal struggle play out on his face.

"I met with Jim Rovinsky when I was down in DC a few days ago," he finally said. "First off, Jim doesn't work for the State Department, as you probably have guessed. He's the head of clandestine operations at the CIA. He's also the one who recruited me years ago to work for the agency. The reason he wanted to meet this time was not related to my regular work at the CIA."

Andrew continued, "Jim wants to create an agency within the agency. He calls it the Unit. Completely isolated. Black ops within the black ops, if you will. No congressional oversight, which would give it an unbelievable efficiency."

"No congressional approval either then," she interjected, "which means they, and I'm assuming you, would be hung out to dry if things were to go wrong."

"Correct." He nodded. "But what he's found is staggering. You've heard all the conspiracy theories, and there are books and movies about the select few who rule the world from the shadows. The Freemasons, the Illuminati, the Knights Templar and so on. All of it fascinating and all of it complete fiction. Until now."

"There is a secret society that rules the world?" she asked, incredulous. "What does it even mean?"

"Well, like most of those things, in real life it's less dramatic, more practical, and yet, more profound. Rovinsky thinks—and after reading what he's given me and doing my own research, I believe him—that there are some international corporate interests who secretly joined forces a couple of decades ago. We've identified four main centers of influence—China, the Middle East, the UK, and the US. But I don't know for sure, so there might be more and for now we have no idea who is pulling the strings. All we know is that there are people who are pursuing some common goals."

Andrew fell quiet for a few moments, collecting his thoughts.

"But you must have some suspects. You said that you thought those were large corporations?"

"No. Not yet. Of course, a few of those players who Rovinsky's been able to identify were affiliated with some corporations, but we don't know if the companies themselves are involved. But when you have multiple actors who share the same goal although they are not associated with one another, you must draw the conclusion that they have the same masters. For now, we're trying to figure out if those corporations are actively conspiring or are just used by high-ranking people for their own nefarious agenda."

"It makes sense."

"I think initially they built the alliance for mere economic collusion. To help a few already powerful multinationals dominate the markets even more and enrich themselves in the process. But as it proved to be successful, they grew bolder. They bribed politicians; they infiltrated law enforcement. At some point, it became so effective that they actually created some sort of governing entity that transcended businesses and international borders."

"An actual alliance?"

"Correct. And once that happened, it was no longer a loose affiliation built for economic benefit but rather a quasi-state with its own government and its own army. They are killing people off who stand in their way. They are using terrorist organizations as their military proxies or to launder money. This is huge."

"So, this new task force is going to do what exactly? It's going to combat this shadowy corporate monster without the approval of the US government, right? But why? Why can't we do it the same way things like these are always done? The FBI, the CIA, Interpol?"

"In a way, that is how it's going to be done." He shrugged. "It's just Rovinsky is convinced that it's too late to do this the usual way because many of those agencies are compromised. So, the Unit will create little secret pockets inside of all of those agencies. We'll do it quietly through a network of reliable people we can trust. And even then, we will keep things compartmentalized and limit the information we share to need-to-know only."

They sat in silence for a few minutes, both digesting the importance of what was said and its implications.

"At first, when Jim approached me with this, I balked at the idea of doing something off the books," Andrew continued. "It's one thing to be an analyst for the agency and limit the excitement to finding suspicious financial behavior. It's quite another story when you're asked to be a part of an organization, however noble its cause, whose mere existence is illegal and should things go awry, to get prosecuted for, I don't know—conspiracy? Treason? You pick."

Audrey reached out and put her hands on top of his. "He asked you to run it, didn't he?"

"How—" He looked at her, surprised. "How could you possibly know?"

"You know," she said, "when I first realized that you were working for the CIA, I was angry. It meant you must've lied to me; had to, right? But what happened in the school..." She trailed off. "I mean, there was a high chance I was going to die. I accepted that. But I also knew that the moment I called the State Department, somewhere across the globe you'd find out I was in trouble and move mountains to save me."

She looked at him, seeing the moisture collecting in the corners of his eyes.

"I think Jim asked you to do this because he knows the same thing that I do—that you are the perfect man for this job."

15

August 2007
New York

"Hiroko?" Chen said.

"Yes?" The woman looked up and stretched in her chair. The dragon on her chest moved as if it were alive.

"You said on the phone that you wanted to help me."

Since their meeting in the park a month ago, Helen had been busy traveling the virtual labyrinth of Guardian Manufacturing servers. It wasn't an easy task. Guardian's security was top-notch, and Chen had to move slowly to avoid detection. After weeks of work, all she had was a single email from Simon Engel, Guardian's CEO, that had one sentence in it that drew Chen's attention.

I need you to take care of RS, the email said. *She's been a problem. Enough is enough.*

RS, Chen figured, stood for Rapid Science, and the *she* referred to her sister, Mary Chen. Helen had learned by now that the board of directors of Rapid Science was in favor of being acquired by Guardian, and her sister was the sole voice who strongly opposed it.

And it looked like Simon Engel was losing his patience waiting for her to come around.

After the brief meeting in Manhattan with the Japanese woman, who acted as Delgado's intermediary, Chen thought she saw the last of her. To Chen's surprise, a few weeks later the woman called her cell phone, and without bothering to explain where she got the number, introduced herself, and offered assistance.

"So, what gives?" Chen asked, looking at the mysterious woman. "My understanding was that our meeting was going to be a one-time thing."

"We have common interests," the woman replied. "At least, for now."

"I'm planning to leak this to the police," Chen said, referring to the email.

"No, no cops." The woman put up a hand. "Involving the police would be a mistake."

"Bullshit," Chen spat. "I can't sit here and let them get away with this because you happened to be uncomfortable with the law."

"Hold your horses, lady. It has nothing to do with my relationship with the law," the woman replied coolly.

"What does it have to do with, then?"

"There are many cops who are on Simon Engel's payroll. I suspect some of the feds are as well," the woman said. "Many of them are in high places. Best case—your tip will end up in the trash. Worst case— you'll join your sis."

"But how…" Chen searched for words, "how am I supposed to get some justice for her, if what you say is true?"

"I told you to walk away," Hiroko said, "and I still think it's the sane thing to do. Think about it. They've killed your sister, and the broker, and the broker's mistress just to be sure. If you get involved, you'll put yourself in their cross hairs as well. They've killed three people so far that we know of. What do you think will happen if they see somebody else messing up their plans? You think they'll say—*oh, this woman seems nice, let's give her a break, shall we?* You think that's what's gonna happen?"

"No. Of course, not."

"And you still want to get involved?"

"Yes." Chen furiously nodded. "Absolutely. I have to do something. But if I can't go to the police, what *can* I do?"

Hiroko stayed silent for a while, her dark eyes studying Chen's face.

"There's still something you can do, though it might fall short of your expectations," Hiroko finally said. "I don't think you can put Engel in jail. It's not realistic. He's too protected to pull off something like that. Maybe, in the long run, we can find a way, but not now. Still. There's something else you could do. You could hurt him financially."

"How?"

"Now that your sister is out of the way," Hiroko continued, "Guardian will make a move on Rapid Science in the next few weeks. To maintain proper optics, after your sister's death, it's going to be a hostile takeover, paid in stock, as usual. But considering there's no real opposition now, the board of Rapid will fold and let the chips fall where they may."

"How does it help us?"

"This is where you can hit them," the woman said, her face unreadable. "By preventing the merger."

"I don't understand," Chen said. "How can we do that?"

"Think about it," Hiroko continued. "What is a takeover? Rapid Science is worth a quarter billion dollars. Guardian spends that much on pencils every year, so they will come and offer, say twice or three times that much for the company, paid in Guardian stock instead of cash. That would make all big shareholders of Rapid Science twice or three times as rich just by saying yes."

"Okay, but I still don't understand," Chen said. "All I hear is the reasons why it will happen."

"Well," the woman smiled for the first time, "it only works if the math works. Guardian always pays for acquisitions in stock, and it makes sense—they can print money as long as the price of their shares stays stable or appreciates. For a small acquisition like that, they can simply issue more stock, and it will cost them virtually nothing."

"Okay." Chen thought she finally understood where the woman was going. "And what can change the math?"

"A couple of things." The woman's smile grew wider. "If Rapid Science's stock appreciated, it would make the acquisition more problematic. Or if Guardian's shares took a dive."

"Or both." Chen exhaled, suddenly realizing that she stopped breathing for a few seconds. "Then the transaction would become much more expensive than they'd originally anticipated."

"Precisely," Hiroko said. "If Rapid Science's shares appreciated enough, and Guardian's fell low enough, at some point the math would stop working. Simon Engel might own Guardian Manufacturing, but there are still a lot of large shareholders who would put the brakes on the merger if the math got completely out of whack."

"Okay. Let's say prices go up for one and down for another the way it makes the math prohibitive. But if things go back to normal, at some point, won't they try to do it again?"

"They might," Hiroko shrugged, "or they might not if they get burned badly enough the first time. It's like petting a dog who bites. Some will give it another go, but some will pet a different dog. All you can do is try. Hit them where it hurts and protect your sister's legacy."

"You still haven't told me what would need to happen to make it possible. We can't wish the stocks to change prices the way we want them to."

"No," Hiroko's face was an unreadable mask again, "but you know what the answer is."

"Targeted disinformation campaign? We could disseminate some fake news releases and try to influence stock prices that way."

"That's not a bad idea, but that alone wouldn't be enough. You need something more disruptive than a string of fake news. You need something to make real waves."

Chen thought about it for a moment. It'd never been done. Ever. And there was a good reason for it. And it wasn't like nobody ever tried. They had. But no one, ever, was able to pull it off. Of course, any system was hackable, at least in theory. But many factors defined the effort and cost, and—most importantly—time that was required to prepare such an attack.

Only in Hollywood blockbusters could a smart hacker break into any system in a matter of minutes. In reality, the preparation time could take weeks, or even months, depending on the amount of available information and resources at the attacker's disposal.

"Can it be done?"

"I don't know." Hiroko shrugged. "It's a tall task for sure, but you won't find the answer unless you try. You can stand in front of a mountain and keep guessing for eternity if you're capable of reaching the top, but unless you start walking and get your hands dirty, you'll never know the answer."

"I can't help but feel that the moment I say yes, a large army of FBI agents will storm this place and whisk me away to spend the rest of my days in a solitary cell."

"Well, I can't help you with that, can I? But I will help you with this crazy venture, should you decide to try it."

Chen looked at the strange woman calmly sitting in front of her, seemingly unperturbed by what was being discussed. "Are you saying what I think you're saying?"

The woman shrugged again, her face a mask of a painted doll.

"All right," Helen said, "let's hack the New York Stock Exchange then. Where do we start?"

16

September 2007
New York

When Audrey woke up, her husband was still fast asleep. The clock on her nightstand read 5:45 a.m. It had been a tough week. They traveled back and forth between Washington DC and New York four times, and they were both exhausted. But it was Sunday, and they finally had a day to themselves—nowhere to be, and no reason to get up at some ungodly hour.

Yet there she was—up, and without a trace of sleep. She looked at him—his hands were thrown about as if he were a bird, ready to take flight, his chest rising and falling with each breath slowly and steadily. She smiled—Andrew Hunt always slept like there was not a worry in the entire world.

It was still dark, but the sky was already taking on the lighter hues of blue, and she could see the outlines of the buildings outside of their bedroom floor-to-ceiling windows.

Quietly, so not to wake him, she pulled on a bathrobe and went to the kitchen to make some coffee. Then, fresh brew in hand, she climbed the stairs, stepped outside to the terrace and settled at the small table by the pool.

It was even brighter now, the first rays of sunlight hitting the green dome of the Police Building Apartments to her left—the imposing Beaux-Arts building that once served as the police headquarters. It reminded her of the Dome of St. Peter's Basilica in the Vatican that she'd seen on a European trip many years ago and the view was one of the reasons she liked the penthouse so much.

They'd been calling it their home for almost twenty years now. She first saw it in some ostentatious magazine when they were sitting in the waiting room at her gynecologist's, ready to see the ghostly image of their son for the first time. She loved the layout, but chuckled at the astronomical price and showed it to Andrew, who only glanced at it and smiled. They could barely pay the rent of their tiny studio at the time.

But a few years later, he pretended to be invited to a party at that very place, and when they got to the door, instead of ringing the bell, he produced the key.

"You're up early." She heard his voice, and a second later he joined her, settling his cup with a steaming liquid on the table next to hers.

"Oh no, did I wake you? I was trying to be quiet. You looked like you needed some sleep."

"No, I didn't even hear you getting up," he said and took a sip of coffee, squinting at her. "Quite a week, huh?"

"Yeah." She stifled a yawn. "It was intense."

"Regrets?" he asked.

"I have a few," she said, and smiled. "No, I want to do this. And if things go south, at least you'll have a roommate at Gitmo."

"I'm pretty sure you can't have roommates there." He smiled back.

When he first suggested that she should join him at the Unit as his deputy, it surprised her. Nothing in her not-for-profit resume screamed *black ops.* The only remotely relevant experience that she had was from her corporate past working for a logistics company. She told him as much, but Andrew was relentless.

"First off," he said to her at the time, pacing back and forth across the room at the army base, "you don't give yourself enough credit. The work that you've done—all over the world—that takes a lot of savvy. Negotiating with local governments, figuring out logistics for something that is happening thousands of miles away. These are precisely the skills that you would need."

"But I have no military experience," she protested.

"Me neither," he shrugged, "and that's exactly why Rovinsky wanted me to run this in the first place. Military men are trained for war, and there's a reason why the president, although possessing the ultimate authority over the armed forces, remains a civilian. If the framers of the US Constitution wanted the military to be under civilian control, then who am I to argue?"

She considered it for a moment. There were many times since she'd realized that Andrew had been working for the CIA that she wished they could discuss things openly. But now, presented with such opportunity, she was overwhelmed.

"Listen," he said as he kneeled next to her and took her hands in his, "I need you there, and not just for your experience. Perhaps it's selfish of me to ask you such a thing, but I need you because I want to be able to tell you what decisions I must make. To ask your opinions, to bounce ideas. I would've never been able to build the company the way we did had you not been by my side the entire time, you know that."

She took the job, and the fact that Rovinsky, instead of fighting Andrew's suggestion tooth and nail, embraced it from the beginning, certainly made her feel more confident.

They sat in silence, drinking their coffee and watching the sun rising over Manhattan. The tops of the high-rises were colored in rose and gold and the air shimmered above the rooftops, making the buildings appear phantasmal, illusory.

"It's still warm," she said, pulling the lapels of her bathrobe higher, "but you can already smell fall in the air."

"Yes, you can."

"Do we need bodyguards?" she said, changing the subject. "I feel awful thinking about them sitting by our building all night in that van."

"Jim wanted to do it, and I don't want to argue with him over it."

"So, what's next?"

"Well, we need to establish the infrastructure first. Jim and I will be going to Southern California next week to look at some sites for the training facility."

"That makes sense," she said. "There's already a naval base in Coronado. If we are geographically close, we wouldn't have to reinvent the logistics for a lot of things."

"You see," he smiled at her, "that's why I wanted you there."

"Here's the thing, though." She put her cup on the table and fixed her eyes on him. "I've thought about this for a while, and it just makes sense to me."

"What is it?"

"We need to tell the president." She put up her hand, silencing his objection before he had a chance to respond. "We can't be hiding from *everybody*. Congress, sure, that makes perfect sense—they've been incapable of working together for God knows how many years. But we can't run a truly efficient organization if there's literally nobody in the government who we can turn to. The secrecy is great for a venture like this, but at some point, more secrecy stops translating into more efficiency. It's a classic case of diminishing returns."

"But the political risk for him would be enormous," Andrew objected. "And his party is in the minority. If the genie ever gets out of the bottle, he'll get impeached and convicted in five seconds. He'll never go for it. And what happens when he's not the president?"

"You're wrong," she said. "If this secret society's agenda is what we think it is—which is world domination—doesn't it pose a direct threat to the president? Think about it. The phrase 'the leader of the free world' is one of those corny things that everybody says and nobody cares about, but in this case, it actually matters. If you want to be in charge of something, say a company, and there happened to be a person who is already considered the leader—the company's CEO— doesn't it put you at odds with that person?"

"You might be right," he conceded, "but think about the ramifications. What if he doesn't agree with us? That would end the Unit before it ever began. We'll never have a second go at this."

"Well, we'll have to present a compelling case then. Besides," she shrugged and patted Andrew's hand, "whoever said saving the world was going to be easy, eh?"

September 2007
New York

"Hi, Helen."

The man was wearing a custom-made beige suit, a white shirt with a European-style spread collar unbuttoned at the top, and no tie. His smooth jet-black hair, dark eyes, and high cheekbones that betrayed his Asian heritage made him look like a famous actor on the set of a Wall Street drama. He sounded like someone who was born in the United States, but the way he articulated his consonants gave away the years he'd spent in the UK—first in a private school, and then as a business major at Oxford University.

"Hi, Vic." She smiled and planted a peck on his clean-shaven cheek.

They looked at each other for some time.

"Are you planning on coming in or you gonna stay in the doorway?"

"Sorry." He kicked off his shoes and followed her to the kitchen. "How are you? How was the trip? You should've called—I would've picked you up from the airport. I just flew back myself last night."

"Oh yeah? Where from?" She feigned interest. She'd known he was in Hong Kong for the last month.

"Hong Kong." He smiled his easy smile. "Had to check on a few things in that office."

She studied him for a few seconds. They'd been dating for two years now. Casually at first. She'd met him at her sister's fundraiser, of all places. She wasn't a regular at upscale things like that; she found them intimidating. Almost a thousand people crammed into a fancy restaurant leased for the night, tasting expensive wines, eating finger food and bidding on ridiculously overpriced items.

A cathedral-like ceiling made for horrible acoustics and the place was as loud as a nightclub. She found herself shouting every time somebody tried to have a conversation, and by the time the evening was drawing to a close she was so hoarse, she could barely talk.

To her annoyance, it also turned out that most people used the event for two reasons—one was to help the cause, but the other to network, to promote themselves and whatever service they provided. She guessed it was fair, getting something out of helping someone else, but it still made her uneasy. It was like taking money off a corpse. The dead didn't care, but it felt wrong anyway.

They were lawyers and doctors and business people, and most lost interest when she informed them that yes, she was just a programmer, and no, she didn't own a company. So, people either moved on or, in case of some single A-type banker bros, tried to score and then moved on as well, when it became painfully obvious that she wasn't interested.

She met Vic at the coat check when the fundraiser was nearly over, and she was reasonably sure she wasn't going to offend anyone by leaving. They arrived at the counter almost at the same time, him ahead of her by a fraction of a second, but he ushered her in front of him with a gesture that was almost old-fashioned and the *Go right ahead ma'am* with that sexy accent of his was the last nail in her pride's coffin.

He was the first serious boyfriend she'd ever had whose Social Security number she didn't know before he gave it to her of his own volition. In fact, he was the first serious boyfriend who she didn't research at all and took him at his word.

Vic was as sharp as they came but not overbearing, and Chen found it easy to be geeky with him. He was estranged from most of his family, but apparently, his biological father saw that his son was taken care of and had set up a trust fund that paid for Vic's education and then supported him for the first few years after college. The man seemed to be painfully aware of the fact that he had a leg up early on and worked harder than most people.

But this was going to be a test of their relationship, she decided. Perhaps she was making a crazy mistake by even considering telling Vic about her plan, but Chen needed someone to weigh in on the dangerous journey she was about to undertake. A small part of her wanted him to persuade her not to do anything in the first place.

"Sit down," she said in a tone that made him pay attention. His dark eyes watched her pacing the small kitchen back and forth, as if trying to read her mind.

"Are you breaking up with me?" he finally offered. He sounded calm, but there was an edge to his voice.

"No, no, no," Chen said, for the first time realizing that her prelude must have sounded like a clichéd break-up routine. "Not at all. Quite the opposite. When I tell you what I'm about to tell you, you might want to break up with me."

His face didn't betray any emotion, and he sat there, waiting for her to continue.

"I've lied to you," Chen continued, "about my trip. To be honest, I didn't really have to, but I was in a weird place. I was here the entire time, taking care of something. My sister's dead."

"What? Mary's dead?" He stood up and took her shoulders in his hands. "How did that happen? When?"

She told him the chain of events, starting from the call she received from the detective and the subsequent search that led her to believe in Mary's murder. She could see the number of questions Vic wanted to ask was multiplying, but he kept quiet and let her finish the story.

"This is..." he paused, looking for words, "a lot to process."

"Yep."

"So, you cannot use the evidence you've found because you got it illegally?"

"That's correct."

"And that lady you've met was the one who got it for you? How do you know you can trust her?"

"She didn't get it for me," Chen said, tensing up. "I hacked into Guardian's servers myself. She helped, but I did all the work."

"I thought you worked for a data mining company. I never once took you for a black hat. Did you hack me too?"

His tone was light, but his eyes said otherwise.

"I'm not a black hat," she said. "Those are the guys who cause mayhem for fun or to steal. Identities, money. They usually call people like me gray hats, but that's the term the general public uses, not the actual hackers. Most hackers are driven by the desire to understand how systems work."

"And then what?"

"Some use it for good, some not so much." She shrugged. "Just like everybody else."

"So, what is exactly your plan? You said you cannot take it to the police. Then what? Call the media? Send it to a newspaper?"

"No," she said and looked him in the eye. "I want revenge. I want to spoil this guy's party. Humiliate him. Deny him what he shouldn't have asked for in the first place."

"But how? I don't understand."

"I'm going to hack the New York Stock Exchange, manipulate the prices of both companies, and ruin any chance he has of a takeover. They'll know it was artificially induced, but it'll bring so much news and scrutiny they will never be able to accomplish it."

"You think you can hack the Exchange?" He looked at her as if seeing her for the first time. "I'm not sure if I'm impressed or terrified. *The* New York Stock Exchange?"

She pondered the question for a minute.

"I think I can," she finally said, "but I will need some help."

1 8

September 2007
New York

"Okay." Vic grabbed a chair, turned it around and straddled it. "Walk me through it. From a layman's perspective. Something I can actually understand."

"Are you sure?"

"I have no idea," he said and rested his elbows on the back of the chair. "Call it a simple curiosity for now. You don't often hear that somebody wants to hack the stock exchange."

Chen studied him for a moment.

"Okay," she finally said. "Let's start with the basics. Most corporate infrastructures, if not all of them, are built like medieval castles. A wide moat, tall stone walls, fortified gated entries, archers at every window checking for trespassers and so on. There's something valuable in the castle and there're mechanisms in place to protect the goods. To make it even more challenging, inside of some networks, especially as important as the stock exchange, it is common to find other mini castles, called sub-domains, that control access to more critical elements of the infrastructure."

"So, in that case, you have to break in more than once?" Vic asked.

"Not quite, but that's a good question," she pointed at him, "and this is why this would never work like you see it in the movies. To get into those sub-domains, you would use what they call a jump box."

"Like a shortcut?"

"Not exactly. It's an internal hardened system with some form of remote access, also not easy to get a hold of. They would have some tight access-control rules and a limited number of trusted users who can access those systems."

"I'm not sure I follow."

"Think of them as messengers who are allowed on the castle's grounds. These systems have a dual network card—one that is connected to the usual corporate network and another to the protected network. To continue our castle analogy—you don't want to open the main gates every time somebody comes to the castle with a simple question. You want to have a system that allows you to communicate with the inner tower without jeopardizing security."

Chen paused for a minute, collecting her thoughts.

"Of course," she continued, "in a place like the exchange, there will be multiple secure sub-domains and jump boxes, like onion layers. Whoever is allowed to use them will have to jump and log in a few times before they can even reach the critical core network."

"Perhaps it's me," Vic said with an expression she couldn't interpret, "but so far all I've heard is why it would be impossible to do the hack."

"Difficult," she said, "but not impossible. The path of least resistance is to identify those trusted individuals, impersonate them and follow their paths. There are many penetration testing tools designed for a task like that."

"But how do we find them, though?"

"Well, surprisingly, I've found those users are the worst security offenders. There's even a term—*security fatigue*—for people who are dealing with complex security day in and day out. People make mistakes. Sometimes they store passwords in plain-text files. Sometimes they save links that have session tokens to favorites tab in the browser, config files with credentials, SSH private keys without restrictions—you name it. We would just need to find the person who made that mistake."

"Hang on," Vic said, extending his hand out like a stop sign. "Let's say you're even able to find such a person, which, by the way, sounds like a long shot. I'm no expert, but I'm sure if this happens and you hack the system, the feds will be all over this. And the feds can afford the best forensic tools. They will eventually find you. Isn't it easier to use the news cycle? Plant some fake news that would affect both companies?"

"I thought about it," she said, "but a fake news campaign would work much better if we were targeting only one company, not two. There're way too many variables, and the effect might be too fleeting to make a material impact. But as far as hiding tracks—it's a complicated issue. They could find anything with enough time and effort but whether it becomes a concern for me is another story. If they dig deep enough, they'll find the files that I planted and the changes that I made, but as long as they can't trace them to me, I don't particularly care. It just would mean we might not be able to do that again."

"Why did you say you needed help?"

"There might be an easier way to do this," she said. "There was a rumor about a year ago that when IBM was hacked, someone lifted the specs for traders' handhelds."

"What are those?"

"It's a small computer that the floor brokers use. You might've seen them on TV. A small, black, rugged-looking rectangular box. They produce only a limited number of them, custom hardware internals and special adaptors for the high-speed wireless within the exchange floor. Those are impossible to hack. They have what's called a trusted protection module inside, a tamper-proof key storage for sensitive crypto operations. You won't break those in a million years even if you had a supercomputer."

"But you said someone stole the specs?"

"Well, officially, they weren't stolen," she said, "but I know for a fact that they were. And if I had them, I'm certain I could get into the network."

"How do you know it was?"

"I've seen a part of it. Whoever stole it was fishing for buyers, but it was like trying to sell a highjacked space shuttle. It's surely worth a lot of money, but who the hell is going to buy it?"

"And do you know who that person was?"

"No," she shrugged almost apologetically, "but I know how to find him. I thought about reporting him to the feds at the time but didn't do it in the end. Out of solidarity, I guess. He—at least, I'm reasonably certain it's a *he*—lives right here in New York. Chinatown, to be exact."

"So, let's say we find him," Vic said. "Then what? Ask him nicely?"

"Pretty much," Chen said. "And if that doesn't work, I'd have to break into his place and try to hack him from the inside. I don't think I'd be able to hack him remotely."

They sat in silence for a few a minutes, digesting what was said.

"I don't like this," Vic said. "Think about it. He's not going to help you if we contact him anonymously. I mean—why would he? He would need some kind of incentive, which I'm guessing you don't have. And if you would want to make an appeal to his human side and tell him the entire story of why you need this, you would put your entire life at risk. He'll know your identity. You'll be at his mercy and would have to hope for the best that he doesn't sell you to the feds or worse, blackmail you for the rest of your life."

"I understand that. But what are my options? I don't think I can steal it from him in time. If I had a month or two to prepare, then maybe, but I'm afraid it'll be too late, and the merger will go through. But I can't sit on my hands and do nothing. This is my only shot."

"Listen," he said and looked up at her with an expression she'd never seen before, "is there any chance I can talk you out of this?"

"No." She shook her head and looked at him with stubborn determination. "I have to do this. I have to talk to that guy."

"Okay then. But I have a better idea," Vic said, standing up. "Tell me how to find him."

19

September 2007
Washington, DC

The suite, as all other rooms in the hotel, presented sweeping views of the Potomac River and historic Georgetown neighborhood. The Ritz-Carlton Georgetown wasn't the closest hotel to the White House. If someone were to set out on foot to the most well-known address in the country, it would take them at least forty minutes as they would have to go north first, across the canal and then turn west onto M Street and then merge on Pennsylvania Avenue.

But what it lacked in proximity, the hotel made up in privacy as it was well known for an exceptionally high standard of discretion to all of its guests. From behind the wide panels of bulletproof glass, that was installed to entice important diplomatic guests and dignitaries, Audrey Hunt looked on as the setting sun shone through the trees of Theodore Roosevelt Island. She watched the river make a gentle turn around the island, past the white rectangle of the John F. Kennedy Center for the Performing Arts and under the Roosevelt Bridge.

It was too early for the leaves to start changing from green to red and gold, but perhaps because the sun was so low, Audrey felt as if the autumn was already here. Usually, this time of the year brought her some gentle sadness. She thought that fall was nature's way to remind humans of their mortality. To show them that everything was bound to end, no matter how vigorously they tried to fight the passage of time.

But now, as she watched the river running its course, she felt strangely alive. Fall wasn't the harbinger of death and winter wasn't the end of things. It was a time of cleansing, a rebirth, after which the strongest would emerge like a butterfly from the chrysalis toward the brightly shining summer sun.

They'd arrived at the hotel the night before, and an hour after they checked in, Jim Rovinsky knocked on the door. They had been brainstorming the upcoming meeting with the president for the entire week, and yet they ended up discussing it into the wee hours in the morning, drinking coffee after coffee and trying to cover every angle, every rebuttal, every possibility.

Now, while the two men were trying to convince the most powerful person in the world that there was a global conspiracy—a threat not just to the presidency, or even to their country, but to the world order—she was left with the hardest task of them all—waiting for the result.

Audrey watched as a white split sternwheeler, its paddles foaming the dark waters behind it, chugged past the island. The double-decker boat looked as if it was transported from the late 1800s. The irony didn't escape her. A trailblazer her entire life, an equal partner in all family endeavors, and a fearless emissary of her nonprofit that built schools and hospitals in some of the most dangerous places on Earth, now she was forced to be playing the role of an obedient wife. She should be wearing a puffy dress and a modest bonnet, she mused. Waiting for someone else to make a decision.

She wondered what was going to happen if the president were to say no. Were they supposed to go back to their ordinary lives and pretend that nothing else had happened? Could they do anything? Or were they bound to watch from the sidelines as the drama unfolded before their eyes? A small part of her still didn't quite grasp the magnitude of the task they were about to undertake.

Her imagination conjured up the images of the president throwing her husband and Rovinsky out of their meeting after listening to the tale of global conspiracy that was about to take over the world. But, of course, this wasn't the first time somebody had an aspiration to bring the world to its knees, bend it to their will, and enjoy the fruits of other people's labor.

It had happened many times before: the Roman Empire, the Mongols, the British Empire, Nazi Germany. In a strange way, she realized, arguing that nothing was about to happen right now was not unlike sitting in a sunlit hotel in Poland on the eve of the German invasion, drinking hot linden tea and enjoying a piece of *kolach,* while explaining to your peers why there was *absolutely* not going to be another world war.

The only true difference this time was the fact that the aggressor didn't have a familiar and instantly recognizable face. It didn't fly banners with bold red colors and a creeping black spider of a swastika. Instead, it was a faceless hydra with multiple tentacles slithering their way into the very fabric of modern society. If anything, that made it only more dangerous.

She heard a key swipe on the door lock and turned around in time to see Andrew Hunt walk into the room. There were dark circles around his eyes, but there was a smile on his lips.

"He said yes," he announced. He walked across the plush rug and collapsed on a sofa, not bothering to take off his shoes. "We're getting a fifty-million-dollar budget, at least for now, some key personnel shuffled around for the Unit to use, and an old installation out in California for a temporary training facility."

"You know, it's a shame," she said.

"I have to admit," he said, a puzzled expression on his face, "this is not the reaction I expected. Are you having second thoughts?"

"No." She shook her head and sat next to him. "Not at all. This is obviously great news. And I'm going to tell you that I am not going to be bringing coffee to your office. I want to be included in every decision."

"I never intended to have you bringing me coffee." He smiled, throwing his hands in the air in a defensive gesture.

"But what I was trying to say was that it's a shame that this needs to be done at all. We should be living in a golden age right now. No wars, no diseases, no poverty. Instead," she made a sweeping gesture with her hand, "we are in this giant mess."

"What do you mean by golden age?"

"The US military budget this year is almost seven hundred billion dollars, that's what I mean. And then you have other countries doing the same thing on a smaller scale. Imagine what you could do if you spent this much money *every year* on things like renewable energy and disease research. We could conquer the deadliest diseases within a decade and solve the energy crisis for the entire world at the same time."

"That's my dreamer." He pulled her into a bear hug and planted a kiss on her lips.

"And kids." She gently pushed him away. "Why are there kids like Dalmar, who have to grow up surrounded by poverty and violence and so much despair? No adult should experience what that kid has already seen in his short life. They should be able to experience life to the fullest, surrounded by happy peers instead of grimy, angry men carrying automatic weapons."

"I know," he said, "but I'm afraid it's human nature. Tribalism is part of our DNA, our internal survival mechanism. Us versus them."

"Bullshit," she said. "We don't live in lean-tos anymore, where you need to ride your horse for two hours to get to the next village. We are way past the point where this kind of mentality is necessary or even useful. You can fly around the world on a commercial airplane in a couple of days."

"So why do you think we are who we are?"

"Greed. That's the only explanation I have," Audrey said, "and this is the biggest conspiracy of them all because it has so many faces. The military industrial complex, the oil companies, big pharma. It all comes down to a bunch of people concerned with lining their own pockets above everything else."

"Well, if that's the case," he said, "then we're doomed. You can defeat even the most powerful enemy if you know who they are. But how do you defeat greed? It's like fighting the mythical hydra when every time you cut one of its heads off, it grows two more."

"I don't know yet," she said, "but this whole experience was a real eye-opener for me. It made me think—what if we are not ambitious enough?"

"How so?"

"Think about what we are doing here and why our organization is being established. There's an actual conspiracy out there to take over the world. That's the craziest thing I've ever heard, but now somehow it makes total sense. And if someone's convinced they can accomplish that, obviously for all the wrong reasons in this case, perhaps it's actually possible."

"I'm not sure I understand what you're saying here," he said.

"I'm saying, we need a conspiracy of our own. I'm not sure how to do it yet, but if we get to create this agency, we can do more than battle the villains. We can change the world."

20

September 2007
New York

*I*t was past ten in the evening when Chen's doorbell rang. She logged out of her laptop, walked to the hallway, and peered through the peephole. A distorted image of Vic waved to her through the curved glass of the lens.

"Hey." She opened the door and stepped back, letting him in. "I didn't expect you tonight."

"Is there a naked man holding on for his dear life on the outside of your bedroom window?" His tone was light, but his eyes were not smiling.

"Two of them, in fact. Don't you know cheating on boyfriends with one man is so twentieth century?" she said, studying his face. "Is everything all right? You seem on edge. What are you doing here?"

He seemed to hesitate for a few seconds, his dark eyes scanning her up and down.

"Vic?"

"I came here to ask if you still want to find that hacker fellow," he finally said. "I might have a lead."

"Of course I do," she said. "You said you might know someone who can help. Why are you acting so weird?"

"Get dressed, then. I need you to come with me."

"You've found him?"

"Please," he pleaded. "Don't ask me questions now. Let's go."

"You're weirding me out," she said, putting a pair of sneakers on, "but okay."

They went down the stairs and through the front door. A black stretch limo with tinted windows was parked by the hydrant next to the house, gleaming in the light drizzle. The engine was running, and Chen could see the silhouette of the driver behind the wheel. Vic went ahead and opened the door for her.

"What the hell?" She stopped and looked at him quizzically. "A limo?"

"Get in."

She hesitated for a moment and then climbed inside the long vehicle. Vic climbed in after her. The driver revved the engine and the locks on the doors engaged. A glass partition between the passengers and the driver rolled down, revealing a middle-aged Chinese driver. He threw something soft on Chen's knees.

"Good evening, miss," the driver said. His accent was a weird mix of a first-generation Chinese immigrant sprinkled with hard Brooklyn consonants.

He probably came to the States as a youth, she thought. Old enough not to lose his accent completely, but young enough to assimilate.

"I apologize for the inconvenience," the man continued, "but you have to put this on. Please."

She puzzled over the object for a few seconds. It looked like an oversized hat and she turned it this way and that, trying to understand what it was. Then it struck her.

"You're shitting me." She grabbed the door handle. "Open the door. Right fucking now."

"Helen, wait." Vic grabbed her hand, turning her to face him. "I didn't want to do it. At all. But you said you needed that guy and there was nothing that was going to change your mind. I'm trying to help. Just do it. Please."

"And then a few days later, my dead body will turn up somewhere downstream in the Hudson River?"

"No. Nothing like that. Please," he said. "I've broken so many rules to find him. At this point, it would be a terrible waste not to see this through. C'mon."

She looked at him for a few seconds and then pulled the hood over her head without a word. Then she leaned back and defiantly crossed her arms. The car started to move.

It was a strange experience to be driven in the back of a limo with a dark hood over the head. After a minute or two, when her eyes adapted to the darkness, she realized that she could still see the ghostly silhouettes outside as the soft, diffused light penetrated the black fabric. She could make out the outlines of the buildings lit up in the night, the bright multicolored traffic lights, and big glowing islands of street lamp posts. Adrenaline coursed through her veins, heightening her senses. Chen could hear the sound of Vic's breathing, the crunching sound of gravel under the heavy car's tires, the swooshing of the windshield wipers.

She wasn't truly scared, at least not yet. But it was ironic, she thought, that the first time she hadn't hacked her boyfriend to make sure there was no weird shit in his closet, he'd show up with a limo with an empty-eyed driver and put a hood over her head.

After what she thought was thirty or thirty-five minutes of driving, the limo slowed down to a crawl and then came to a full stop. She heard the door open and Vic exited the car.

"Can I take this off now?" she asked without too much effort to hide her irritation.

"No ma'am, I'm sorry. Not yet," she heard the driver say.

A strong arm took her elbow and guided her out of the car. The rain was coming down harder now and the cold drops were softly drumming on the top of her hood. She shivered as biting wind found its way under her blouse and hugged herself, trying to keep warm.

Chen let them guide her on an uneven path to some kind of structure and then she was inside a building and out of the rain. Somebody pulled the hood off her head, and she squinted against the bright light.

She was standing inside of a small warehouse next to the limo driver. There was a row of garage doors on her left, a few smaller offices on her right, and a large empty area in between with regularly spaced spotlights illuminating the room. A low rumble of machinery working somewhere nearby filled up the air.

"Where is Vic?" she demanded. "I want to see him."

"Please follow me," the driver said, ignoring her request. "It's this way."

He started off toward one of the garage doors, and after a moment she followed after him.

"Before I'm allowed to let you in," the driver said, his tone almost apologetic, "I was instructed to ask you one more time if you were firm on your intention to proceed."

"I'm getting a little sick of these games," she said. "Yes, I want to proceed. It's not my thing to be driven in black limos with a hood over my head for no reason at all."

"As you wish." The driver bowed and started walking away. "I will open the door for you in a minute, and once you go in, I will close it behind you. There will be another door inside that you will have to go through. The light is configured to turn on when you close it."

"Whatever," she said angrily. "Let's get this over with."

The man opened one of the office doors with a keycard and disappeared inside. After a few seconds, the metal door in front of her rolled up, opening up a dark, cavernous space. Chen stepped in, and the gate slowly rolled back down, leaving her in pitch black.

Her heart started to race and her adrenaline spiked up again. This was the end of her relationship with Vic, she realized. There was no way to go back to normality after this. Whatever explanation there was for her ride in the limo and the secrecy, there couldn't be anything good about it.

Vic must've employed illegal aliens, she reflected, hence the machinery hum somewhere inside of the building. Probably even participated in smuggling them into the country. That would explain his frequent trips to Hong Kong and mainland China. Her mind raced. She'd always felt he stayed there for longer than necessary for a regular business trip, but never bothered to press him on it.

The lights turned on, blinding her for a moment. When her eyes grew accustomed to the light, she saw a small metal door at the end of the empty space. Uncertain, she took a few steps and pulled on the door. A loud creaking noise startled her, but not as much as the horrible stench that hit her like a punch to the gut. As in a nightmare —terrified, but not able to stop herself—she took a step inside the room and closed the door behind her.

A naked man was tied to a rough wooden table, his arms and legs spread so hard it made his entire body taut with tension, like a thread on the bow of a cello. As under a spell, Chen made two more steps and stopped next to the table, not able to look away. The man turned his head to her, revealing an empty socket in place of one of his eyes and missing skin on half of his face.

"Please," he whispered. "I'll tell you anything you want to know."

21

September 2007
New York

Jill Cooper checked her watch for the third time. The guard was supposed to leave more than twenty minutes ago, which should have given her the opportunity to enter the building. Yet the rugged-looking rent-a-cop was still standing in front of the squat four-story structure and showed no signs that he would be departing any time soon.

It should have been an easy job. The ugly red-brick building with two gated entrances in the front and an attached garage on the side had no internal surveillance and the streets leading to the address were devoid of traffic cameras or any other video equipment. The three guards watched the place in eight-hour shifts, right outside the main entrance, but the one with the graveyard shift always left the place for a few minutes to repark his old Subaru closer to the building.

She put down the pair of Night Owl Pro infrared binoculars and reclined in her car seat. It didn't matter if he left now. At some point, sooner or later, he'd have to take a leak, and that was going to be her cue. For now, all she could do was wait.

It was a puzzling mark. The man Jill Cooper was hired to eliminate wasn't a hot-shot CEO of a big company, or a star acquisition attorney making big waves in deep corporate waters. He was an owner of a small specialty welding business that operated out of two locations, one in the southern Bronx and one in Long Island. The only anomaly she spotted during her routine research was that the company had a few dozen patents on welding techniques, but Cooper wasn't able to find anything that would suggest they were of any significant value.

The man traveled between the two shops most of the days, but every Friday night he stayed in the Bronx location overnight, catching up on some paperwork. There was a small apartment on the top floor of the building and Cooper was certain that's where she would find her target at this hour.

A small bright light of a match illuminated the guard's face as he lit up a cigarette and a moment later, he headed away from the door.

"Finally," Cooper said out loud. She slid out of her Toyota Camry and started walking toward the building, staying away from the street lights. By the time she got to the front door, the guard was nowhere to be seen. She glanced around and, not seeing anyone in a two-block radius, Cooper squatted by the lock and took out her tools.

A simple deadbolt lock gave up in less than a minute, and Cooper stepped into the dimly lit workshop and closed the door behind. The place looked neat and well organized. There was a row of machines by the windows facing the street, a line of red lights silently blinking on top of each one. There was another row of large rectangular desks situated by the inner wall. She started to move toward the stairs when something gleaming on top of the desk in the farthest corner caught her eye.

Cooper hesitated for a moment. She shouldn't be wasting any time here on the main floor, exposed if anyone was to walk in. Her job was to get in, take care of business, and walk out before anyone ever knew something was wrong. But there was something unnatural in the way the light reflected off the object on the dimly lit desk.

Curiosity killed the cat, she thought, crossing the open space as quickly as she could without making any noise.

The polished wooden surface of the desk was covered by neatly arranged piles of drawings pressed by horseshoe-shaped paperweights. A few sharp HB2 pencils were lined up next to a protractor and an expensive-looking draftsman's compass. But that's not what attracted her attention.

The easiest way to describe the object that was casually left next to a pile of blueprints was to call it a prosthetic arm. But as Cooper looked at it gleaming in the low light as if it were made of liquid mercury, she instantly knew it was no mere artificial limb. It ended at the elbow joint with a cluster of multicolored wires, and there was a cutout at the wrist that exposed some gears inside of the limb that were made from similar but darker metal.

When Cooper leaned closer to take a look, she could make out thin geometric lines punctuated by tiny square dots under the surface of the metal. It looked like a computer board.

She examined the arm for a few seconds. The illusion of liquid metal was so strong that she finally gave in to the temptation and touched the surface with the tip of her index finger. The metal was cold and felt hard as a diamond. Somehow, Cooper was sure that if she were to try to scratch it with a knife, the blade would bounce off the strange metal without leaving a mark.

"Fascinating, isn't it?"

Cooper heard a voice behind her and spun on her heels, the heft of the Glock 19 miraculously migrating from the small of her back to her hands.

The man in his mid-sixties was standing in the front of the room by the stairs. He wore a pair of worn-out jeans, a simple flannel shirt, and a pair of workman boots. His dark face was hard and creased in a way people's faces get creased when they spend a lot of their life doing some hard, physical work. The man didn't seem to be afraid of her, or the fact that she was pointing a weapon right at his face.

"It's as hard as a diamond but becomes pliable when you run a small electric current through it. You can make it more flexible than a real hand without compromising its integrity."

Cooper didn't answer and moved closer to the man instead. The sights of her gun remained trained on his face the entire time.

"Is this why you are here? To steal the prototype?"

"I'm here for you," she answered and pointed with the barrel of the Glock toward the stairs. "Let's go back up."

"I see." The man didn't move an inch, his impression unreadable. "You're here to kill me. That means your employer miscalculated a great deal."

"Let's go."

"You see," the man continued, ignoring her request, "while our shop does some exceptionally good welding, I don't think that's the reason you're here. There's no life-or-death competition between welding shops. The only logical conclusion I can draw is that you're here because of this." He pointed at the prosthetic with his chin.

"I'm going to shoot you right here," Cooper said, getting in the old man's face, "if you don't start moving right this second."

"It doesn't matter where you shoot me," he said, unperturbed, "here, upstairs, or anywhere on the street. Unless you know how to create this alloy, and I'm going to go out on a limb here, pun fully intended, and assume that you don't, you're screwed."

"Move."

"You know I'm right," the man said stubbornly. "Think about it this way—you got lucky because you saw it before you had a chance to kill me. I'd say you're still a step ahead, but you have to listen to me if you want to stay there."

She looked at him for a few seconds, weighing her options. What he was saying made sense. *It had to be the damned prosthetic,* she thought. There couldn't be any other reason why she was here. But if he was telling the truth, killing him was the opposite of what her employer would have wanted.

If he were her first target provided by her new boss, this conversation would have been long over, and she'd be at least a couple of miles away from his cooling body. But having worked for the same employer on a few jobs now, she pieced together at least in broad strokes that their agenda was domination and acquisition of their rivals, not annihilation and total wipeout.

She had to make a decision and quick before the night guard found a perfect parking spot and returned to his post. Cooper looked at the man standing in front of her and holstered the gun.

"I'm going to offer it to you only once," she finally said. "If you want to live, you're going to have to come with me."

2 2

September 2007
Camp Unit, California

ndrew Hunt looked through the one-way glass. The man he was about to interview was sitting in an empty room behind a desk. The place looked like an interrogation room from a cop drama —a square, empty space with a sturdy, cheap-looking aluminum desk, and two chairs. The only things missing to complete the set were a bright lamp to shine into the suspect's face and a built-in hook for a pair of handcuffs.

The guy didn't look anything special, Hunt decided. He seemed to be in his late thirties, or early forties. Fit, but more in a wiry rather than in-your-face bodybuilding kind of way. He was on the short side too, five eight at most, with a balding head and a plain, pockmarked face.

"Every time I see guys like that, I feel cheated by Sean Connery and Pierce Brosnan," Hunt said. "I still haven't met a spy-looking spy."

"If they looked like James Bond, it would defeat the purpose, wouldn't it?" Rovinsky said. "You want someone who blends in, not someone who stands out."

"So, you're saying he's one of the best."

"No," Rovinsky disagreed, "that's not what I said at all. I said he was *the* best. He's been in all the hot zones that we cared to admit we were in, and pretty much every place where we were not supposed to be but were there anyway. We *need* this guy. Don't think for a moment that you're interviewing him. He'll be interviewing you, my friend."

"No pressure then."

"None at all." Rovinsky patted him on the shoulder. "Go get him, tiger."

When Hunt entered the room, the man stood up and walked out from behind the desk to shake his hand. His posture was straight, but relaxed, and the movements were graceful and soft like a cat's.

"Rick Porter," the man said. "It's a pleasure."

"Andrew Hunt."

Porter's handshake was firm, but not excessively strong, and there was no discomfort in his calm brown eyes looking up at Hunt's six-foot-five frame that he was accustomed to seeing in people significantly shorter than him.

"Rovinsky speaks very highly of you," he said, taking a seat and gesturing to Porter to do the same. "He went as far as saying that you'd be interviewing me, not the other way around."

"Not at all, sir," Porter said, his expression neutral. "It's an honor to be considered."

"Appreciate you saying that. I'm sure you've read the docs, so you're aware we'll need at least a couple of dozen operators within the next two years. I'd like to know your thoughts on the selection process, if you don't mind."

"If we want to keep it under wraps and get those numbers, I'd suggest starting with one hundred men," Porter said without missing a beat. "SEALs have about a ten percent graduation rate, so I'd say we should aim for the same."

"Even though a lot of them will be coming from elite units, to begin with?"

"Yes, sir. It's never about the physical ability alone. The vast majority of guys who start BUD/S training are also capable of finishing it, but not everybody does. And here you have a different dimension thrown in the mix—you want them to be operators *and* intelligence officers at the same time. And you'd need them to be able to switch back and forth. Not everybody is capable of being both."

"That's a fair point. What else?"

"It will be important to do the first group right," Porter said. "Traditions are valuable. Being the first class is going to give them something to brag about later on, but I wouldn't want them to feel like guinea pigs during the course."

"What would you suggest?"

"I'd say we keep it secret until graduation," Porter said. "Tell them it's class number five or six, so they feel they are a part of the community. We can give those who graduate the bragging rights of being the first, later."

"You don't think they'll be able to tell?"

"Not if we play it right." He paused. "And if somebody does figure it out, they deserve extra points, in my book."

"Interesting. What else?"

"I know the project is going to be on a need-to-know basis, but I'd suggest we make friends with the ISCD. Not necessarily tell them everything about who we are and what we do, but some kind of relationship with them wouldn't hurt."

"ISCD? I've never heard of them," Hunt said.

"International Serious Crimes Directorate. They're loosely associated with Interpol, with headquarters in Paris. They are in a similar business—investigation of political crimes. Coups, kidnappings of government officials, corruption, political assassinations and so on."

"That sounds right up our alley."

"They don't have a whole lot of resources for the actual ops, so they do more of intelligence gathering and research than anything else. They punt the action to other law enforcement divisions."

"You think we could leverage them?"

"Absolutely. They're already working with some of the CIA groups and understand the need for compartmentalization." Porter shrugged.

"They've been doing it for a long time. They can save us a lot of legwork."

"Have you worked with the ISCD yourself?"

"Yes, on more than one occasion. I was on a mission in Bogota once that would've gone south if not for them. It turned out that we had bad intel, but those guys saved the day."

"All right. You can reach out to your contacts and establish a link, but I'd like to be in the loop."

"Roger that."

"One more thing," Andrew said. "We aren't in a position to wait for everybody to graduate. We'd need a small team almost right away. Is it going to be a problem for the ongoing class? We'd have to have an explanation for people coming in and out."

"That happens on the Farm all the time. Part of the training, actually, to get out and test the skills," Porter said. "This is not BUD/S. I'd say that wouldn't be a problem at all. I'll put together a four-person team for you ASAP."

"That would be great," Hunt said and then paused for a second. "Can I recommend someone? The name's Michael Connelly. He was instrumental in my wife's rescue operation in Kenya. Seemed like an outstanding soldier."

"Only if he fits," Porter replied at once. And then added, after a slight pause, "All due respect."

"I wouldn't expect anything different."

The interview went on for almost two hours, and by the end of it, Andrew Hunt was sure of one thing—Rick Porter was worth his weight in gold.

"I think he's coming on board," he told Rovinsky when they reunited in what would become a chow hall to snack on cold pizza they'd brought with them.

"Good," Rovinsky said, opening the box and putting slices on paper plates. "I never doubted he would. He's a good guy and he can teach, which is a rare quality."

"I have to say," Hunt said, "I'm still struggling with the *why* you thought I'd be the right choice to run the organization. Why not someone like Porter? Or yourself? I've never even served."

"You gotta stop doing that," Rovinsky said with his mouth full. "Sorry, I'm starving. Tons of people, including station chiefs *and* agency directors, never served. Nobody gets training before they become presidents, either."

"Presidents get elected," Hunt interjected.

"They do, sure. But presidents are salespeople first; everything else is secondary. You sell the town, you get to be the mayor. Sell enough folks in the country, and you get to be the president. But these jobs, the way I see it," he licked tomato sauce off his fingers, "you need to have what they used to call *the right stuff* back in the day. The straightest of arrows. That is not a trick you can learn, not something you can acquire with enough practice."

"Is that so?"

"I think so." Rovinsky threw the last piece of pizza in his mouth and got up. "You either have it, or you don't, and you do. And for what it's worth—the president thought you did too. Otherwise, we wouldn't even be here."

23

September 2007
New York

The sound of the ringing phone that lay on the stone floor, just outside of the shower glass, brought Chen out of the stupor. She looked around in confusion. She couldn't remember how she got home or how long she'd been sitting fully clothed on the floor under the warm running water. At least it looked like when she arrived there, she was aware of herself enough to take out her wallet and the phone before she got in the shower.

Chen slowly got up, stretching her sore limbs, took off her sneakers, undressed, and dumped the wet pile of clothes in the corner. Then she stood there for a few moments, letting the water pour over her head and run down her body. An image of a mutilated face with an empty eye socket flashed in her mind, and she doubled over and fell to her knees as she sprayed the contents of her stomach over the shower panel and the bathroom wall.

Chen stayed down, waiting for the spasms to stop, and then turned the water as cold as she could bear. After a few minutes, she was shivering uncontrollably, but at least her stomach backed away from her throat. After a while she got out of the shower, wrapped herself in a warm towel and shuffled to the kitchen, taking her cell phone with her. There was an empty voicemail from a blocked number, which was the preferred method of the Department of Defense telling their contractors to call back. Chen stared at the phone for a second, deciding if she wanted to be bothered, and then dialed the memorized number.

"Please enter your authentication code," the automated message prompted and Chen typed a ten-digit password they had given her for the assignment.

"Your contract has been discontinued. Thank you for your services. Good-bye," the automated female voice informed her, and the call terminated a second later.

"What the hell," Chen murmured and then dialed Hiroko's number.

"Do you know what time it is?" the woman said, as the call connected.

"Um, no," Chen said and pulled her phone away from her ear to look at the clock. "Shit. I didn't realize it's four in the morning. I'm sorry. I can call you later. What day is it?"

"It's Thursday, obviously, and I wasn't sleeping, so it's okay," Hiroko replied. "Is everything all right?"

"Thursday? No." Chen thought about it for a moment. "Nothing is all right. First of all, the DOD dumped me from the project. And I got the info that should help us do what we decided to do."

"That bit sounds like good news."

"It would be," Chen said, "if not for the part that it came from a naked guy tied to a table with half of his face missing."

"Hang up the phone," Hiroko said with steel in her voice. "Go make some coffee. I'll be over in thirty minutes."

Helen was on her second cup of coffee, spiked with a fifteen-year-old El Dorado Special Reserve for good measure, when Hiroko showed up at her doorstep. The woman marched past her to the kitchen, helped herself to a cup of coffee and took a seat at the table.

"So?"

"Want some rum in that coffee?" Chen asked.

"No," the woman said, "but I do want to hear the story."

"There's not much to the DOD story," Chen began. "They left me a message saying that I was fired. The other story, though—"

Hiroko listened to the tale of Chen's blindfolded trip to the unknown warehouse and the consequent visit of the chamber of horrors that she'd discovered there. The woman's face remained unreadable the entire time, and her eyes studied Chen as if trying to decipher if she were telling the truth.

"Do you have any pictures of him?" she asked when Chen finished the story.

"Good grief, of course not. Why would I—"

"Not the naked dude," the woman interrupted her. "Your boyfriend."

"Um, sure." Chen looked around, then left the kitchen and came back a moment later with a faded Polaroid. She and Vic could be seen hugging on the pier in front of a three-masted sailboat in the background.

"Some kid took it by Pier 11. We took a boat around Manhattan there once like a pair of tourists." She smiled at the memory and then shivered. "The first guy I've ever dated whose drawers I didn't turn inside out before getting serious. Jesus."

"This," the woman pointed to the man in the picture, "is your boyfriend?"

"Yes."

Hiroko threw her head back and let out a hearty laugh, which unnerved Helen even more. She'd never seen the calm and measured woman laugh this way before.

"Victor Ye Junior was your boyfriend," the woman said, looking at Chen. "Helen, you must be the dumbest smart person I've ever met."

"Stop this." Chen raised her voice. "I just came back from the place where I saw a naked guy who was skinned alive. Then I apparently slept under a running shower for almost twenty-four hours with my clothes on. I'm not in a fucking mood to play games. Who is Vic?"

"He's the estranged, well—" Hiroko stopped herself. "I guess not that estranged. He is the son of Victor Ye, the mobster in charge of the

Red Dragon, the most powerful Chinese gang outside of mainland China. Or as the mobsters call him, the *Master* of the gang. They do all the usual mobster stuff—money laundering, racketeering, and so on. But their primary business is high-quality street drugs. They are giving the Colombians quite a run for their money. And they also got a reputation of skinning people who crossed them, which, judging by your story, is warranted."

"Jesus," Chen buried her head in her hands, "what the fuck am I supposed to do now? I guess I should disappear for a while."

"I don't think you're in any danger right now," Hiroko said. "They wouldn't let you out of there alive if they considered you a threat. They probably figured what you saw would persuade you to keep quiet."

"They figured it right." Helen looked up. "It would be suicide."

"If anything, I might be in danger," the petite woman added. "For all we know, your house is being watched. But for what it's worth, I think they won't touch you or anyone you're with unless you start making noise."

"Wait." Chen stood up and started pacing back and forth. "Tell me if I'm going crazy here, but don't you think it's weird that first I get whisked away to see a horror show and then in the middle of the night, less than twenty-four hours later, I get canned by the DOD? What if it's not a coincidence?"

"Yeah," Hiroko said, "I'd say you're going crazy. One hundred percent."

"I don't even know if the DOD has a full grasp of what's going on," Helen insisted, ignoring the woman. "Otherwise, why the secrecy? They want us to find the hacker, but won't even give us the names of people who had access to their shit? And someone stole something, but we can't know what? I mean—fifteen hundred computers get hacked and I only communicated with three dudes during my entire stint there. They write a press release, but then never actually release it. It should've been a bigger deal. That makes no sense, unless—"

"Unless what?"

"Unless they didn't know what was stolen, because they didn't know they had it in the first place."

"I've called you the dumb one, but I have no idea what you are saying right now," Hiroko said.

"What I'm saying," Helen stopped pacing and looked the woman in the eye, "is that someone is using the Department of Defense for the cyborg project and the DOD has no idea about it. Not a single goddamn clue."

2 4

September 2007
New York

The safe house where Jill Cooper placed her captive was a dump. An abandoned three-story red brick with a garage door covered with obscene graffiti was squeezed on both sides by public housing buildings. The sun was shining through the gaps of the two-by-fours that covered the gated windows and reflected off the pieces of broken glass on the dusty floor. An old twin bed with a stained bare mattress, a desk, and two plastic chairs were the only furniture in the room.

"It's a nice area," the man said. He was tied to one of the chairs, but his voice was calm and his features relaxed.

"Did you see outside?" Cooper asked without looking up from her laptop.

"Yes," the man continued. "There's a lovely church right in front of this building, and the street is lined with linden trees that bloom every summer. And of course, there's quite a bit of history in this neighborhood as well."

"Stop talking, man," Cooper said, refusing to look at her prisoner. "I'm busy."

"The name's Arthur, but I guess you already know that," he said. "Do you know why they call this neighborhood Morrisania?"

"Why?" Cooper said before she could stop herself.

"Once upon a time, this was part of the Manor of Morrisania, the massive estate that belonged to the powerful aristocrats, the Morris family. Ever heard of them?"

"No." She stopped typing and looked up.

"You should." The man smiled. "At some point, the family owned most of the Bronx and a large part of New Jersey."

"There were a lot of families who owned a lot of land back in the day," she said.

"That may be true," he continued, "but that's not the best part. What makes it interesting is that the family included a New York senator named Lewis Morris, who signed the US Declaration of Independence."

"Huh," Cooper said, genuinely surprised. "It is interesting, I'll give you that."

"It also included another man named Gouverneur Morris I, who I hope you're familiar with."

"I'm afraid not. Who was he?"

"He was one of the Founding Fathers of the United States," Arthur smiled, "though of course not as famous as some others. Both of them, Lewis and Gouverneur, are buried in the crypt right here in Morrisania at St. Ann's Church."

"The place's changed quite a bit, I suppose," she said.

"Yeah. Now," he pointed with his chin toward the windows, "predominantly populated by Latin American and African American families, it's considered to be one of the poorest neighborhoods in the country."

"How do you know all this?"

"I wanted to be a historian," the man said, "but there weren't a lot of choices for a kid with my skin color living with a single mother when I was growing up. My uncle had a small welding shop, and when my mother passed, he took me in as an apprentice. Lucky for me, it turned out I liked welding and was good at it."

"You seem to have done well for yourself."

"It's unclear." He turned his wrists around as if to show that he was bound to the chair. "It'll depend on how you and I part ways, I guess."

She closed the laptop and looked at him for a few seconds.

"It's out of my hands at this point," she finally said. "I made a case, and now we wait. One thing's for sure—I'm not getting paid for this, and that's the best-case scenario."

"From where I'm sitting—everything is in your hands. You could let me go, and then walk away right now."

"It's not that simple, Arthur." Cooper walked over to the bed and lay down. The rusty springs squeaked in protest. "But since I'm waiting, why don't you connect some dots for me. Who hired you for the prosthetics?"

"Actually, I don't know," Arthur said, "and that's the truth."

"How's that possible?"

"The man who approached me said he worked for the government. Showed me the ID and the papers, the whole nine yards. Made me sign some non-disclosures as he said the work would be deemed classified."

"So, you don't know what department he was from?"

"That's the thing," Arthur said. "I don't think he worked for the government at all. I actually did a few small jobs for Uncle Sam in the past, also classified. Some research for the parts of the Abrams tanks. This guy wasn't it."

"But you took the job anyway?"

"What can I say?" Arthur's face stretched into a grin. "A man needs to pay his bills. Sometimes people come to me, and after we do the work, all I have is a first name and a cash receipt. As long as you don't ask me to do something illegal, that's going to come back and bite me, I don't care if your name is real or fake. As long as the Benjamins you're paying with are real, we'll be your best friends."

"How long ago did you start?"

"The work?" The man shrugged. "I don't know—six, seven months ago? But he came to me because he saw a few patents I'd filed, and I got those a few years back."

"What about the alloys that you mentioned?" Cooper asked. "I didn't see patents on those."

"You've done your research." The man smiled. "Very impressive. No, I didn't file patents on those. You see, patents are a double-edged sword. On the one hand, they protect you, but on the other, they tell the whole world how you did what you did. That always makes it a tricky decision whether to file one. Because if someone steals your idea, then you will have to enforce your rights—hire a law firm, sue them and so on. Might work for a big company with an army of lawyers already on a payroll, but I'm just a small guy with a small business."

"So, you reckoned it'd be harder to figure out your formula than to enforce the patent if somebody had stolen it," Cooper said, almost to herself.

"That's right," Arthur said. "Now I have a question. How does one get a job like yours? It's not like you get people to visit your college campus and leave booklets with potential prospects. If I had to guess, you must've served in the military at some point, but I always thought that people like you only existed in the movies."

"Keep guessing, old man," Cooper said, "and you will talk yourself into trouble before I hear from my employer."

Her phone beeped as if on cue, and she sat up to read the message. When she looked up at Arthur again, his face was still calm, but she could see that his body was now rigid with tension.

"You're one lucky bastard," she said. "Here's the deal. I will let you go and, in a few days, someone will contact you. All you have to do is to start working for that person. You'll be compensated handsomely. But if you breathe one word of this encounter to anyone—well, you're a smart guy. You know what it means."

Cooper cut the bonds holding his left hand and left the rest untouched. It would take him at least five minutes to free himself, she decided, and by then she'd be long gone.

"I still stand by what I said." She heard his voice as she was leaving the room. "Everything's in your hands."

Cooper didn't answer and took the stairs to the first floor. She cracked the door open and stood there for a few moments, peeking out through the gap to make sure there was nobody outside the building. Then, satisfied, she opened the door, slid outside, and started walking. As she did, her hand slipped into her breast pocket and produced a faded wallet-sized, laminated photograph.

A young girl, her face beaming with a smile, was sitting on top of a circus pony, her hands clutching the reins of the animal.

"It's not that simple," Cooper said to the picture. "You know that, don't you?"

The girl on the photograph remained silent, a moment frozen in time, never to be seen again.

Cooper put the picture back in her pocket and held her hand over it for a few seconds.

"It's not that simple," she repeated as she continued to walk.

25

September 2007
New York

Vic sniffed what was left of the Scotch on the bottom of his tumbler, groaned, and then poured it out into the sink. He was starting to think that drowning one's sorrows was a misplaced idea for those who didn't drink that much to begin with. He worked the cork back into the bottle and set the bottle on the counter.

It was late in the afternoon, and he had spent most of the day indoors. He'd called in sick first thing in the morning and then stepped outside to do some grocery shopping, which somehow resulted only in a bottle of Johnnie Walker, a bag of peanuts, and a container of blueberries. He then spent the rest of the day flipping channels on the TV. He watched a reality show where a fight broke out between two plus-sized women, a real estate channel that taught him about the nuances of wall insulation and different types of roofing materials, and a baking competition on a cooking network.

Nothing seemed to be helping, at which point he turned off the TV and decided to graduate to Scotch, peanuts, and blueberries. It worked, but only for a short time and soon he gave that up too. After dumping the leftovers of Scotch into the sink, he dragged himself back to the bedroom, lay down without taking his clothes off and closed his eyes. The doorbell didn't register in his mind until the ringing stopped and the pounding on the door began.

"No one's home," he said out loud and covered his head with a pillow.

The pounding persisted, and he got up and walked to the door, determined to tell whoever was there to go straight to hell.

"Open up. NYPD," the voice said, and the pounding continued.

Vic looked through the peephole and, to his alarm and surprise, saw two uniformed cops standing outside of the door. He turned the lock and opened the door just far enough to see the policemen behind it.

"Can I help you?"

The cop standing closer to the door gave it a hard kick, crashing it into Vic and sending him tumbling back. Vic let out a yelp of pain as something cracked in his right side.

The cops forced their way into his apartment and then another man, whose familiar face sent Vic into a fit of blind rage, stepped into the hallway as well.

"You bastard," he breathed. "How dare you show your face in my home. Get the hell away from me."

"You don't think I have the right to check on my son?" the man said. He closed the door behind him and then nodded to the cops. "Bring Junior inside, will you? I don't want to have this conversation in the hallway. And tie him up."

Vic tried to fight back, but the two cops were stronger. The broken rib in his right side didn't help either as it sent hot searing pain through his torso with every move. They dragged him to the living room, and Victor Ye watched as the cops tied his son to a chair.

"There's a reason I stayed away from you for all these years," Vic spat. "I knew you were a thug, but you're even worse than I could've possibly imagined. Torturing people? Who does that? What kind of a monster are you?"

"And yet, when you wanted to get information from someone, you had my people get it from him," Victor Ye observed coldly. "Lied to them too, pretending I was okay with your plan. Doesn't it make you a monster too?"

"I had no idea they were going to torture the poor shmuck," Vic cried out. "I thought they'd scare him; rough him up a little, but torture?"

Victor Ye bent over and slapped his son in the face with the back of his hand. The force of the impact was hard enough to make Vic feel the whiplash.

"Stop the hysterics, you bloody idiot," Victor Ye said and nodded to the two cops silently standing on either side of the chair. "Teach some respect to this young man."

Vic cringed and pulled his head closer to the chest, as a boxer dodging a hard hook, but there was nowhere to escape. The shower of hits came from both sides, the hard punches landing on his torso and the head. Within seconds, he was disoriented, the primal part of him trying to break the bonds and run. The pain quickly reached a crescendo and then Vic started to drift away.

The beating stopped as suddenly as it had begun and Vic groaned as the sweet darkness that was about to envelop him disappeared. He couldn't open one eye, and his nose was bleeding profusely, the bright red pouring over his white shirt and light-blue pants.

"Now," the man standing in front of him said, "you and I haven't been on speaking terms for many years. How long has it been, eh?"

"Not long enough," Vic breathed out.

"You have some spirit, I'll give you that, but next time you want to use my resources, I'd like you to get permission first. It's not too much to ask, is it?"

Vic looked up and tried to spit at the man, but his swollen lips refused to comply.

"What were you looking for?" his father asked. "What information did you need from that man?"

"Wouldn't you like to know," Vic said. "It's a pity nobody will tell you as I'm assuming the guy's dead."

"You're not dead," his father observed. "Not yet."

"Well," Vic shrugged, regretting the gesture at once, as the sharp pain pierced his ribs, "you can kill me, but I'm not going to tell you anything."

"You have no idea how many times I've heard people say that," Victor Ye said, "and yet, they always spill the beans in the end. It's human nature."

"Go to hell. I'm not afraid of you, asshole," Vic said. "If you think you can use your mind tricks on me, you're wrong."

"You see," the man bent over, putting his face close to Vic's, "everyone has a pressure point. Some people are terrified of physical pain and will tell you anything because you *say* you're about to hurt them. Others aren't afraid of pain at all, and yet start jumping out of their pants to tell you what you want to know when you bring up their loved ones."

"Fuck you."

"Oh. This is amusing. You think I don't know about your little pet? What's her name?" Victor Ye snapped his fingers a few times as if trying to remember. "Helen? Helen Chen?"

"Don't you dare—" Vic started, but his breath caught as one of the cops struck him in the stomach. It took him a few agonized tries to pull some air into his lungs before he finally succeeded.

"So, which one are you, I wonder?" his father continued. "Will you tell me when I start breaking your bones, or will you rather wait until I start breaking the bones of your girlfriend who you so foolishly brought to my warehouse?"

"Don't you fucking touch her," Vic screamed. "Don't you touch her, you fucking monster."

"I think we have a winner," Victor said and made a sweeping gesture as if he was presenting in front of a large audience.

"It has nothing to do with you," Vic screamed. "Please, don't hurt her. It has nothing to do with you."

"Tell me, then."

"People working for some corporation killed her sister," Vic said. "She wanted to make them lose some money, that's all. I swear, it has nothing to do with you. Please don't hurt her, I'm begging you."

"I promise." Victor Ye straightened up and raised his right hand. "Tell me what she was trying to do, and I will not touch her."

"She was just trying to hack some company," Vic said, hot tears running down his face. "I told you—they killed her sister. I swear, it wasn't about your stupid gang."

"What was the name of the company, son?"

"Guardian Manufacturing," Vic said. "You promised. Please."

"I believe you," his father said and nodded to the cops. "Let him go. And don't you worry—I will not touch your girl."

26

September 2007
New York

"I thought, at least during that conversation, that you were speaking figuratively," Andrew Hunt said as he watched Audrey pace the kitchen. "As in we bring the bad guys to heel, and make the world a better place. I didn't realize you actually meant something else."

It was five in the afternoon, and the low-hanging sun shining through the kitchen's floor-to-ceiling windows set her blonde hair ablaze as she walked. She looked like a prophet, preaching to a skeptical crowd, he thought. Convinced of her higher truth, but in need to translate it into simpler words for those who were reluctant to follow.

They returned from the camp the night before, where Rick Porter was taking charge and starting to build what would become the special operations teams for the Unit. It wasn't going without hiccups —one of the recruits, Sean Young, a baby-faced favorite on Mike Connelly's team, was killed by a ricochet during a live-fire exercise.

They all knew there were risks of people getting hurt or even killed, but seeing a young man, a father of two, go into a body bag was a sobering sight. It rattled Andrew, and he could see that Audrey was taking it hard, too.

"No, I wasn't hypothetical at all," she said. "We're fighting with one hand tied behind our backs. The cabal doesn't follow the same rules that we do."

"Well," Andrew interjected, "that is not exactly true. The whole purpose of setting up a black ops division is *not* to follow the regular rules. We have the power to eliminate our enemies, to be what they call *the judge, the jury, and the executioner.*"

"Yes," she agreed, "but that's only a part of it. Our similarities end with the notion that neither we nor the cabal operatives want to get caught. Even the outcome of getting caught is almost the same—for them, it means jail; for us, it means the end of funding, and, well, also jail. But what follows is completely different."

"Different how?"

"For us, if we get caught, or the president changes his mind, or if the funding runs out for any reason, that's it—that's the end of the road. For them—they dispose of their apprehended operatives and hire somebody else. How's that a level playing field? We get only one shot of getting things right, where they can do it over and over again."

"So, what exactly do you propose?"

"We need independence—from everybody, including the president." Audrey stopped pacing and climbed on the stool at the breakfast bar. "To get that, we'll have to be ruthless, and we actually have a good example to follow—our own government."

"Go on." Andrew took a seat opposite her, planted his elbows on the marble table, and rested his chin on the back of his hand.

"The War on Drugs, for instance," she continued. "What do we do with all that seized money? Billions of dollars. Do we burn it? Bury it? Give it to orphans?"

"No," Andrew volunteered. "It goes back to the agency that seized it in the first place."

"Exactly." Audrey pointed a finger at him. "All we have for now is a measly fifty million dollars a year. A trickle that can dry up at any moment for some reason or for no reason at all. Is this how we're planning to fight an international conglomerate that's made up of companies whose combined value is greater than a GDP of a developed country? We are bound to fail if this is our plan."

"I know where you're going. But they'll hang us for treason if we get caught," Andrew said, "and Jim will never go for it, nor will the president."

"Jim will understand," she said with passion he never saw before, "and we can keep the White House in the dark about this. May I remind you of something—you didn't want to bring them in at all in the beginning. But to fight a successful criminal enterprise, we need to almost become one ourselves. Self-sufficient, multifaceted, well-funded."

"You've seen the report from the ISCD about their possible drug operations in Afghanistan," Andrew said. "Is it what got you thinking?"

"Yes. You said it yourself—we have to follow the money. It's the right approach. All I'm suggesting is that instead of pulling on the thread to see where it leads, we hit them hard and appropriate whatever we can find. If it works—we can kill two birds with one stone: hurt their operations and finance ours."

"We'll have to launder that money if we get it," Andrew said, watching her face. "We can't bring it to the States and deposit it in our local bank. Not if we're planning on keeping it a secret."

"Um, I know this guy." Audrey threw him an impish smile. "He's a financial genius. If we can convince him to do that, he'll launder that money so clean it'll smell like roses."

"Very funny," Andrew smiled back, "but in reality, it's much harder to move dirty money through the banking system than it used to be. They've tightened things up quite a bit since 9/11. There's a reason why a lot of drug money that goes back to South America from the US is now smuggled out the same way as the drugs were smuggled in —in bundles, hidden in secret compartments of cars and false floors of trucks crossing into Mexico."

They sat in silence for a few seconds, looking at each other. Weighing the possible consequences.

If he wanted to be honest with himself, the idea of what she had proposed was appealing to him. Excited him even. And on a lot of levels, it made sense—what they were setting out to do was bigger than the failed War on Drugs. And if the entire US government couldn't bring down the cartels, how on earth were they supposed to achieve an even greater goal with a few dozen men and a few million bucks?

Of course, they could concentrate on strategic points and try to deliver precision strikes to the joints of the colossus in hopes that they would be enough to make it crumble. But at the end of the day, he thought it was likely going to be a game of whack-a-mole. A deadly game where right after they cleared up one target, another would pop up, and then another.

"Can it be done?" she finally asked and put her hands over his. "Can we pull it off?"

"I think we can," he said, "but I guess we won't know for sure until we try. One thing that keeps coming back to me, especially after seeing that young man in a body bag, is the danger we're putting ourselves in and by extension—our son."

"Yeah." She let his hands go and hugged herself. "I struggle with it too. But it's probably for the best not to tell Jason anything we do."

"I talked to him once."

"You did?"

"Yeah. In a roundabout way. Wanted to see if he'd take an analyst position, but he wasn't even remotely interested, so I left it alone. He can't help us now, and all we would do by disclosing it is give him another burden to carry. Let's make sure he never needs to find out."

"Agreed."

"Here's what we need to do," Andrew said, standing up, making a decision. "Let's start with that report on Afghanistan. See if we can identify where the money's coming from. If we can do that, then we can try to hit them where it hurts and put some of that dirty cash for better use."

"Are you sure?"

"Yes." He walked around the breakfast bar, picked her up in his arms, and started walking toward the bedroom. "I'll talk to Jim today. In an hour or so."

"Where are you taking me?"

"To the secret lair where I devise my plans of taking over the world."

"This is the most desperate line I've ever heard," she said, laughing.

"Desperate times," he said, walking into the bedroom and placing Audrey on top of the pillows. "Desperate measures."

27

September 2007
New York

"You said that there was a reason you wanted to do it on this Friday?" Hiroko asked.

It was a quarter to nine in the morning, and the markets were going to be open in the next forty-five minutes. Chen set up a battle station of two powerful laptops on her kitchen table the night before and now was on her third cup of coffee, reading the news.

She was up since four o'clock in the morning, not as much because she needed to do anything that early, but mostly because she was too anxious to sleep. The Asian markets closed with steep losses earlier after a volatile session, and their major European counterparts weren't having a good day either.

"Yes," she said. "For two reasons. First off—any extra volatility helps, and Fridays are more volatile as you have a lot going on. Short-term traders will implement exit strategies so they don't have any positions open over the weekend when the exchange is closed and they can't react to the news cycle. You also have options expiring this weekend, so whoever holds those contracts will have to make some moves before that happens."

"What's the second reason?"

"The actual news cycle," Chen said. "I want to amplify the effect as much as I can. The fact that it wasn't a normal trading pattern will be obvious before the end of the day. Everybody's going to be talking about the hack of one of the biggest pharmaceutical companies in the world. But I want everybody to *continue* talking about it over the weekend, so it doesn't get buried by some celebrity break-up gossip mid-week."

"To maximize the damage," Hiroko said thoughtfully.

"Exactly. The markets will be closed, no one will be able to step in and buy a perceived bargain—it'll get just worse and worse. We can't stop the actual merger, but if we bring enough scrutiny, we can stave it off indefinitely."

"Where did you learn all that stuff?"

"I took a few courses back in college," Chen said, "but mostly I learned this from the ramblings of my father. The markets always fascinated him, and he made some savvy investment moves that helped our family in the long run. It also made him insufferable every time the conversation touched upon the greatness of American capitalism. He always preached that this was the best system in the world and refuted the mere notion that it could be improved in any way, shape, or form."

"Oh, I know the type," Hiroko smiled, "but let's do the rundown one more time, to make sure we're on the same page."

"All right," Chen said and looked at her notes. "Let's talk about Guardian first. First, we let the markets run their course for thirty, forty-five minutes. It looks like the market's going to open down, so if Guardian's shares fall on their own that would help us, but at the end of the day, it's irrelevant. Then, at some time after ten, I get in. Once I'm inside, I send you the paths to establish the mirror terminal."

"Right," Hiroko checked her notes as well, "so when the trades come in, they go to me, that way the system thinks they are still going through, but we pick and choose which ones get executed."

"Remember, though," Chen held up a cautionary finger, "we have to keep the rate of decline under ten percent within a rolling five-minute time period, so we don't trip the circuit breakers. We don't want the party to be over before it properly begins. We'll have to play some tug-o-war with it—bring it down some, then let it recover. Then bring it down more."

"Understood," Hiroko said. "We can stretch it out through the day. As long as you're routing the trades to me, I can make it flow like the real thing. I'll let it recover a few times to make it look like buyers are stepping in to snap up some of it at bargain prices. People will start getting suspicious anyway since we can't let everybody fill all of their orders, but we can keep the charade all the way to the closing bell."

"Which brings us to the next stage," Chen said. "The news. You got the files?"

"Yep." Hiroko smiled. "Every negative keyword I could find, in a nice little package. I can feed it to four networks at once."

Chen saw some parts of the file that Hiroko had compiled in the last couple of days. It would be painfully obvious to any human who happened to see the text that it was a nonsensical mix of strung together references to Guardian Manufacturing stock and some trigger words such as *fraud, a significant drop in value, unsustainable,* and so on.

Fortunately for Chen, the markets were now largely driven by trading algorithms of giant financial firms, and those were the first intended consumers of their text file. The keywords would trigger the selling mechanisms of the AIs, and the market would dutifully do the rest.

"How long do you figure it'll take them to realize it was planted and stop it?"

"It's hard to tell for sure." Hiroko shrugged. "Two, three minutes, tops. Then, if we are lucky, another one or two minutes to shut it down. But the damage will already be done. It'll be shared and forwarded and by then it'll take some time and effort to completely debunk it."

"Right," Chen agreed, "and the last two or three minutes before the bell, we don't have to worry about circuit breakers anymore. We can drive it down as hard as we can."

"It works for me," Hiroko said, "and we do the same thing for Rapid Science, just in reverse."

"Yes," Chen said and then looked at Hiroko for a moment. "Unless—"

"Unless what?"

"Unless you see the orders, either *buys* or *sells*, coming from the same brokers for both companies at the same time. It didn't occur to me before, but now I think it's important."

"I can see that," Hiroko replied. "If your orders are not getting filled for one company you will find it weird, but if that's happening for two companies then you're calling your prime broker and start demanding answers. I can handle this."

"Great."

The two women sat in silence for a few moments, checking their notes and making sure everything was ready to go.

"You know what's the worst?" Chen said. "I didn't want to hear anything when I saw him. I just wanted to go home."

"What are you talking about?"

"The poor guy in that warehouse," Chen continued, almost choking on her words. "I didn't want the info from him, but he begged me to listen. He said they'd keep skinning him alive if I didn't. But if he talked to me, they'd let him die."

"Jesus," Hiroko said. "But it's unfair to put this on yourself. You didn't see it coming, and nobody's going to blame you for the impossible choice you had to make. C'mon, your boyfriend of two years takes you out of town, well, in a hood over your head, yeah. But if I were in your place and had to speculate what was waiting for me at the end of that road, I'd say some confused romantic gesture would be higher on my list of guesses than a naked guy half-tortured to death."

"I know. But it doesn't make it any easier." Chen wiped her eyes with the back of her hand. "This better be worth it."

"It is," Hiroko said. "Wait. What's this? Have you changed the IP masking? I thought we were going to be endlessly bouncing through proxy servers, but I see a closed loop that ends with a New York IP address."

Chen typed something on her keyboard and then moved the laptop so Hiroko could see the screen.

"I don't understand," the petite woman said, looking at the set of numbers. "Where is this?"

"This is the IP address of the Guardian Manufacturing IT department." Chen smiled through the tears. "Might as well."

Hiroko looked at her for a few moments and then gave out a hearty laugh. "Serves them right."

2 8

———————————

October 2007
Kabul, Afghanistan

"I will never get used to this goddamn air," Doug said. "I spent two years here last time, and the whole time, I felt like a fish out of water."

"You ever been to Denver?" Martin asked him. "Same exact altitude. It doesn't bother me at all."

"Of course, it doesn't." Doug snorted. "You're what, a mile and a half tall? The air is always rarefied up there."

The four operators were flown in the night before to the Bagram Airfield and then driven to the safe house in Kabul crammed in a rusted-out Toyota Corolla. What should have taken them less than an hour under normal circumstances took almost three.

Part of the reason was that most of the way they drove at crawling speed without running lights. Twice, however, they also had to pull off the road, kill the engines and wait when a supporting drone spotted large convoys of vehicles approaching them.

The safe house, where Mike Connelly and his teammates were

staying, was part of the network of special operations sites situated in different parts of the ancient city.

"What bothers me," Martin continued, "is that this place screams *Americans*. I mean, there's an actual open sewer running down the length of the street next to the houses made of shit and straw while we have a bunch of satellite dishes on the roof, Jersey barriers in front of the house, and local guards walking the perimeter. What was the point of sneaking us in?"

"The point was not to let anyone know who we were," Doug said. "Now we're just another bunch of CIA assholes on a reconnaissance mission."

"The locals will always know who you are," Patrick chimed in, "especially if you're staying for a while. Once you leave the house, though, it's another story. It's a big city, and as long as you don't let anyone follow you, you can always disappear and get things done. How's it that you never ended up here before anyway?"

"How am I supposed to know." The giant shrugged. "I go where the brass tells me to."

"Ain't that the truth."

"Connelly," Patrick turned to Mike, "how do you want us to play this?"

"Well, for now, we are a bunch of assholes on a recon mission," Connelly said and handed three manila folders to his teammates. "Our friends at the ISCD identified a seller for one of the local Taliban groups that control the opium production. The word is—he is set to meet a potential buyer tomorrow at the bazaar next to the Gardens of Babur. Our goal is to identify the buyer, see what he's up to, make sure he isn't followed, and grab him before he leaves the city."

"Malik Zubair," Doug said out loud, looking at his dossier. "That sounds familiar. Isn't he the guy who used to be a part of one of the al-Qaeda cells in Iraq? An Iraqi, running a Taliban drug deal? This is a bit odd."

"He's Afghani, actually," Connelly said, "but he's been all over the place—the Stan, Iraq, Somalia, all the good places."

"What about the buyer?"

"Him, we don't know much about. No pictures, no real description, except that he is believed to be in his mid- to late-fifties. All we know for sure is that he is an American. The guys in Paris think that he's pretty high up in the organization, so if we squeeze him hard enough, he'll be able to give us some solid leads."

"What's the time frame? Do you wanna grab him tomorrow or should we give him a longer leash to see if we can pick up some more intel?"

"No long leashes," Connelly said. "We shouldn't stick around here any longer than we need to, but we'll have to play it by ear. If he's running around the city, shaking hands with a lot of strangers after the meeting, we can watch him for a couple of hours, snap some pictures, listen in if we can. But the second he looks like he's about to skip town, we bag him."

"Exfil?" Doug asked.

"We have a CIA contact here who will provide us with transportation tomorrow, so when we get the guy, we pack him nicely in the trunk, and then off we go."

"Seems pretty straightforward to me," Martin said. "Too bad your guy Sean can't be here. I said it before, but I'm sorry, guys."

"You shouldn't be sorry. It's not your fault that you're replacing him," Connelly said as Doug and Patrick nodded in agreement, "but it is a shame what happened to him. He was a good dude. Had kids, too. But things like that happen, even in training. Could've been any of us. Ricochet doesn't choose targets."

"How are the locals who are guarding us?" Patrick said, changing the topic and breaking up the awkward silence. "Are they trustworthy? I hate being guarded by locals. You never know if they're gonna save your ass or stab you in the back."

"I don't mind the locals," Martin said, visibly relieved that the conversation had moved on. "I was once stationed in Kenya. We were looking for a bunch of kidnapped girls the local warlord wanted to have for his private harem and we'd been going round and round and couldn't pick up the trail. To make things worse, there was a local shaman who said that whoever talked to Americans would be forever cursed."

"You're shitting me." Doug chuckled. "I've heard a lot of stories in the teams, but none ever included shamans."

"Swear on my mother's grave," Martin said and crossed himself. "It was getting pretty bad, and we were starting to get concerned that the girls would be done for. So, one night me and my buddy are talking to this local dude. Nothing serious, just shooting the shit. He spoke English a little bit, and it made him feel good to practice it."

"Was that the shaman?" Patrick asked.

"No, just a villager." Martin continued, "So we're talking, and it's pitch black, and my bud, without any warning, breaks a chem stick to get some light and this dude freaks out. I mean like if the sky opened and God himself delivered this holy light from Heaven to Earth freaks out."

"Holy shit, no way."

"Yeah, so me and my buddy, we seize the moment and tell him that these glow sticks are magical and will protect from any curse that shaman would want to put on them. But they would have to lead us to the girls first. Guess what? We got two guides the next morning and found the girls in a village fifteen clicks from where we were right before the asshole could send his guerillas to round them up. Not a single shot fired."

"A win's a win," Connelly said when they stopped laughing, "and I'll take an easy win any time of the day."

"Quiet, guys." Martin held up his hand. "Can you hear this?"

Connelly gestured to his teammates to get weapons and picked up a two-way radio that they used to communicate with the local guards.

"Team one, this is castle. Please report, over," he said into the black brick and switched it from *transmit* to *listen,* but there was only static.

"Team one, this is castle," he repeated as the four of them spread out through the house, weapons at the ready. "Please report, over."

There was no answer, and Connelly put the radio down on a table and moved the safety switch on his HK MP5 submachine gun to line up with the red notch, unlocking the weapon.

Then the night erupted in fire.

29

October 2007
New York

Chen folded the *Wall Street Journal* and boarded the Queens-bound N train at the West Fifty-Seventh Street and Seventh Avenue station. It was two in the afternoon, and at this hour it was almost empty, save for the family of four at the other end of her car and two teenagers glued to each other by the door in the middle. She took a seat in the empty corner of the car and looked at the folded newspaper as the train pulled out of the station.

"Wipeout," the headline said.

It'd been almost three weeks since the hack, but the story still dominated the news cycle with almost daily updates as the investigation continued. The results of her plot exceeded Chen's wildest dreams. At the end of the day of the hack, they drove the price of Guardian Manufacturing shares from forty dollars to just above ten, wiping out over eighty billion dollars of the company's worth. During the same time, the value of Rapid Science quintupled.

As she and Hiroko anticipated, the cat was out of the bag right after the market's close. Every major news outlet was reporting that a hack took place and the four studios that disseminated Hiroko's text file were also issuing apologies and scrambling to scrub the false information from being shared through third-party sites and social media.

But the damage had already been done. The massive sell-off had triggered limit orders and margin calls, leaving investors scrambling and once the sales were completed, not everybody was rushing to jump right back in to repurchase the shares.

What the duo didn't anticipate was that the New York Stock Exchange would remain closed for two more days after the weekend, its first shutdown since 9/11, as an army of technicians and forensic teams descended upon the trading floor servers, trying to understand what had happened.

When the market finally reopened the next Wednesday, the shares of Guardian didn't bounce right back either. After a modest uptick in price at the beginning of the day, they continued the slide as worries mounted over the company's ability to meet its debt obligations and continue to pay dividends.

Rapid Science, on the other hand, though it lost some of its artificially inflated market cap, gained some nation-wide attention that brought fresh buyers and when the prices stabilized, the small company found itself at triple its original value.

Chen and Hiroko decided to lay low for a while, limiting their communications to emergencies only as the hunt for the potential perpetrators intensified. Some of the morning shows went as far as calling the attackers *terrorists*. As a sister of a former founder of one of the affected companies, Chen suspected that she might be interviewed at some point, and to be on the safe side, the laptops used in the attack were now nothing more than two fried bricks resting on the bottom of the Hudson River. But so far, no one came knocking.

Her phone vibrated, and she looked at the screen.

SOS, the message from an unknown number said.

"Shit," Chen said out loud. She must have missed the message when she was still outside.

When the train stopped at the next station, she ran up the stairs and went outside. Then she crossed Fifth Avenue, sat on the bench by the short stone wall separating the street from the edge of Central Park, and dialed a number.

"Don't go home," Hiroko said, skipping the small talk. "Do you have cash?"

"Yes," Chen swallowed hard, "but I'd have to go to the bank. It's in a safe deposit box here in the city. Is it okay to go there?"

"The bank's fine," Hiroko said, "but don't go to your house under any circumstances. How long will it take you to get the money?"

"I don't know—an hour, an hour and a half? What's going on?"

"Okay," the woman said, "let's call it two hours. Let's not discuss anything over the phone. I think this line is secure, but I don't want to take any chances. Do you remember where you and I met for the first time?"

"Sure."

"Great. Meet me there at four o'clock sharp. Leave your phone in the deposit box too. You can get a burner phone later, after we meet. And make sure you're not followed," said Hiroko and then the line went dead.

Chen closed the phone and put it in her jeans back pocket. *To make sure she wasn't followed?*

That sentence alone made her skin crawl. That didn't sound like the feds. The FBI was not in the habit of following people they were trying to arrest—they showed up, served you papers, and took you away with a shiny pair of handcuffs. This was something else. Something much worse.

She praised the hacking gods for a job she'd done four years ago. A small IT firm had hired her to test their security system and promised to pay a nice bonus if she finished the job ahead of the schedule. She did, and when she showed up to pick up her pay, the CEO gave her a check for the work and, to her great annoyance, a small brown paper bag with three stacks of one-hundred-dollar bills.

First, Chen wanted to deposit the money right along with the check but then realized that the bank would report the transaction to the IRS, which would create the need to get a proof of payment from the IT company and file taxes on the income.

After some consideration, she opened a safe deposit box and stashed the money there.

Just in case, she told herself then, thinking that she'd end up taking the cash out a few months later and slowly spending it on groceries and MetroCards. She was glad she never did that.

Chen arrived at the park at quarter to four and took a seat on the bench facing the statue, like the last time. It was getting cold, and she wrapped herself in a jacket as she watched the pedestrians going about their business, most having their hands in their pockets, casting quick glances at the overcast sky that threatened to come down with the rain at any moment.

Though the conversation with Hiroko made her heart race, Chen decided not to jump to any conclusions yet. There could be many reasons why her friend was being cautious. After all, neither of them was getting arrested yet, so there was no need to panic. But Hiroko could have gotten a tip from her hacker friends about the feds' investigation, or she might have observed some unusual movement from the Guardian Manufacturing security team—something they'd been monitoring lately.

Whatever the case was, her friend had her reasons to act this way, and with a little patience, soon she would be up to speed as well.

It was five after four when Chen saw the petite woman with jet-black hair crossing the street. Hiroko rushed across Third Avenue, trying to beat the changing traffic light and started toward Cooper Triangle, but then stopped before she entered the small park.

Chen was already on her feet ready to meet her friend as their eyes met and Hiroko shook her head ever so slightly as if saying *no*. In horror, she watched as two stocky Asian men peeled off the side of the building on the north side of the park and approached Hiroko. They flanked the woman on both sides, and then one man pressed something to the small of Hiroko's back. The second man whispered into the petite woman's ear, and as Chen looked on, the trio started to walk away from the park.

As they turned away, the woman looked at Chen, and her lips formed a word that was impossible to misunderstand:

"Run."

3 0

October 2007
Kabul, Afghanistan

*M*ike Connelly and his teammates took cover as the deadly staccato of bullets hitting the walls filled the house. The sour, pungent smell of nitroglycerin and sawdust hung in the air.

"They're jamming the radio," Patrick shouted between the shots. "We gotta get the fuck out of here."

"Boss?" Doug called. "What's the plan?"

Connelly stuck the business end of his MP5 through the broken window and let out a short burst of bullets, but a hail of return fire forced him to duck for cover.

"We're gonna need to punch through," he said. "They are every-where. I see three—no, at least four guys on this side. What about you, Pat?"

"Four or five," came an immediate reply. "Maybe more. I can't tell —it's dark as fuck."

"Nothing's in the back so far," Martin's voice boomed, "but if I were them, I'd be crawling through the neighbors' right now. If we're making a run for it, we should do it now, before we're encircled."

It wasn't a good place to be in, Connelly observed. The house had a few layers of defense—the first line was the local guards who had been patrolling the streets, walking around the perimeter in pairs. Then there was a row of concrete Jersey barriers that were supposed to stop any approaching vehicles and serve as a cover should someone try to mount a ground assault.

Now, however, as the local guards seemed to have been dispatched, and barriers overrun, the situation had been reversed, and the stronghold became a trap. All Connelly's team could do for now was to preserve ammo and try to keep the enemy from entering the house.

"Sooner or later this is gonna attract local cops," Pat said between the shots.

"Yeah, but it might not be soon enough."

Then, as abruptly as it had begun, the shooting stopped. Connelly risked a quick peek through the window, but now as the assailants took cover behind the roadblock, it was impossible to tell how many of them there were.

The silence lasted only for a few seconds and then came the high-pitched feedback of a bullhorn.

"You're surrounded," the voice said in heavily-accented English. "Surrender, and you will not be harmed. Resist, and you will be destroyed. You have three minutes. Put down your weapons and come out with your hands up in the air."

"What the fuck's that?" Doug said.

"I've no idea," Connelly responded, "but I'm not gonna wait for three minutes. We gotta split up. Pat, Doug, take the side exit. We'll get some smoke grenades out and lay suppressive fire so you can get through the yard. You can hop the fence there."

"What about you?" Patrick said. "We ain't leaving you behind. Why don't we throw some frags out there and then go out the front door?"

"Civilians," Doug grunted. "Those houses across the street are made of straw. Too high of a risk we're gonna kill some families with kids."

"The walls should hold," Patrick protested. "It'll blow the windows, but that's just tough luck."

"No time to argue, guys," Connelly said, peeking through the window. "Martin and I will booby-trap the place and get out as those assholes start moving in. At least then the blast will be contained. We'll meet you tomorrow at eight at the bazaar. Leave all your heavy gear behind. I'm sure our CIA friend can hook us up with whatever else we'll need. We gotta move. Now."

"We can climb out through the big window in the back," Martin said. "It's a little high, but at least it's wide enough. Even I can fit through there."

There wasn't enough time to get creative, so Connelly decided to play it straight. He fixed a pair of grenades on either side of the front door and Martin tied a wire to their safety pin rings. Then, they stepped back to the room at the far side of the house.

"Are we ready?" Connelly asked, looking at his teammates.

"You have thirty seconds left," the voice amplified by the bullhorn bellowed. "There will be no more warnings."

"Let's go, boys."

Connelly and Martin lobbed two smoke grenades through the side door, and as the smoke started to envelop the patchy lawn, their submachine guns roared to life, laying suppressive fire. They watched as Doug and Patrick dived under the gray curtain and disappeared into the night.

The sounds of automatic fire intensified and then, without a warning, the house shuddered as if it were a great living beast that drew its last breath. The shockwave of the fragmentation grenades knocked Connelly to the ground and showered him with pieces of broken glass and small debris.

He shook his head, trying to get his bearings. A thick sheet of dust hung in the air, leaving a tangy taste in his mouth and getting into his eyes. Two massive hands reached out to him through the cloud of dust and lifted him off the floor as Martin's pale pockmarked face came into his view—the giant's lips moved, but the world remained silent.

"What?" Connelly asked, and the sound of his own voice cut the blast-induced deafness as the cacophony of the firefight returned.

"Let's go," Martin bellowed into his ear. "We gotta move."

A bearded man rushed through the door, his AK-47 ready to spit out hot lead. Connelly lifted his submachine gun to meet the attacker, but before his weapon could finish its deadly arc, Martin jumped. The giant soldier moved so fast, it looked as if he teleported from where he stood, magically appearing next to the assailant.

His left hand slapped the rifle out of the insurgent's hands and his right struck out, burying a fist the size of a watermelon into the man's midsection. As the insurgent collapsed, Connelly watched in shock as the man's torso folded in half at an unnatural angle.

Another man appeared in the doorway and Connelly squeezed the trigger twice—his bullets connecting with the man's cheek and jaw.

"Do remind me, never to piss you off," Connelly said to Martin, as the second dead body fell on top of Martin's prey. "C'mon, buddy, let's get out of this dump."

He dashed to the window in the back of the house and peeked out, trying not to be seen—if there was any activity, he couldn't see it. Connelly looked around and then dug out a dusty frying pan from the debris on the floor.

He picked it up by the handle and, keeping his face away, he stuck the pan out of the window and kept it there for a few seconds while moving it up and down. No shots came and satisfied, he threw the skillet to the floor.

"We're good," Martin said, moving away from the door. "You go first, Mike."

Connelly placed his hands on the high windowsill and jumped up, pushing with his palms down and propelling his body forward. He was halfway through the window when he heard the clanking noise.

He knew what it was before he had a chance to turn his head back and look at the source of the noise and when he did, his eyes only confirmed what his ears had already told him.

Two Soviet-made F1 grenades were spinning on the floor a few feet away from them—too far to get them in time to throw back, but close enough to vaporize anything more tender than concrete inside the entire room.

"Sorry, Mike," Martin said, moving between Connelly and the grenades and, before Connelly could try to protest, in one fluid motion, Martin's giant hands shoved him up and out of the window.

The moment stretched as in a slow-motion film, as Connelly's mind protested at the speed his body could not match. As he fell, his body instinctively turned toward the ground, preparing to roll on impact to soften the shock.

Before he made contact, the night above him was split by the brilliant light of the blast. For a moment, it looked as if a portal had opened and the heavens themselves were revealed to the realm of the mortals in all their glory. Then it was dark again.

3 1

October 2007
New York

As she watched Hiroko being led away by the two goons with a gun to her back, Chen felt her heart pounding in her chest. She'd grown fond of the enigmatic woman over the past three months. Her razor-sharp wit, her biting sense of humor, and, more than anything else, her *nothing-can-scare-me* attitude helped her navigate the craziness of the world where her sister had been murdered in cold blood, and her boyfriend turned out to be the son of a skin-flaying mobster.

Chen looked around, scanning the area for a cop or anyone else she could call for help, and that was when she saw them. Another two thugs, identically dressed, were running toward her from the southern entrance of the park.

"Oh shit," she swore and, fighting her suddenly jelly-like legs, Chen started to run.

She dashed out of the park and across the street, narrowly avoiding getting hit by a pickup truck, ducked under the scaffolding running alongside the building, and crashed into a muscular young man in a hoodie stepping out of the coffee shop, almost knocking him off his feet.

"Help," she pleaded, grabbing the man's arm. "Those two guys are trying to hurt me."

"What's your problem, fellas?" The man stepped forward, putting himself between Helen and the two approaching thugs. "Stop right there."

The two men slowed down just long enough for one of them to extend his arm. A blue arch of electricity jumped from the black box in the thug's hand and the young man cried out in pain as he fell backward, his hoodie sliding over his face.

Chen turned to run, but one of the attackers swept her leg, tripping her and sending her crashing head first into the metal pipes supporting the scaffolding. The impact knocked the air out of her lungs and before she could recover, another man bent over and touched the black box to her neck, sending fifty thousand volts of electricity into her body.

Hot, pulsating pain traveled the length of Chen's entire body, paralyzing her head to toe. Through the fog, she heard the squealing of a car's brakes and then she was carried a few feet to the side of the road and thrown onto the dirty floor of a large van.

As the vehicle accelerated away, the man brought the Taser to her face.

"If you misbehave, I will zap you again, and again, until you start listening. Do you understand?" he asked in heavy-accented English.

"Sure," Chen said. "I understand."

Then, pushing herself off the floor, she kicked the man in the face with all her might. There was a cracking sound, and the man staggered backward as blood gushed out of his broken nose.

"You bitch," he wailed, and charged at Chen, as his partner tried to grab Chen's hands. She scratched at his face, digging her nails as deep as she could as the man howled in pain and surprise.

Chen scrambled for the door handle and pulled it down, swinging the door open and pulling herself out, ready for a jump.

The gray surface of the road looked hard and unforgiving as it sped by and she hesitated for a moment. Then one of the men crashed into her side, knocking her on the floor and before she could catch her breath, another man stabbed her with a Taser in the back.

The fight went out of her as the liquid fire of the electric shock spread out through her body. Through the red mist of pain, she felt as they flipped her on her stomach and tied her hands and feet with some rope. Then, they turned her on her back again and stood there, looking down at their captive.

"I'll come to watch you scream," the man with a broken nose said.

"Me too," the other one added, gingerly touching the deep gashes on his cheek with the back of his hand, and spat. "Even play with you a little."

"How's your face, asshole?" Chen managed through the pain. "Untie me, and I'll play with you right now."

As she lay on the floor of the van, watching her captors and awaiting her fate, an awful realization dawned on her—whoever these people were, they were not planning on bringing her back. This was going to be a one-way trip. There was no other explanation for this.

After a while, the rumbling of the gravel road replaced the low hum of wheels over asphalt, and finally, the van came to a stop.

The two men opened the door, jumped out, and then pulled her outside. She was standing inside of a small warehouse, and to her left, there was a row of familiar garage doors on one side and offices on the other side of the area. The low rumble of machinery wasn't there now, but she had no doubt they were in the same warehouse where she'd met the lone hacker—the man who had met a gruesome end because she needed a piece of information that only he could provide.

One of the men bent down and cut the rope around her ankles, and the moment her bounds came undone, Chen tried to knee him in the face, but this time he was prepared.

He dodged the knee and stabbed her stomach with the Taser. Chen collapsed as the ball of fire exploded in her midsection. Strong hands grabbed her feet and somebody unceremoniously dragged her listless body across the floor, inside one of the offices and then to the metal door at the end of the empty room. The door squeaked, and Chen bumped her head as the man pulled her body over the threshold.

As dark panic enveloped her, she started thrashing about, trying to free herself, but another pair of hands grabbed her wrists and then the two men lifted her in the air and slammed her down on the wooden table.

Before she could do anything, they slapped restraints on her wrists and ankles, and she heard the wheel turning as they stretched her in four directions. The man kept on going until she could not move a single muscle and her body was so taut with tension, she had difficulty breathing.

Then one of the men produced a pair of scissors and proceeded to cut away her clothes, moving around the table with surgical precision. Chen found herself paralyzed with fear; even her vocal cords refused to work. All she could do was watch as the two collected the pieces of her clothes off the floor and headed for the door. The lights turned off, plunging the place in complete darkness.

As she lay there in the dark, cold sweat forming on her naked skin despite the cold, Chen's consciousness started to slip away, the fragile net of normalcy being pulled apart by the madness of her predicament. She was going to die a nasty death in this awful place, the logical part of her brain told her. A primal, guttural wail escaped her lips, the sound of a wounded prey with no means of running away, cornered by a terrible predator.

Then, without warning, the door squeaked again, and the bright light flooded the room, making her squirm, trying and failing to cover herself from prying eyes.

A short, broad-shouldered man with a big mane of jet-black hair was standing in the middle of the room. His suit was perfectly tailored to accentuate his athletic frame. His black eyes scanned her head to toe without a trace of shame, his face relaxed and content.

"Oh my, Miss Chen, what a pleasure. You're such a spirited fighter," the man said, a humorless smile on his lips, his polished British accent sounding out of place in the chamber of horrors. "But I have so many questions."

3 2

October 2007
Kabul, Afghanistan

By the time Mike Connelly reached the river bank, the stars had already all but disappeared, and the sky in the east started to change from the inky black to hopeless gray. Connelly had shaken the pursuers off his tail a long time ago, but he kept zigzagging the city for a while longer until he was confident that no one was going to catch up. On one of the quiet streets, he climbed the roof of a brick house and left his submachine gun jammed inside of a chimney, leaving only the MK23 pistol tucked into its appendix carry holster. Then he made his way to the Artal Bridge by the Kabul River.

The word *river* hardly applied to something little more than a dirty brook, Connelly thought. Though it swelled during the hot summer months when the high temperatures melted the snows up in the Hindu Kush mountain range, the dams and the changing climate kept the riverbed, choked on both sides by piles of garbage, almost dry during the bigger part of the year. Now, as the temperatures dropped into the mid-sixties, and at night even going as low as the mid-forties, the putrid smell wasn't as strong as during the summer, but even now, Connelly could smell the river long before he could see it.

The road by the bridge, usually packed with walking people going in and out of the shops, delivery boys running errands, and slowly driving cars trying to navigate the crowds and ignoring every traffic law, was almost deserted at the moment. The few men and even fewer women hurrying about their business at this early hour were giving Connelly curious looks, whose tall, muscular frame, clean-shaven face, and light complexion were sticking out like a sore thumb.

It was only a short walk from here, over the bridge and past the local hospital, that would take him to the bazaar where the meeting was going to take place. But he had two more hours to kill, and he wondered for a moment if he was better off spending them somewhere where he was less likely to attract any attention. He walked a few blocks in a circle, trying not to stay in one place for too long. He was passing the bridge for the third time when he saw two familiar silhouettes leaning over the stone barrier by the river. Like him, they were wearing civilian clothes and yet just like him, they looked decidedly out of place.

"Gents," Connelly said as he approached them, "it's good to see that you've made it."

"Where's Martin?" Doug asked.

"He didn't make it. Saved my ass," Connelly replied, meeting his teammate's eyes. "I was halfway through the window when two frags rolled in, and he tossed me out of the room as if I were a child. I didn't even have the chance to react. It's fucked up."

"That kid was strong," Patrick said and sighed. "Geez, what a shit show."

"Strong is the understatement of the century. Fast too," Connelly said. "When one of the assholes got through, he punched him, before I could place a shot—broke the guy in half. For real—I've never seen anything like that."

"It's almost like we're cursed," Doug said, turning back to the river. "First Sean, now Martin."

"Let's make sure it's not for nothing," Connelly said, looking at his watch. "Our CIA contact should meet us at the bazaar in about thirty minutes. It's about a fifteen, twenty-minute walk from here, so I'd suggest we start going."

"Sure, boss," said Patrick. "We're way too visible here anyway."

"But let's be on the lookout when we get to the rendezvous point," Connelly said. "Nobody was supposed to know we were at the safe house and the moment we get there, we get a fucking army as the welcome party. I don't want to take any chances."

The sun was creeping up higher and as they walked, the crowds grew thicker as people started heading out to work, the shop owners started to put their fares out, and shoppers descended on the market to haggle over spices, produce, jewelry, and clothes.

The CIA contact who was supposed to meet them at the bazaar was working at a small stall, selling spices. A picturesque collection of colorful bags was crowding a small foldable table, and a jovial-looking bearded man was hustling about, setting up price tags on his fares and arranging his product. While Patrick and Doug took positions to keep watch on either side of the row where the merchant's stall was located, Connelly approached the trader alone.

"As-Salaam-Alaikum," the man said, looking up at Connelly and flashing a wide smile.

"Wa-Alaikum-Salaam," Connelly replied, and added in English, "I'm looking for some traditional spices."

"Ah, someone who appreciates quality," the man said in accented English. "The best spices you'll find in all Kabul. Turmeric, saffron, cardamom—anything you want. What are you cooking, my friend? Palaw, qormah, or maybe mantu?"

"No. I wanted to make some Chapli kebab."

"With rice, I assume?" The man smiled, as he continued to busy himself.

"Not with rice. I hear that proper Chapli kebab is always served with naan."

"A proper meal, then." The man smiled again. "Let me give you an address where you can buy some good beef. The beef is as important as the spices you put in."

The merchant threw a quick glance around the row of stalls and then disappeared into the back of his kiosk. A few moments later, he returned, holding a small paper bag.

"Here you go, my friend," he said, handing the bag to Connelly. "I threw some spices in there for you to try. When you try them, you'll come back for more."

"Thank you," Connelly said. He threw some banknotes on the table that promptly disappeared in the trader's hand, and then made his way out of the row.

"How's it looking?" Patrick asked when the operatives made their way through the crowd.

"Got the keys for the van," Connelly said, looking inside of the bag, "and some instructions."

He took out a small handwritten note and read it in silence as they walked.

"Change of plans," he finally said, putting the note back into the bag.

"Oh, Christ. I don't like this already," Doug grunted in disapproval. "What's happening now?"

"The meeting's been rescheduled. We've got the coordinates for the house where the buyer and the seller are going to be. The brass is also aware of last night's events, and we're getting a new weapons cache. That's the good part."

"And the bad?" Doug asked.

"The house belongs to one of the local mid-level drug lords, so it'll be heavily guarded—a dozen guards at least. Also, now they want us to grab Malik Zubair as well. While they still want the info on the buyer, the primary objective has changed—we need both of them and alive."

"I'd prefer we had more guys, but it sounds doable so far. It's the grabbing them alive part that might be difficult," Patrick said, voicing what was on everybody's mind.

"Yes," Connelly said, "but I'm afraid grabbing them alive is imperative. The main objective of our mission is now to locate and retrieve the money that was going to be used for the drug purchase. And since the buyer's already paid half of it as a deposit, we won't be able to locate or retrieve all of it unless we have both of them alive, awake, and answering our questions."

3 3

October 2007
New York

"**B**efore my men start working on you, Miss Chen," the man in a tailored suit said, "I'd like you to know that I take no pleasure in doing this to you. In fact, I'm a gentle person when it comes to people I care about."

He walked closer to the table and stopped when he was a foot away from Chen's head.

"However," he continued, "I have a vast empire to protect, and thousands of people depend on me. Do you understand that, Miss Chen?"

Chen didn't answer as she watched the person who had her abducted, brought her there against her will, and tied to a table for torture. A small part of her decision not to engage him was pride. The bigger part, however, was the fear that should she open her mouth, the only sound that would come out would be an incoherent wail of terror.

"I'll make you a deal, Miss Chen," the man said and bent over to bring his face next to hers. His breath smelled of mint and cinnamon. "If you talk to my people and answer their questions truthfully, your ordeal will be painful, but quick. But if for a moment you start playing coy, I can promise you this will feel like an eternity."

"What do you want from me, you crazy fuck?" Chen screamed, as for a moment, the anger overwhelmed her fear. She spat in Victor Ye's face. "I can promise you one thing. I will make it my life's mission to destroy everything you own, you hear me?"

"You are too smart for your own good, Miss Chen," Victor Ye said, straightening up and wiping his face with a pocket square, "and that will be a short mission indeed, though you will not feel it that way."

The door into the room burst open, and a short man ran in, breathing hard, his shoulders heaving up and down with every raspy breath. He stopped a few feet away from them and bent in a deep bow in front of Victor Ye.

"What is it?" Victor snapped at the newcomer.

The man shuffled closer and whispered something into Victor's ear and then stepped away again, bowing as he went.

"I'm afraid I have to leave you, Miss Chen," Victor said, "but don't despair. Someone will be here shortly, and they'll keep you company."

He turned around and briskly walked out of the room, his entourage in tow. As the door slammed, the lights switched off again, plunging the place in total darkness.

Chen tried to shift, desperately looking for a more comfortable position, but it was no use. Her shoulders and hips were hot and sore, and the muscles on her back and buttocks were starting to get numb. She was cold now too. The strain her body was under was making her sweat profusely, and as the liquid evaporated off her bare skin, it took away the precious warmth. Shivers ran down the entire length of her body.

She tried to bend her wrists as much as she could, feeling with her fingers for the restraints, but her fingertips only scraped on the edge of the cuffs, too far from the locks. Desperation started to settle in again, its dark tentacles reaching into the farthest corners of Chen's mind. She couldn't tell how much time had passed, torn between wanting the darkness to end and dreading what the arrival of any visitor would mean.

The door squeaked, and the room exploded in harsh light, blinding her. Chen thrashed in her restraints, certain that the torturers were finally here, ready to deliver on Victor Ye's terrible promise. A raspy wail started to build in her throat.

"Shh," somebody said, and a soft palm covered her mouth, smothering her scream. "Please don't make any noise, I'm begging you."

As Chen's eyes focused, getting used to the bright light, the familiar face came into view. The mixture of anxiety and relief washed over her as she looked at her ex-boyfriend's features distorted by the colorful bruise covering half of his face.

"Let's get you out of here," he said, walking around the table, undoing her restraints. He favored one side as he moved and took extra care not to bump into anything.

"Are you okay?" she asked before she could stop herself.

"Only you're capable of this." He gave a soft chuckle. "You'd think they tied *me* to a table and got me ready to be tortured. My father thought I needed a lesson, that's all."

He finished untying the restraints and helped Chen off the table.

"Here." He offered her a pile of clothes. "Not sure if they'll fit you, but it's better than nothing."

She stood there for a few seconds without moving, and then her hand lashed out, striking him across the face.

"I guess I deserved that," he said, wincing, and then turned away to spit. A trickle of blood ran down from his nose, and he wiped it with the back of his hand. "I made a terrible mistake, but you have to believe me, I had no idea any of this would happen."

"Oh yeah? What did you think was gonna happen after your driver put a hood over my head? You thought he was going to buy me popcorn and show me a movie?"

"Helen, I'm sorry. The guy you were looking for..." He trailed off. "I thought they were going to rough him up, scare him, you know? And I had no clue they would try to hurt you, I swear."

Chen didn't answer as she put on a pair of worn-out pants, a sweater, and a pair of old sneakers. A dirty jacket completed her outfit. The clothes were baggy and foreign but it was a welcome change from feeling exposed, and Chen wrapped herself in the jacket, trying to warm up.

"We have to go," Vic urged her, pulling her outside of the room and softly closing the door behind them. "I don't know how much time we have before the guards come back."

"We're not going anywhere yet," Chen said, pulling away from him and stopping him in his tracks.

"What?" He looked at her in disbelief. "Have you lost your mind? I always thought that the flaying business was a bullshit story meant to scare my father's rivals, but they actually do it. Do you understand what I'm saying? We've got to go."

"We're not going anywhere until we get Hiroko back," Chen said, standing her ground. "I'm not leaving without her."

They looked at each other for a few seconds, and finally, he gave up.

"Fine," he said. "Follow me. I think they are holding her in the southern building. C'mon."

They jogged through the warehouse, trying to keep the noise to a minimum, and stopped before the door leading outside of the building.

"Hang on," Vic said, motioning to Chen to stay behind.

He cracked the door open and peeked outside for a few seconds.

"Stay here," he told her. "I'll be right back."

He disappeared outside before Chen could say anything. She stood there alone, anxiously listening for any sounds that might indicate her tormentors were coming back. After what seemed like an eternity, Vic's bruised face appeared in the doorway. He was holding a short piece of metal pipe in his hands. One end of the pipe was sleek with someone's blood.

"Here," he said and handed her a car key. "There's a Bimmer parked in the back of the parking lot. Let's grab your friend, and you should get out of here."

"What about you?"

"I'll be fine," he said, urging her on. "He's not gonna kill me, but I have to buy you some time."

They snuck outside and ran across a small yard to what looked like a carbon copy of the warehouse where Chen had been kept. A crumpled shape of a body was sprawled out next to the door. Vic fumbled with the keys for a few seconds, and then the door opened, letting them in.

Vic pulled her toward one of the office-like doors and swung it open. As the lights came to life, Chen saw a naked body of a tattooed woman tied to a wooden table, thrashing wildly against her restraints. As the woman's eyes grew used to the light, she stopped struggling and stared at Chen with disbelief.

There was a bruise on the woman's face, and she sported a large scrape across her ribs and abdomen, but otherwise, she seemed to be unharmed.

"I'll be right back. Hold on to this," Vic said, giving her the pipe. "I'll go get her some clothes."

"Hello, girlfriend," Chen said, as she started to work on Hiroko's restraints. "Let's get you out of this wonderful place."

3 4

October 2007
New York

"Are you okay?" Chen asked as she put a wool blanket around the petite woman's shoulders.

The two women were hiding in a basement studio apartment in Brooklyn that belonged to one of Hiroko's friends. After they'd left the warehouse, Chen drove Vic's BMW to the city. There, they left the car in an underground parking garage and then jumped the turnstile to get into the subway station.

After surfing the subway for a couple of hours, Chen felt safe enough to let Hiroko take the Q train and lead them all the way to their destination. The townhouse built at the turn of the twentieth century was sitting in a sleepy part of the Kings Highway neighborhood and was only a short walk from the subway station.

Their host was a short, wiry kid with shifty eyes behind thick glasses, who introduced himself as Eugene in a light Eastern-European accent. Eugene used the semi-finished basement with a foldable sofa and a bathroom in desperate need of an update for visiting relatives and friends. Despite the lack of amenities, however, Chen found their accommodations downright luxurious compared to the house of horrors they'd escaped from.

"No," Hiroko said. She shook her head and wrapped herself tightly with the blanket. "I'm most certainly not okay and, to be honest, I'm not even sure how not okay I am right now."

"I'm sorry—"

"Sorry?" Hiroko interrupted her. "What are you sorry for? We may have broken the law, but sure as shit, we don't skin people alive."

"I know." Chen put her hands on her friend's shoulders and held them there. "I'm not okay either, but all I can think of right now is how I can hurt that monster."

"All I can think of right now is a nice juicy steak with some French fries and a bottle of ice-cold beer," Hiroko said. "I might be fucked up, but I'm starving. PTSD's gonna have to wait."

"Geez, girl." Chen couldn't help but smile. "I don't know about steak, but I saw some ramen noodles as I was rummaging through the cupboard. There's a kettle in the kitchen. Hopefully it's not broken."

"Works for me," Hiroko said. "But listen—we will need some money. I can borrow some, but that's not gonna last long. You don't have any cash, do you?"

"I had thirty grand on me when I was coming down to meet you," Chen said as she put the kettle on. "I mean, I have some savings, but I'd need to go back to my house to get my cards and then go to the bank to get the cash."

"Forget it," Hiroko said. "They'll be watching our places so I wouldn't risk it. It's all right, we'll figure something out about the money. But we'll need some help too."

They sat down at a round wooden table, and Chen poured the boiling liquid into the Styrofoam cups.

"What kind of help are you talking about?" she asked.

"We need allies," Hiroko continued as she held the steaming cup in her hands. "Someone with some serious resources. We can't take these guys on by ourselves. We can harass them here and there, but it's only going to get us in more trouble."

"That's easier said than done," Chen said, "but it's not like we can assemble a team, right? I know a bunch of people online who I've collaborated with over the years and I'm sure you do too. I doubt, though, anyone would jump on the opportunity to take on a criminal enterprise with the penchant of skinning people alive. Do you have anything specific in mind?"

"Eugene can help some," Hiroko said, "but we need something bigger than a ragtag team of hackers."

"How do you even know this guy? He doesn't strike me like someone from your circle. He looks shady, if you ask me," Chen said. "But I guess in our situation, I can't be too choosy."

"Well, he is shady." Hiroko laughed. "Funny you should say that. I'd met him at the club once, and we had a casual on and off thing going on for some time."

"Those pesky Russians," Chen snorted. "Wow, definitely not the type I pictured you with."

"He's Ukrainian, actually," Hiroko said, "and hey, a woman has her needs."

Chen threw her hands up in surrender as she looked at her friend with amusement.

"More importantly, though," Hiroko continued, "he is one of the best code breakers I've ever met. Maybe even better than Delgado."

"Speaking of," Chen said, "have you heard from him?"

"Not since our first meeting, but it's not like we were close or anything," Hiroko said, shaking her head. "He was using me as a messenger, and I'm pretty sure I wasn't the only one."

"I see."

"Eugene…" Hiroko trailed off. "He's shady, no doubt, but mostly because he doesn't concern himself with things like the law. Eugene's weird. Most of the time he just wants to understand how things work. And he hates when the powers that be hide secrets from the rest of us and use them to their benefit. Once he hacked one of the biggest electric companies in Canada, because he read an article that made an allegation that they were overcharging their customers for electricity."

"An idealist then?"

"Nah." Hiroko smiled. "I wouldn't call him an idealist. Another time he found out a local bank in South Carolina had a vulnerability in their network. It allowed people to wire the money out, circumventing the approval process. So, he went ahead and sent a detailed report to the bank describing how to fix it."

"I feel a *but* coming up," Chen said.

"Oh, you got that right," Hiroko continued. "He also wired out a hundred grand to show them it was for real and, well, let's just say he forgot to return it."

A knock on the door interrupted their conversation.

"Speaking of the devil," Hiroko said as she got up and walked to the door.

"Girls," the man said as he entered the apartment with takeout bags in his hands, "please tell me those are not the noodles from the cabinet. Throw them away, for Chrissake. They are ten years old."

He marched to their table and started unloading the bags. "Here's some steak, some fries, and if anyone feels particularly healthy, I got a salad too. Sorry, love." He turned to Hiroko. "They don't sell beer to go, and I'm out, but I thought you were hungry, so I figured that beer could wait."

"I think we should keep him," Chen said. "At least, for the time being."

"He grows on you." Hiroko smiled. "Also, he and I were talking about the need to bring in some help before you and I got taken, so he's practically up to speed."

"Practically?"

"I didn't have the opportunity to tell either of you, but there was something else," Hiroko added. "As they dragged me to that room where you'd found me, we passed an open door to a larger area. I guess nobody counted on me getting out of that place alive, so they didn't care. I saw a few shiny things hanging off the ceiling that looked like some crazy spacesuits."

"Spacesuits?" Chen asked incredulously.

"Yeah," Hiroko said as she took a French fry from the plate and took a bite, "but I don't think those were spacesuits. I think those were whatever the hell project Nyctalope was developing. The prototypes for the cyborg army."

35

—————

October 2007
Kabul, Afghanistan

The sun was setting over Kabul when Mike Connelly and two of his teammates parked the van on the corner of the street of the target house in the neighborhood of Sherpur.

It was a strange place. Once dotted with poor mudbrick houses, it was now the local version of Los Angeles' Beverly Hills—the home of so-called *poppy palaces.* Drug lords, gun dealers, money launderers, and corrupt bureaucrats occupied the glittering extravagant mansions sitting behind roadblocks and concrete barriers.

The target house, sitting in the middle of the street, was a red-and-white brick villa adorned with a glass-lined balcony and an ostentatiously large statue of an eagle carrying a snake in its beak perched on top of the sloping roof. Two guards were stationed outside of the heavy iron gate and a few more sentries walked the grounds on the inside.

"There're two tangos outside of the main gate," Connelly said, pointing to the satellite image on a small tablet. "Two more are sitting on the roof, and the rest of them are positioned throughout the villa."

The team had picked up the van at the location given to Connelly by the CIA contact. Inside, there was a weapon case stocked to the brim, three bulletproof vests, and—to the delight of the team—a large bag filled with water and fresh local food. The smells of kebab and qormah, a rich stew with caramelized onions, filled the van, making their mouths water.

"We should take the guys on the roof first," Doug said, his mouth full of food. "Is there a place we can climb around here?"

"Unfortunately, there isn't," Connelly said. "At least, not close enough, so we'll have to take the guys out front first. But the gate is pretty high, so if we hit them fast and stay close to the walls, those two dudes on top will not be able to see anything until we're gone. It looks like they check in via radios every ten minutes or so, but that should give us plenty of time."

"What about the neighbors?" Patrick chimed in. "Any guards out?"

"Not on this block," Connelly said. "The house to the left of the entrance is for rent, but for the moment it seems to be empty. The house on the right seems abandoned. There's, of course, a bunch of video cameras on the other houses, so there's a risk that someone's monitoring those feeds in real time. If they see us, they'll call the police or some other reinforcements, but that's what we have to work with."

"Where do you think Zubair is going to be?"

"There's a second-floor balcony in the back, facing the backyard and the pool. It looks like they'll be throwing a party tonight and they've set up a table with the view of the pool. My guess is Malik Zubair and the buyer will be watching the festivities from there, while they discuss the transaction."

"A party?" Patrick said with concern. "That means more people."

"I don't think so," Connelly said. "They've brought some dancers before in a bus, but it looks like a private event for the buyer."

"Frontal assault then. In this case, it looks like speed's our best friend here," Doug said, turning the image this way and that. "Hit them hard and fast. Get them before they realize what's happening.

Ideally, before they start shooting. This is a bad neighborhood to be in if the neighbors hear the gunfire."

"Agreed. Also, the entire backyard is under a glass dome, like a giant greenhouse, so let's try not to get any stray bullets flying, or else everyone in a mile radius will know something's up."

"Nice. And they say that crime doesn't pay." Patrick chuckled. "My girl's been chewing my ear off for over a year to build a pool in our backyard, 'cause apparently, she thinks I shit money."

As the night descended onto the city, they stayed in the back of the van for the next two hours, keeping tabs on the house and watching the neighboring streets. The area seemed to be deserted, with only a handful of people passing their van during that time. A few cars sped by, but none stopped at the house's main entrance. It seemed that not too many ventured to the neighborhood populated by the rich and the powerful, as if repelled by some invisible force field.

"It looks like the party's started, boss," Patrick said, putting down his binoculars. "Look."

Before Connelly even had a chance to look through the window, he could hear it—the booming vibrations of bass speakers, pumping out a dance rhythm. As Connelly peeked through the back of the van, he could see the house awash with colorful lights, pulsating with the music.

"All right," he said, turning to his teammates. "This is our cue. Let's crash this party."

The guards at the front entrance went down in unison as the nozzles of Connelly's and Doug's submachine guns flashed fire.

"Pat, get the door," Connelly whispered as they rushed toward the gate adorned with intricate iron designs welded onto the massive brass frame.

Patrick dragged the corpse of one of the guards who'd collapsed near the entrance and then kneeled in front of the lock.

"Mukhtar?" A voice came from behind the gate, followed by something that sounded like a question in Arabic.

"Shit," Connelly whispered, motioning to his teammates to move back as he trained the business end of his gun at the door. The guard on the inside must have heard the commotion despite the blaring music in the back of the house.

"Mukhtar?" the voice repeated, this time with some urgency. The lock clicked, and the gate swung back ever so slightly to give the person behind a view of the street without exposing them.

Connelly squeezed the trigger, placing the bullet into the man's left eye, and kicked the door before the dead body had even started to fall, sending it tumbling backward.

As he rushed through the door, he scanned the front yard, the business end of his submachine gun looking for targets, but the area was empty.

Connelly motioned to his teammates, and they dragged the two bodies from outside of the gate and hid them along with the third guard behind the manicured bushes.

The front door to the mansion opened up into a wide hallway leading into separate staircases on each side of the building.

"You two, take this one." Connelly pointed to the left staircase and started toward the right. "We'll converge on the second floor."

As he jogged toward the stairs, a pair of military boots appeared in his view. Connelly paused, hugging the rail as he waited for the guard to come down, and then placed two bullets in the side of the man's head before he had a chance to see him.

A pair of quiet pops came a second later after he pulled the trigger.

"Two down, boss," Patrick said in his earpiece. "Coming toward you."

"I got one," Connelly responded.

They met by the door to the second-floor rooms and Patrick went down on his knee to look through the keyhole.

"There are two guards, right outside of this door," he whispered as he turned back, "and there are two more by the balcony. I can see two dudes sitting at a table out there, and two girls are sitting on their laps. I don't see anyone else."

"The door?"

Patrick touched the knob and gingerly turned it back and forth for a few seconds. Then he gave Connelly a thumbs-up.

"Do it," Connelly mouthed.

Patrick swung the door open and before the guards could react, the two bursts of suppressed automatic fire cut them down. The scantily dressed Asian-looking women who had been sitting on two men's laps on the balcony jumped up, alarmed by the commotion, but then froze in place as they saw Connelly gesturing them to stay quiet. He could see the dancers by the pool continuing their rhythmic gyrations, seemingly unaware of the deadly developments on the second floor.

"No one will hurt you," he said to the women in English. "Get your stuff and get out of here."

"You," he barked at the two men sitting at the table, "get the fuck up and move. We've got a long ride ahead of us."

3 6

October 2007
New York

"Listen, love. You'd expect me to be the last person to say this, but this is the time to go to the cops or perhaps even to the feds," Eugene said as they picked on the leftovers. "The guy has a torture chamber installed in his warehouse and apparently is building a cyborg army. I can't imagine the police, as slow as they are sometimes, will pay no attention to something like this."

"I've tried to have this conversation with her," Chen said, "but she thinks that there are high-placed cops, and even some high-placed feds, who aren't going to be happy if we do. Besides, I've given some information to the NYPD and never heard back. What I don't understand is how a mobster like Victor Ye and a pharmaceutical giant like Guardian Manufacturing are connected. I thought that Guardian was building cyborg prototypes and somehow used the DOD resources without them knowing. Now, I'm just confused and can't connect the dots. What did Victor Ye want with us in the first place and how did he get the suits?"

"Well," Hiroko said and shifted uncomfortably in her chair, "Victor Ye's been working with Guardian for a long time. He was quite chatty when he came to visit me in the warehouse, and now the pieces are kind of falling into places."

"Shit," Chen said and hid her face in her hands. "I can't believe this. It's all my fault. If it wasn't for my stupid idea of revenge, we wouldn't be here. I could have gotten us both killed. I still might."

"Don't be ridiculous. It's not like Victor Ye had been running a bunch of nonprofits for orphans and rescued animals before we showed up. And in any event, it's too late to engage in a shoulda, coulda, woulda kind of a conversation," Hiroko said. "Let's concentrate on what we know and what we can do going forward. I've been following this hornet's nest for a while, but until now I had no idea they were interconnected. By hacking Guardian, we forced their hand, and now we know something that I bet even the law enforcement agencies don't."

"I should have bought beer," Eugene cut in. "It sounds like it's turning out to be one of Hiroko's infamous brainstorming sessions."

"You should have." Hiroko smiled at him. "So. There are at least three players in this group. One is the Red Dragon gang, led by Victor Ye. Another's Guardian, with Simon Engel at the helm, but some are saying that his son, Alexander, is more and more active in the day-to-day operations. I can only assume that it involves whatever shady shit they're in as well. And there's also Otomo Corporation, run by Takeshi Yamamoto."

"But how are they working together?" Chen asked. "Hearing about Otomo is news to me, but in some way, it makes sense. Though it's not their bread and butter, they do have a large pharmaceutical arm, and I guess by colluding with Guardian, they can split the markets better and help one another, rather than compete. But how does Victor factor in? As an enforcer?"

"That was my first thought, but now after listening to him talk and seeing the spacesuits in the warehouse, I'm starting to think I was wrong," Hiroko said. "Victor is the number one guy in this alliance, or whatever you want to call it. He's the one calling the shots. How did he get there—I've no idea. Perhaps he blackmailed Guardian and

Otomo, or maybe he offered them something they couldn't get otherwise. Ultimately, it doesn't make any difference. Somehow, he got in the position of power to lead this alliance, and we have to take it as a starting point."

"Should we go to multiple agencies then?" Eugene interrupted. "Let's call all of them—the NYPD, the FBI, the Department of Homeland Security. Someone's got to be honest in those places."

"No, I don't think so. There're plenty of honest people who work there but all it takes is one crooked cop for us to end up dead before they can help us," Chen said, "and I have a better idea. We should go to an agency, just not the cops or the FBI. We should find a way to get the CIA involved. For starters, they are much less likely to be compromised by Victor Ye and his ilk. And also, they'd be in a better position to do something about it."

"The CIA? I thought they didn't have jurisdiction over the things that happen within our borders?" Eugene said and then shrugged. "What? Stop looking at me like that. That's what they say in the movies. Besides, to do this right, we'd need someone on the inside and do we know anyone who works for the CIA? Don't answer—that was a hypothetical."

Hiroko raised her hand for a moment and then made a dramatic gesture of pointing at Chen.

"Love," Eugene said, "you brought a spook to my own house? Now I most definitely need a drink."

"I *worked* for the CIA, as in past tense," Chen corrected, smiling at the man's exaggerated reaction, "and I was a one-time contractor for a project that later landed me a gig for the Department of Defense, so not even like a permanent position or anything. So, no, sorry, not a spook."

"Do you still have any contacts?"

"Yes," Chen said. "Well, kind of. I built a door when I was there, so I could come back and look up a few things, if I needed to, but it's gonna be a one-time access. It will deactivate itself after being used. So, we better know exactly what we're looking for. There'll be no do-overs."

"Okay, I can't have this conversation without two things—a laptop and something with alcohol in it," Eugene said as he stood up and headed for the door. "I'll be right back."

"Is he always this..." Chen paused, looking for the right word. *"Theatrical?"*

"More or less." Hiroko smiled and stretched. "God, I'm tired. He's worried about me, that's all."

A few minutes later, there was a knock on the door, and Eugene barged in carrying a laptop under his arm, a small box of glasses and a bottle of Remy Martin.

"I thought you were going out to get some beer?" Hiroko said.

"No, love," the man said, setting up the glasses on the table. "We're past the beer time now."

He poured everyone a drink, threw an empty box to the corner of the kitchen, and opened a laptop.

"First of all," he said as his fingers flew over the keyboard, "what exactly does your door allow you to do?"

"Not much," Chen admitted. "Look up contact information within the agency, read some top-level folders and files in them. Nothing too deep."

"Can you send a secure message to someone within the agency so they would see it as if it was coming from the inside?"

"Sure," she said, "that could be the way to do it. Make a compelling case and leave it there. Let them figure it out."

"The question is," Hiroko interjected as she sipped on her drink, "who do we send the message to?"

"Look." Eugene turned the screen of the laptop so the two women could see it. An organizational tree chart dominated the bigger part of the screen. "This is the organization structure of the CIA. The unclassified part of it, of course."

"I guess it's safe to say we can skip Support and Science and Technology," Hiroko said, looking at the diagram, "which leaves us with Intelligence and National Clandestine Service. Any of the subdivisions of those, I suppose?"

"Let's see." Eugene scrolled down the list of subdivisions within the two departments, reading out the likely candidates. "There's crime and narcotics, corporate resources, terrorism analysis, weapons intelligence. These are all within the Intelligence department. What's HUMINT?"

"Human Intelligence," Chen said, "but when you said *unclassified*, it got me thinking. Maybe the best place would be actually the *classified* guys. The ones who run the black ops. The National Clandestine Service. They'll have the biggest pull and more freedom to follow up leads wherever they come from. Can you look up who's the head of the Service?"

"Can't look up things like that on Google," Eugene said as he typed, "but hang on."

Chen took a sip of her brandy as she watched Eugene work. She concentrated on the warmth as the liquid traveled down her throat. She let herself relax, the fear-induced tension finally leaving her body. It'd be a long time before she'd feel normal again, but she was in good company, and they were going to make sure that Victor Ye regretted ever crossing their path.

"Found it," Eugene exclaimed, plucking her from her daydream. "This is our guy."

Chen studied the picture of a man in his early fifties. His gray eyes, an effortless smile, and a shock of gray hair cropped on the sides gave him a distinguished appearance of a university professor.

"All right." She looked at the bottom of the photograph to read the small inscription. "Mr. James David Rovinsky. Let's send you a message."

3 7

October 2007
Unknown location, Afghanistan

The mountain road was flanked by a heart-stopping cliff of crumbling gravel on one side and a nearly vertical wall of jagged blue-gray limestone on the other. The path was an offshoot of the Kabul-Jalalabad road that ran through the Tang-e Gharu gorge in the Hindu Kush mountain range. It started as a proper gravel road as it separated from the main artery, but as they continued on north, getting deeper into the mountains, it'd gotten narrower and steeper with every mile.

This was the Taliban's backyard and spending more time here meant a greater chance of running into some of the heavily armed groups roaming the area. But after coming too close to sliding off the road one too many times, Mike Connelly finally ordered to abandon the van. On the section of the road where it was still wide enough to allow a U-turn, he maneuvered the vehicle around. From there, the group continued on foot.

To his surprise, when they had started to question their prisoners, neither Malik Zubair nor the American buyer, Erik Hanson, put up any fight. They were mercenaries, driven by the sole desire to sell their services to the highest bidder, and for the moment Connelly was it.

"We should have handed Hanson over to the CIA," Doug said to Connelly as they marched on, keeping the captives a few yards ahead of them. "If he's telling the truth, the other half of the payment hasn't been even cashed out yet. And now, since we got him, we'll never know when and where it's gonna be."

"Doesn't matter. Money's only one part of the equation. We need to find out who his bosses are. Besides, once our guys are done with him, they'll hand him over anyway. I don't think Hanson will be a free bird ever again."

"I don't like the fucker." Doug spat on the dusty surface of the road. "If it was up to me, I'd put him down like the rabid dog he is. You gotta be something to work with those assholes."

"Don't you think they're going to guard it like Fort Knox?" Pat interjected. "Twenty-five mil is a lot of dough to leave unattended."

"It'll be guarded, all right. But there's no love lost between the different factions here and putting up a large garrison is going to attract some unwanted attention. Secrecy is a much better protection than a few extra AK-47s."

In front of them, Malik Zubair slowed down, and then stopped as he examined the rocky wall.

"What's he doing?" Doug said, pointing at the man with a barrel of his MP5.

"We need to climb up here," Zubair said.

For anyone continuing up the road, the path would have been almost invisible. But now, as Connelly knew where to look, he could see a trail weaving through the boulders and disappearing up the hill. It zigzagged first, climbing steadily up for a couple of hundred yards and then ran parallel to the ground around the mountain.

"How far?"

"It's about three kilometers around the mountain, but we'll have to make a loop to come from above, so it'll add another one, maybe one-and-a-half."

"I need you to tell me where the guards are."

"There are usually two guards by the cave. And there's a cliff about three hundred meters before the cave. They'll have another guard or two watching the path from there."

"Can we get to them unnoticed?"

"That's why we need to make a loop."

"Go on, then."

Connelly watched as the man started to climb up the steep path.

"You, go after him," he nodded to Hanson, "and let's pick up the pace. We don't have all day."

"I don't like this," Doug said. "I feel like we're being led into a trap."

"Let's keep our heads on a swivel."

They trekked the path up and around the mountain for half an hour. When Zubair started to head up again, looping around the cliff where he said the insurgents would be keeping watch, Connelly stopped the group.

"You two, sit down back to back and don't move until I return," he commanded to the detainees. "Pat, you're watching them. If they as much as blink funny, shoot the motherfuckers."

"You got it."

He nodded to Doug and together they continued on the path until Patrick and the two prisoners disappeared from the view.

"What's the plan, boss?"

"We climb first." Connelly pointed straight up. "I think two guys by the cave and another two dudes three hundred yards out sounds too easy."

"Yeah. He's up to something."

The climb turned difficult just after the first few yards. The surface was a treacherous mix of loose pebbles and dry soil. More than once they found themselves sliding back, unable to stop the descent, digging their bleeding fingers into the ground as anchors. After what seemed an eternity, Connelly crept out onto a rocky bluff hanging above the path that Zubair was leading them on.

"Fuck me," Doug whispered as he crawled next to Connelly. He rolled on his back, facing the sky, and took a few long breaths. "I hate mountains."

"Yeah."

Doug rolled back on his stomach, took out binoculars, and scanned the hillside under their position.

"That little shit. There," he whispered, pointing down. "A guy with a Dragunov."

As Connelly looked in the direction of Doug's hand, he saw it—a slender silhouette of a Russian-made sniper rifle peeking out from behind a boulder, just a hundred yards below them. Another fifty yards down the mountain, under the sniper's nest, he could see two more guards laying prone on the cliff above the entrance to the cave.

"How do we get this fucker?" Doug whispered.

Connelly scanned the area. The sniper's body was almost entirely hidden behind a gray boulder, leaving only the top of his turban above the surface of the rock, a pair of boots sticking out on one side, and the end of the rifle on the other. As far as he could see, there was no way to climb around the man without attracting his attention, and an altercation with the sniper would alert the two guards below him. Connelly turned back to Doug.

"How well can you throw?"

"I dunno." Doug shrugged. "Well enough."

"I can see the tip of his turban," Mike pointed down, "but he's too low. I need him to look up. Can you hit that boulder from here?"

"I think so. But what about the guys below him? They'll hear the shot."

"Don't worry." Mike stood up on one knee and took a careful aim. "Just make the fucker look up. Let me know before you throw."

He slowed down his breathing and rested his cheek on the butt-stock of his MP5.

"I got a good pebble," Doug said.

Connelly aligned the sights of the submachine gun and placed the tip of the turban dead center of the front sight holder. His index finger slid inside the trigger guard and rested lightly on the serrated surface.

"Three," Doug said behind him in a hoarse whisper. "Two, one. Go."

A pebble went too left and instead of hitting the boulder, flicked the man's boot, startling him. A surprised face popped in Connelly's sights and he pulled the trigger. Red liquid splattered the rock, and the turban disappeared as quickly as it showed up. Connelly swung the weapon and let out two short bursts as the guards below reacted to the commotion, cutting them down. He kept the gun trained on the crumpled bodies down below, but there was no other movement. The boots behind the boulder were not stirring either.

"Good shootin', boss." Doug patted him on the shoulder.

"Thanks. You can tell Pat to start moving."

"Can I tell him not to bring anyone else?"

"No," Connelly said. "I'm afraid we're gonna have to keep those two for a bit longer."

By the time Connelly and Doug made their way down to the cave, Patrick already had the two prisoners clearing out the entrance. Big boulders that were blocking the entry were rolled aside, and loose tree branches that served as camouflage were now piled next to the dark, gaping hole.

Connelly turned the flashlight on and stepped into the cave, keeping his MP5 at the ready. The narrow corridor widened after a few yards and then opened up into a large rectangular place with a low ceiling and a pair of hefty wooden torches affixed to the walls on the opposite sides of the cavern.

"Jesus, Mary, and Joseph," Pat said behind him. "Do you see what I see? Is it what I think it is?"

Connelly walked to one of the torches and flicked a Zippo. The fire licked an oil-soaked rag for a moment and then spread around with a soft whoosh, throwing long shadows around the cave. Connelly turned back and walked to the center of the room.

There were what appeared to be large boxes sitting on top of wooden pallets. They were covered with a heavy tarp, and someone placed a few rocks on top of the rough material to keep it from moving. Connelly walked around the pallets and swept the rocks off, then picked up the corner of the tarp and, in one motion, pulled it off to the side.

"Yeah," Connelly said, looking at the five-foot-tall stacks of one-hundred-dollar bills wrapped in plastic. "I think it is. And I'm certain it's more than twenty-five mil."

3 8

October 2007
New York

"This is huge, Jim," Andrew said, looking out the kitchen window. "This is not normal."

"Of course, it isn't normal," Rovinsky said, as he poured himself a glass of water and settled on a couch. "My entire house can fit inside your kitchen. I need to stop and take a break every time I take a walk to the bathroom because I get winded. How's that normal?"

"Stop it."

"I'm serious, Andy. You should give your guests a scooter. You know why I never bring Susan to New York? Because if I do, I'll have to bring her over when you and Audrey decide to host a dinner. I'm convinced that she'll divorce me right after the visit."

"You give her too little credit," Andrew said. "Susan's one of the loveliest people I've ever met."

"I wouldn't know," Jim said. "We've only been married for thirty-two years, so I haven't decided yet if I'm going to keep her. Talk to me —why are you so glum? We've struck gold in Kabul. We had some losses, it's true, but the operation's been a massive success. I thought you'd be happy? You wanted a war chest? You've got a massive one. Or you're still jet-lagged from your flight back from the Stan?"

"I'm not jet-lagged anymore, and I was happy," Andrew said, "until yesterday's news about Rosario Jones."

"They've briefed me on the attack, just like everybody else," Jim said, "but I haven't seen anything different from what's been reported by the media. It sounds like some white nationalists who were unhappy with her agenda did it. She's been driving at them pretty hard for the last couple of years."

"Yes, she has," Andrew agreed, "but I don't think those were white nationalists."

"But she's been targeted by those guys before," Jim said. "A few months back, somebody sprayed a swastika on her car and then there was an incident when she found a KKK hood in her office."

"That may be true," Andrew said, "but I think those assholes were just a useful tool and as far as the actual assassination, it was carried out by someone else. A team of professionals."

"You think it was a paid hit? I don't know," Jim said. "It seems like a stretch. Look, it's never normal when a US senator gets assassinated. This is the first time something like this happened since the Peoples Temple's crazies killed Congressman Leo Ryan in Guyana. What was it? Nineteen seventy-seven?"

"Seventy-eight," Andrew said, "but those were religious fanatics. This is something else."

"Look, I hear you, and I'm as appalled as you are, but can we talk about the operation in Kabul, for a second?" Jim said. "What are you planning to do with the money? On the one hand, I'm excited, but I have to say I'm shitting my pants at the very thought of you laundering over half a billion dollars."

Andrew Hunt turned away from the window, walked back across the room, and took a seat opposite his friend.

"Jim," he said, "work with me here. I know I've been driving everyone insane in the past few weeks and sleep hours have been scarce, but think. Who was Rosario Jones?"

"A second-term US senator from Texas." Jim shrugged and looked up, trying to remember. "A rising star, some people called her. A centrist Republican. Popular with the Hispanics, African Americans, and the younger folks. Why?"

"Can you name one piece of legislation that has caused more controversy in the last year than the—"

"The Public Safety Concern Act," Rovinsky interrupted him. "She was the swing vote against it. Not sure how it is even possible that there's a debate on that issue."

"That's right," Andrew said. "This legislation will make the police response to certain crimes optional. And as the argument goes, any possible rise in crime should be mitigated by installing the Safety Web Network, the all-seeing network of cameras hooked to the massive AI which will determine which activities justify the use of the police force."

"Well, that's how they've been selling it," Rovinsky said. "Not that I'm buying it."

"There's another piece of the puzzle for you," Andrew continued. "Jones is slated to be replaced by no one else but Ron Mulvany, an outspoken supporter of the bill, and the son of the disgraced Phillip Mulvany, who's been married to corporate interests his entire life."

"I didn't know that. You're saying the cabal is behind it? They want the act to pass?"

"Of course they do, Jim," Andrew said. "Let me draw a picture for you. As it stands now, the bill doesn't describe which crimes should be addressed and which shouldn't. Of course, they will position it as something each municipality should define themselves, according to their laws."

"But, to play devil's advocate, that could be a good thing. It could eliminate the need to respond to small offenses. Which should free up the cops to do better on something important."

"Sure. That's the sales pitch. Somebody double-parked a car? Didn't stop for a school bus with flashing lights? You don't need to send a heavily armored SWAT truck their way. Capture them on video and send them a ticket in the mail."

"Right," Jim said. "But?"

"But who gets to decide what should be looked at and what

shouldn't? It can send it down the slippery slope of bigger and bigger crimes that never get reported at all. We know that the cabal controls some of the law enforcement already. Now they get to dictate how they behave and when."

"Turning it off and on, like a cop planting evidence with his dashcam offline?"

"Exactly. A rival corporation starts building a new plant and somebody sets it on fire, but poof." Andrew made a gesture like a magician making his assistant disappear. "Wait, where's the tape?"

"That's science fiction," Rovinsky said. "That would require massive cooperation of different levels of the police department. Some of them might be crooked, but not all of them."

"No, not all of them," Andrew agreed, "but it doesn't require all of them or even that many people. It only requires a tech guy who controls the video feeds, and a person in charge somewhere high enough for the cover-up. To make sure nobody messes with the tech guy."

"Let's say you're right."

"You know I'm right," Andrew said, "but that's not all. It's not just the law enforcement issue. It's also the issue of control."

"Control of what?"

"Everything, Jim," Andrew said. He stood up and walked back to the window. "This is the greatest intrusion into anyone's privacy ever. Whoever controls those cameras will not just control the police response. They will control an unbelievable amount of information and let me tell you, if I've learned anything in my life, it is that information is the ultimate currency. Whoever knows more controls the narrative and therefore wins."

"But the news organizations surely—"

"How will the news organizations find out there's an incident to report on if nobody calls it in?"

"Man." Rovinsky took a long gulp of water, set the glass on the table, and leaned back on the couch. "My head is spinning."

"My head's been spinning since I joined you in that hot car down in DC," Andrew said. "I've been living in a perpetual bout of vertigo ever since. And it's only going to get worse. I've spoken to the president, and he agrees with me. But that news is only half-good, Jim. Those in the government who oppose the measure, notably the president himself, will want to wrestle this tool out of other people's hands."

"Sets them on the collision course," Rovinsky said. "A war."

"That's right," Andrew replied, "and like any other war, those who suffer will not be the people at the top. A war is coming, Jim. Not the likes of which we've seen before, but the results will be similar, nonetheless. It will destroy neighborhoods and some people will die. Poverty will rise, and kids will starve. The very fabric of our society will rip and fray, and we will see it with our own eyes."

3 9

October 2007
New York

Jill Cooper dreamed of Sa Calobra beach at the end of the Torrent de Pareis gorge. The jagged slopes of the Serra de Tramuntana framed the view like a movie shot and the sky over the ocean was a cloudless well of deep blue stretched over her head as far as the eye could see. When she first opened her eyes, the light from the windows, diffused by azure-colored curtains, if only for a moment, let the illusion linger, but then, the night vision slipped away and disappeared into the bright daylight.

She got up and walked to the window and peered through the glass from behind the curtain. The view couldn't be any farther from the Mediterranean shoreline—it snowed overnight in Brooklyn; the first snow of the year. It was still too warm for it to stay on the ground. In front of her brownstone sitting on a quiet block of Prospect Park, the snow had already turned into a gray slush, and from here Cooper could see a few of her neighbors shoveling it away. But the front yard, the steps, and the railings ending with a pair of cone-shaped knobs still looked pristine, and Cooper stood there for a few moments, taking it all in. Enjoying the simple geometric beauty of black and white lines and right angles.

In another place, in another life, Cooper thought. She sighed and let the curtain go. There was work to be done.

She pulled on a tracksuit and a pair of old Nikes and went for a four-mile run around the Green-Wood Cemetery, getting into the rhythm of her step, keeping her breath steady. Then, she followed it by a workout in her basement gym. Some weights and a punching bag, some stretching, and then a few rounds on a punching bag again. She showered and had a quick breakfast and then called a car service. There was someone she needed to talk to.

It'd been a couple of days since she had let Arthur go. By now, he was undoubtedly back at work on the prosthetic arm she'd caught a glimpse of while in his workshop. She should have moved on as well. But what normally should have been just another job—filed, payment received, and promptly forgotten—instead continued to dominate her thoughts. To her surprise, not only had she received full payment on the assignment despite breaking the protocol, but the employer had also given her a sizeable bonus.

Curiosity in her line of work was both necessary and deadly. Prying into your secretive employers' business was sure to draw their ire if noticed. That could lead to a range of consequences, from discontinuation of services to a contract on your own head. But it was also essential for self-preservation. Cooper had heard too many stories about people of her profession who took assignments based on payouts alone, never bothering to check whether their employer was going to keep paying them, or would throw them to the wolves the moment they did their job.

This time, however, she broke her own rules by choosing to work for the mysterious benefactor. The money was the deciding factor when she had been approached for the first time, almost quadruple of her going rate. She did all she could to vet the employer, but the only thing she could find was that the same person, or a group of people who hired her, had hired other professionals in the field and had paid them well.

She took the gamble and so far, it seemed to be paying off, but now, especially after the last job, Cooper was starting to suspect she was entering some uncharted waters. She had to find out who was paying her and what their agenda was.

Aaron Zimmer, the person she wanted to see, lived alone in a six-thousand-square-foot monstrosity that looked like an ugly version of the White House and sported two ten-foot-tall crying angel statues in its front yard. The house itself was located in the heart of Dyker Heights, an affluent Brooklyn neighborhood sitting on top of a hill between Bay Ridge and Bensonhurst, but knowing Aaron's paranoia, Jill had the driver let her go by the entrance to the Dyker Beach golf course about a mile away from the house. Then she covered the remaining few blocks to Zimmer's residence by foot.

She'd known Aaron for the last five years, since her previous banker had introduced them before he retired. A *banker*, of course, was a generous term when it was applied to people like Aaron Zimmer, although he could give a lot of people working for some legit institutions on Wall Street a run for their money. But the term that someone might have used to describe Aaron Zimmer's services never bothered Cooper or even entered her mind. Her only concern was that he charged a reasonable fee and laundered her money well.

This time, however, Cooper didn't need him to launder her illicit earnings. A few days ago, she had given him the details of every money transfer she'd received from her new employer and asked Zimmer if it was possible to trace the origins of that cash.

"For the right amount of money, everything is possible, darling," he said at the time. "It's the right amount of money that is not always possible."

The slush around the house wasn't cleaned, and the path to the house had no footprints on the snow either, but that wasn't what made Cooper's alarm bells go off. Aaron was a homebody and sometimes stayed inside the house for days, getting food and entertainment delivered straight to his door.

What set off the alarm was the steel bar gate leading to the inside of the front yard. The door was ajar, and Cooper couldn't come up with one good explanation of why a remote-controlled entrance to the lair of such a security-paranoid freak like Aaron would be unlocked. She squeezed through the gap and pushed the door back in place until the lock mechanism engaged. The windows of the house had curtains down, and though she couldn't sense any movement, Cooper couldn't help but feel exposed standing in the middle of the open space.

She threw a quick glance around, making sure that no one was watching, and pulled out a compact HK P30SK. Then, she made her way across the yard and up the stairs. The front door was unlocked as well, and Cooper pushed it with the nozzle of the gun and stepped into the house.

The sweet, pungent smell hit her like a truck. There was no mistaking that odor with anything else—it was death's own cologne—a rotting mixture of decaying flesh and human excrements wrapped in one ugly bottle. From the front door, she could see Aaron's body seated in a chair in the middle of a giant living room, facing away from her. His hands were bound behind him and his ankles tied to the legs of the chair. His head was thrown back and rested at an angle no living person would find comfortable.

Cooper circled around the body, keeping the pistol at her chest level. She was ready to engage if someone was hiding in the shadows, but the house stayed still. The only sounds bouncing through the empty house were the creaking of the floor planks under her feet and her own ragged breathing.

Satisfied she wasn't walking into a trap, she put the gun away and walked to the corpse. The man's throat was slit. She could see a ghastly laceration going almost all the way from his left ear to the right, but that's not what caught her eye.

Attached to Aaron Zimmer's chest with a safety pin was a small rectangular envelope with three words on it that made her heart skip a bit.

For Jill Cooper

4 0

October 2007
New York

"I'd say we should be extra careful, that's all," Eugene said, looking at the screen. "This guy is a little too high up. If he gets something that smells even remotely funny, he'll kick it down the chain and we'll be old and gray by the time they decide to make a move on it."

"Didn't we want somebody high up? Someone with enough pull to be able to follow up on this?" Hiroko asked.

The three of them stared at the picture of the Director of Clandestine Service, as if asking for answers.

"You might be onto something," Chen finally said. "Maybe he is too high. It's like if we went to the president himself to tell him about the corruption in the mayor's office of some town in the middle of nowhere. It just doesn't make sense. There's got to be someone more suitable for the dump of info like that. Still high on the totem pole to make a difference, but not too high to freak out about getting an unauthorized message."

"They'll freak out regardless," Hiroko said, "even if you send it to their janitor, but okay, I'll bite. What are our options then?"

"Can you look up his deputies?" Chen asked. "Or you don't think you can do it on the fly? Because if that's the case, I can reach out to some guys who might be able to help."

"I find your lack of faith in my abilities disturbing," Eugene said. "Love, did you hear that?"

"C'mon, show-off," Hiroko said. "Do your thing—give us the names."

Eugene didn't answer as he continued to type on the laptop. A minute later, he stopped and moved it back on the table so they could all see his screen.

There was a page that looked like a scan of a document with four names on it and a small bio underneath each one.

"My vote goes to this guy in Covert Action." Eugene pointed to one of the names. "He's gonna kick some major ass. General Roberts. A two-star general, participated in Desert Storm, a former Marine. I mean, c'mon, it's not even close. I'd say we send it to him."

"I don't think a military guy is a good choice," Chen said. "If anyone is going to be more prone to kicking this down the chain, it's going to be him."

"Why? He's clearly sharp as a whip, and with his military background I'm sure he can think outside of the box."

"His military background is exactly the wrong part of his profile for this. I'm sure he's got a good head on his shoulders, but he's also trained to follow orders. To do things by the book. I'd say we pick someone else."

"All right, you pick, then."

"What about this guy?" Chen pointed at another name.

"Financial crimes?" Eugene shrugged. "I don't see how a guy who analyzes financial crimes can help us."

"Something just occurred to me." Hiroko interrupted him. "Narcotics. It's gotta be narcotics. Think about it."

"I'm sorry, love, I'm not sure I follow," Eugene said. "What about narcotics?"

"The link," she said excitedly. "The missing link we couldn't understand that connected a mobster like Victor Ye and legit businesses like Guardian and Otomo. It all makes sense now. They are not just any businesses that make, let's say, car parts and door handles. They are pharmaceutical companies and Victor Ye produces high-quality street drugs."

"You're right," Chen said. "This is a match made in heaven. Or rather, hell. Each party has something unique to bring to the table. He brings the raw product, and they bring the know-how. I bet the profit margins on those street drugs are a magnitude higher than any prescription stuff you can sell to the general public."

"He also probably acts as the money launderer, who cleans up the profits for them," Eugene added. "It would be much more difficult for them to do that part of the business, but for Victor Ye, it's just another day in the office."

"This is precisely why we need the finance guy," Chen said and pointed at the screen again. "We won't have to sell it to him as hard as we'd have to for anybody else. He'll be able to see that connection himself."

"Well, if that's the guy we're sending the info to, then we don't need to burn your secret door," Eugene said. "We can keep that access point for later. He's got a large footprint outside of the agency. We can contact him through his business, Orion Securities."

"Okay." Chen rubbed her eyes and looked at her friends. "Let's write the pitch. What have we got?"

"Torture chambers," Hiroko and Eugene said simultaneously.

"Yes, besides that, dummies. Never mind, I'll write. Give me this."

She took the laptop from Eugene and opened a new Word document. She didn't have to think—it all came to her now: The murder-suicide of her sister's broker and his mistress. The murder of her sister and the link to Guardian Manufacturing she had found when she'd looked through Mary's apartment. The suspected connection between Otomo, Guardian, and Victor Ye's criminal empire. And finally, the Nyctalope program, where someone was using the DOD's resources to build what appeared to be a prototype of a cyborg.

When she finished typing, Chen looked up and moved the laptop back to the middle of the table. "There," she said. "Please critique away."

She watched as the two of them read the document—Hiroko with the face of a statue, and Eugene moving his lips like a kid as he read.

"Wait. It says you want a meeting too. And it doesn't say anything about how we know all this." Eugene spoke first. "Although it's hard to explain without mentioning how you two hacked Guardian's servers and then the New York Stock Exchange."

"Yeah. Let's keep that information to ourselves. We might be alerting him about some big conspiracy, but I'd imagine this guy still has an obligation to report us if he finds out what we've done. But yes, I want to meet him in person. I want to take Victor Ye down. Writing a letter isn't going to cut it."

"Okay. So, where are we sending this?" Eugene asked. "His business email? A package to his house? I'm game, whatever you guys decide."

"Email, right?" Hiroko said. "Faster."

"Sure," Chen agreed, "and let's see if we can monitor this guy. See what he's up to and if he does anything that looks like he's acting on this information after he gets the message."

"I like it," Eugene said and ran a search. "Got it. Here's the email. Who do you want it to come from?"

"The agency?" Chen said. "Then it's not going to disappear in the junk folder. Can you do that without using the back door?"

"I'll make it look close enough," Eugene promised. "There you go. A couple of letters are backward, but on first glance, it'll look like it came from the right place. Are we doing this?"

Chen looked at Eugene and then at Hiroko and finally gave him a slight nod.

"Yes," she said. "I don't think we have any other choice. Wait. Will he be able to reply?"

"Yes," Eugene said. "I've also set up an alert in case he does. Unless you don't want him to be able to."

"No, let's keep it open. Do it."

Eugene's slender hand hovered above the keyboard for a second and then his index finger punched the button with a decisive stroke.

"It's done."

41

November 2007
Punta Cana, Dominican Republic

As she sat at the bar by the lighted pool, sipping on her cold drink, Jill Cooper contemplated her fate. The message she'd found in Aaron Zimmer's home was without any ambiguity—stop sticking your nose where it doesn't belong. The envelope that was pinned to his lifeless body had a photograph of a girl on a sunny Mediterranean beach. The photographer caught her mid-jump as she was about to hit a volleyball—her wet hair swinging wildly, her face lit by a smile from ear to ear.

She looked happy. Of course, Cooper told herself, she wanted her to be happy. Yet, somehow seeing her like that, having a good time in the sun, surrounded by people she saw as friends, hurt Cooper even more.

The back side of the photograph had instructions for a new banker. Her employer insisted that she was going to have to use their service from now on. That message wasn't vague either—Cooper's money wasn't her money any longer. She only got to use it as long as she played nice and followed instructions. For now, she didn't see any other choice but to play nice.

She came to the hotel a full week earlier than her employer had asked her to for a couple of reasons. The first one was professional—she wanted to learn the lay of the land. It never hurt to do some extra homework, and she spent the first two days walking around the hotel and the surrounding grounds, taking mental notes of cleaning crew schedules, deliveries, and garbage pickup times. The second reason was selfish—Cooper was starting to get burned-out. However crazy that sounded, she wanted to mix the job with a small vacation.

Set on the sugary sands of Arena Gorda Beach, the hotel was a large T-shaped three-story complex. Surrounded with coconut palms and straw cabanas, its long leg stretched perpendicular to the sapphire waters of the Atlantic. A thousand-foot-long pool ran along the entire length of the eastern wall of the hotel and Cooper spent the last four days before her target's arrival doing what everybody else did—drinking piña coladas in pool bars, eating local food, and flirting with other hotel guests.

To her dismay, most people staying at the hotel around this time turned out to be families with kids and married couples, which reduced her chances of having a proper "resort experience" to virtually zero. Cooper watched as the silver-haired executive-type American who she was exchanging pleasantries with was joined by his wife, who shot her a suspicious look. Cooper smiled at her with a dumb expression of a friendly tourist and returned her attention to the drink in her hand.

Cooper was cross, but the picture she'd found in Zimmer's house wasn't the only reason for her sour mood. What also made her restless was the way her employer wanted to carry out this assignment. She had made a name for herself creating elaborate false stories around her hits, where assassinations looked like accidents, random acts of violence that had nothing to do with the real reason behind the killings. But even when her employers didn't need subterfuge, the hits were always professional—clean and quick. Surgical.

This time, it was different. She was instructed to leave a statement —a break-in, signs of torture, and an execution. A local contact delivered to her a brand-new Glock semiautomatic pistol, a silencer, and a fifteen-round magazine stacked with hollow-points. The target—a Japanese businessman—was scheduled to arrive tomorrow morning with his wife and was supposed to stay at the resort for a week. If he was anything like the patrons that Cooper had been observing for the last few days, it would be nearly impossible to separate him from his wife long enough to fulfill the contract.

That added to Cooper's frustration. Sometimes collateral damage was inevitable, but it always bothered her when people who had to be eliminated with the target were there for the right reasons. She'd be much less conflicted if the man was traveling alone.

"Would you like another drink, señorita?" the bartender said, his accented English making him sound like an actor from a telenovela.

"No. Gracias." Cooper smiled back, threw a few singles on the counter and got up. "I think I'll hit the sack."

As she headed toward the paved path along the pool, Cooper felt someone's eyes on her. She paused, pretending to check her purse, and threw a glance back at the direction of the bar. There was a young man sitting at one of the corner tables. His olive skin was smooth and seemed to ripple over hard muscles on his exposed arms. His posture was relaxed, and his eyes fixed on the drink in his hand, but Cooper's adrenaline surged through the roof.

He didn't have to be looking at her or doing anything suspicious. Just like one fox would recognize another inside of a henhouse, Cooper instantly knew that the man sitting across the room was a professional killer.

She closed her purse and started walking, quietly cursing herself for leaving the pistol in the hotel room. As she reached the doors to the lobby of the hotel, Cooper risked a quick look over her shoulder— the man from the bar was now walking along the paved path heading her way, a small satchel in his hands. There was no time for pretending anymore, and Cooper threw the door open and sprinted down the hallway and past the elevator. A gust of warm air brushed her neck, and the wall next to her exploded in a shower of dust and small debris.

"Mother fucker," Cooper exhaled, as she turned the corner and ran up the stairs, taking three steps at a time. Her room was located on the third floor of the hotel and by the time she burst into the hallway, she had a keycard in her hand. Cooper swiped the card and threw herself at the door, diving into the dark room as another bullet bit into the doorframe.

A baseball bat crashed into the door where her head would have been had she walked through the door instead of rolling in. She looked up in time to see another man, a carbon copy of the killer from the bar, raising the bat for another blow.

Cooper rolled into the swing, reached for the man's groin, and squeezed with all her might. The assailant yelped in pain and shock, and she sprang to her feet, delivering an elbow into his trachea. As the man collapsed onto his knees, Cooper planted her thumbs into his eye sockets and pushed. The man made a gurgling sound; his body tensed for a fraction of a second and then almost immediately went limp.

She pushed the body away from her and leaped to the room's door, slammed it shut, bolted it, and stepped away in time to see two ragged holes appear below the peephole. Cooper ran on her fours to the small bag next to her bed, pulled out the Glock and racked the slide, getting a bullet into the chamber. As another two holes appeared in the thin door, she aimed for where the shooter should have been and pulled the trigger.

There was a click as the firing pin slammed on the bullet's primer, but the gun didn't go off.

"You're shitting me," she cursed, racking the slide again to eject the bad bullet, and getting a new one into the chamber. She aimed and pulled the trigger again. There was another empty click.

Something heavy crashed into the door, straining the deadbolt and then slammed again. The door wasn't going to hold for much longer, Cooper decided, and the room was turning into a death trap. She threw away the pistol and dashed toward the balcony, ignoring the rhythmic pounding on the door. She looked down, searching for escape options.

There were two daybeds with thick mattresses sitting on the lawn right under her balcony, but after some deliberation, she decided that jumping on those was too much of a gamble. For all she knew, the frame of the bed would splinter, and she had no intention of helping the assassin by having herself impaled.

Cooper bent over the railing and looked at the level below her. If she timed it right, she thought she could grab the rails of the second-floor balcony as she fell.

There was another sound of a crash behind her and Cooper flung herself over the railing and let go as the door to her room swung open. There was a brief rush of the air and then she reached out just in time to catch onto the wooden balustrade. Hot pain exploded in her shoulders, but she ignored it, pulled herself in, hurled a beach chair through the glass door blocking her way to the room and ran.

A few seconds later, Cooper bolted out of the building and mixed into the group of people heading for the beach. As they passed a few hotel patrons sunning by the pool, she snatched a big straw hat laying on the grass and covered her head. She could hear the sounds of commotion coming from the hotel. Some people were shouting and then a fire alarm went off, drowning all other sounds away.

As she gained some distance from the hotel, she started to relax, her heart slowing to a normal pace, but as the adrenaline drained, the pain in her shoulders returned with a vengeance. The pain was going to have to wait, she thought. First, she needed to find a place to hide, lick her wounds, and regroup. Once she was safe, she'd be able to make plans on how to find those who were responsible. Someone was going to pay for this.

42

November 2007
New York

Simon Engel had been coming to Billy's Steakhouse on Broad Street in downtown Manhattan almost every day since it had opened its doors a few years ago. Something about this place checked all the right boxes for him. He always thought that it was a combination of things.

Part of it was the location, just across the street from the famed New York Stock Exchange. Another part was that the main entrance didn't open into a spacious dining room like in most restaurants, but instead led you to the basement that once housed J.P. Morgan & Co.'s original bank vault, installed by Remington & Sherman back in 1902. Coming here made him feel like he was a part of a secret club—an insider with a special invitation.

And, of course, because they served a magnificent thick-cut applewood-smoked bacon with balsamic reduction.

Simon was enjoying the bacon as he sat in the corner of a paisley tapestry-covered banquette while admiring the original three-feet thick vault door, when his son, Alexander, joined him at the table.

"I'm sorry I'm late," Alexander said as he pulled the chair to sit across his father. "The traffic was atrocious. I don't understand why you insist on keeping this office downtown. Frankly, I don't understand your obsession with this place, either."

"I like being able to keep my hand on the pulse of the markets. And you can't hear the pulse better than being right next to the heart. As for this place—I like this door." Simon pointed to the massive vault door. "It's easy to forget these days the lengths people are willing to go to protect what they think is theirs. This door reminds me of that. And I love the bacon."

"There are places in Midtown that have doors like that, and you shouldn't eat this much bacon."

"Good afternoon, gentlemen." The waiter, wearing a white jacket and a black bow tie, approached their table and gave a slight bow. "Would you like to hear our specials?"

"No, thanks." Alexander cut him off. "I'll take your chicken Caesar and some mineral water, please. And make sure we're not disturbed."

"Of course, sir."

"What was so urgent that you wanted to talk to me about? And why did you have to drag me down here across town when we could discuss whatever it was over the phone?"

Simon cut the strip of bacon into short pieces, dunked it in the inky pool of balsamic reduction and threw it in his mouth. "I wish you enjoyed yourself more. Life's short and being too strict with yourself is about the worst thing you can do."

"I'm enjoying myself plenty."

"Buying things doesn't always count, but it's your life. You sure you don't want to try the bacon?"

"I have a meeting in two hours, and as much as I'd like to chat about nothing, I need to be going soon."

"Well," Simon put his fork down and looked at his son, "it has come to my attention that you've been using some of my assets in a somewhat frivolous manner."

"Assets? What kind of assets?"

"The ones that give us answers when nothing else does."

Simon watched as his son shifted in his chair, but to his surprise he saw no remorse on the younger man's face. The emotion was the one he hadn't expected at all.

Anger.

"You've never told me I couldn't use them and what's the purpose of having them if I can't touch them?"

"It's true—I never said you couldn't use them, but things like that should be used sparingly. Strategically. And most definitely not against our own people."

"She was poking her nose where it didn't belong."

"It's not for you to decide when to write them off. You've made a lot of mistakes lately, and I don't like cleaning up other people's mistakes. Even my own son's."

"What are you saying?"

"What I'm saying," Simon leaned closer to Alexander and lowered his voice to a whisper, "is that we are not in the business of cutting loose threads every time it gets a little bit inconvenient."

"It's not actually a moral lecture, is it? Because I don't need to remind you that the stuff that we sell, well, let's say it affects thousands, tens of thousands, not an inconvenient few. I'd say it is time to move ahead. The landscape's changed, Dad. We have to take what's ours. Do it by force if necessary. We've been hiding in the shadows for too long and why? We don't answer to anyone, and we're finally in the position to assert our rights—"

Simon slammed his hand on the table so hard it stung. The glasses danced precariously, splashing cold water on the white tablecloth. The few patrons sitting at the neighboring tables were throwing them surprised glances, but Simon didn't care.

"Only a fool thinks he doesn't answer to anybody. You are my son and one day you'll have to sit in my place and make those decisions but, by God, you're not ready yet. Do the work for the company you do, get involved with the board, oversee the acquisition team, fine. You're good with those things and I appreciate what you've done for the firm. But I forbid—you hear me?—forbid you from using my cleaning crews."

"Dad."

"Do you understand me? If you so much as want to clean somebody else's car, you come to me first, is that clear?"

Simon stared at his son with a mixture of fury and disbelief, but there was nothing but defiance on Alexander's face.

"What's perfectly clear, Dad," Alexander said and stood up, "is that you don't have the vision anymore. As long as I can remember, you've been the guy who broke the rules and blazed his own trail. I don't have to retell you the stories—you've lived through them. But you're not that guy anymore."

"Son, sit down."

"Did you know that there was a new governmental program that was created with the sole purpose of shutting us down?"

"Yes."

"Oh, you did? And you've kept it from me? You didn't think I needed to be in the loop?"

"That's exactly what I thought," Simon said, his cheeks flush with anger. "Because you don't know how to handle these things. There's a place for brute force, but some things must be handled with finesse and, trust me when I tell you, this is exactly the thing that must be handled delicately."

"Quite the opposite. There's only one way to handle something like this—by force. Remove the threat before it has a chance to blossom."

"You can't fight the government outright. You can't win that war. That will make things worse."

"It used to be the case. But I can't believe you don't see the state we're in. The balance has shifted and whoever takes this opportunity will change the future. It's sad, but you're not a leader anymore. You're just an old man reliving his glory days who thinks he's still in control. Enjoy your bacon."

Simon watched as his son put on a coat and walked out of the restaurant. The waiter, who was observing the conversation from a safe distance until this point, finally moved and waltzed to the table.

"Is everything okay, sir? Should I still bring your entrees?"

"No, thank you. I won't be staying," Simon said. He stood up and threw a few twenty-dollar bills on the table. "I have to go."

"Was it your son?"

"Yes."

"He looks like you." The waiter smiled. "Kids. They always think they know best. My teenage—"

"Get the fuck outta my face before I smash it into the table. And don't presume you know anything about me or my kids."

He stormed past the stunned waiter, ran up the stairs, and burst outside into the cold November afternoon.

The area in front of the exchange was bustling with tourists, taking selfies outside of the fence separating the crowds from the building. A few office workers were striding purposefully to and from their lunch breaks, dodging the crowds with a mix of determination and annoyance on their faces.

Simon looked around for his son, but Alexander was nowhere to be seen.

43

November 2007
New York

"This retirement isn't living up to all the hype," Andrew Hunt said as he turned off the lamp on the nightstand and lay down. "I haven't been this tired since college, and I'm starting to run out of excuses of why I never go out to play golf anymore."

"You should go play a round or two," Audrey said. "It'll help you to clear your head and unwind. As for being tired—you should stop checking your email on your phone after you go to bed. That's why you have trouble sleeping. I've read somewhere that the light excites your brain by tricking it into thinking it's still day."

"That's not what excites my brain."

"Don't even think about it. Not tonight. I'm spent."

"Yes, ma'am."

He scrolled through the company's emails, trying to catch up. Separating himself from the organization he'd build from the ground up turned out to be more emotionally challenging than he'd anticipated, and he tried to mitigate the loss by occasionally checking in and staying in the loop. Most of the emails were the routine day-to-day, and he was ready to retire for the night when he saw it.

The message appeared to have come from the agency, which in itself was strange—he never received any communications from the CIA before, other than on a separate secure phone. Andrew hesitated opening it for a moment, thinking that it might be a scam email and have a virus, but it didn't seem to have any attachments, and it wasn't flagged as suspicious by the server.

He clicked it open and started to read.

"Are you okay?"

"Yes, why?"

"Because you're not in bed and standing in the middle of the room."

Andrew stared at his wife and then glanced down at his bare feet.

"Yeah," he finally said. "Come to the study. You gotta read this."

He walked to the study, powered up his desktop and pulled up the email on the big screen for Audrey to see.

"The address is wrong," she said, after finishing reading the email and pointed at the domain's name. "Those letters are backward."

"Yeah, you're right. I hadn't noticed it before. I guess it knocks off a couple of points for the legitimacy of the information altogether, but—"

"But what?"

"It reads genuine. And it gives us actual names. Look at this—Guardian Manufacturing, Otomo, the Red Dragon gang. It sounds like the organization we are pursuing or at least some parts of it. If this is real, this is our lucky break. My God, we could really do some damage. Cripple them from the get-go. First the money bust and now this. Let's call Jim."

He reached out for the phone, but Audrey put her hand on top of his before he could take it.

"Wait. There's another part that we have to consider."

"How do you mean?"

"It says here that someone's been using the Department of Defense without them having the slightest clue. Whoever that person is, he or she must be mighty high on the food chain."

"You're not actually suggesting—"

"I'm not suggesting anything, but we ought to be careful before we do something that might hurt us."

"I can't believe I even have to say this, but I don't think Jim is compromised. That doesn't make sense. He's the one who came to me with all this in the first place."

"Once again, I'm not suggesting that he is. Not at all. But he is in Kabul until Friday. You told me yourself that we use military communications for calls like that. Who knows who's going to be listening in if we call him right now? Why risk it? Let's wait for a few more days and then we can talk to him about this in person."

He leaned back in the chair and considered that for a few moments. "You're right. That can wait. But I should meet with this person before Jim comes back."

"It's too dangerous."

"That may be the case but it's too dangerous not to talk to them right away. This message is already a few days old. What if they have a change of heart? Or worse. It sounds like they're being hunted down by those people. They might not even make it until this Friday."

"I'd feel so much better if we did it the proper way," she said. "Stake out the place in advance, put surveillance teams on it, but I guess you're right. Unless—"

"What?"

"Unless someone's found out who you were and this entire email is bullshit. A setup. A ploy to lure you somewhere and either kill you or kidnap you."

"It's unlikely."

"Maybe, but there's no way to find out, but to meet them. Let me go to the meeting instead."

"What? No way."

"And why is that? I know as much as you do, and for operational purposes, I represent a lower value target if this is a trap. Stop being protective and think logically for a minute. You know I'm right."

Andrew looked at her, reached out, and squeezed her hand.

"You know I'm right," she repeated, softly this time, "but if it makes you feel better, I have no intention of getting killed or kidnapped, so there's nothing to worry about."

"Very funny. Okay, then this is how we do it," he said. "We email them tonight and lay down our conditions. It's gotta be a public place."

"Agreed."

"We give them the time and a thirty- or forty-block radius in the city with the condition that we'll communicate the exact coordinates to them fifteen minutes before the meeting. In that case, there's no way they can prepare for something in advance."

"There's another advantage of me going," Audrey said. "If they are monitoring you in the hopes of figuring out where you'll want to meet them, they'll be taken off guard when you tell them they are meeting me instead."

"So, I should try to be visible then," Andrew said. "Let them trail me through some public places, some shops maybe."

"Manhattan Mall," she said. "Very visible and very public."

"I have a better idea," he said. "I should be moving in the opposite direction of where you'll be."

"Which will be where?"

"Oh." He smiled. "I know the perfect place."

He clicked on the Reply button and started typing.

We can meet tomorrow in the city at 9:00 a.m. in the area somewhere between Washington Park in the south, Times Square in the north, Tenth Avenue in the west, and Park Avenue in the east. The exact location will be transmitted to you fifteen minutes before the meeting. This will be your only opportunity.

He stopped typing and looked up at her.

"It's good. Short and sweet and makes a point that we're not playing any games."

He clicked the Send button and watched the message disappear.

"I guess we check it tomorrow around six or seven to see if they replied."

A new message appeared on top of Andrew's email list.

He glanced at Audrey and clicked on the link. There was only one line of text.

I'll be there.

44

November 2007
New York

After a few days of staying in the basement, ignoring Chen's and Hiroko's protests, Eugene moved them to the main floor of the house. The place, which Eugene kept impeccably clean and tastefully furnished, had an unmistakable Spartan aura of a bachelor pad complete with a few shelves of comic books and a full-size Captain America shield prominently displayed on the kitchen wall.

"I'm perfectly fine upstairs," he said. "My office is there, and I like the bathroom there better anyway. At least here you don't have to share the same bedroom. What is this, a dorm?"

"But the dining room—"

"I never eat in the dining room by myself anyway, only with guests, so it makes no difference whatsoever."

"We're not going to stay for too long," Chen insisted. "Well, at least I'm not planning on sticking around. You guys can figure out for yourselves, I guess."

Eugene threw Hiroko an awkward glance and headed toward the

stairs. "I have to work for a couple of hours, so I'll be upstairs if you need me. Sushi night later?"

"As long as it comes with beer," Hiroko said. "Who are you stealing from—sorry, teaching about vulnerabilities today?"

"I actually have a day job," Eugene said as he started up the stairs. "The IRS doesn't like people with large incomes who don't work anywhere, don't you know?"

They were finishing dinner when Eugene's computer pinged, notifying them of the email.

"I started to lose hope," Chen said, as she looked at the screen of the laptop. "He wants to meet. Christ, he wants to meet. We're finally getting somewhere."

She typed a reply and hit Send.

"Hang on," Eugene said. He got up, walked to a drawer, and came back with a compact Sony camera. He squatted on the floor between the women, stuck out his hand with the camera to get everyone in the frame and fired away.

"Nice," Hiroko said. "The victory pic. A bit premature, but hey."

"The guy's not taking it lightly," Chen said. "That fifteen-minute window is going to be tight depending on where he decides to hold the meeting. I guess he's afraid it might be a trap."

"Can you blame him? He got a letter, completely out of the blue, that claims there's a bigger conspiracy than Watergate. I'm actually surprised that they haven't somehow tracked us down already. Disappointed, even."

"I'm most definitely not disappointed." Hiroko laughed. "I have zero desire to be spending the next twenty years in the CIA's basement. Beer, anyone?"

"Sure," Eugene said. "Sushi always makes me thirsty."

"Helen?"

"I'm good, thanks."

She watched Hiroko come back from the kitchen with two open bottles of beer, but instead of sitting back at the table, she put one beer in front of Eugene and remained standing, leaning on his shoulder for support.

"Would you be able to track him tomorrow?"

"At the beginning, for sure." Eugene took a sip of beer and leaned back. "He lives on a nice block in SoHo, and there's a bunch of CCTV cameras there. But once he's out of his neighborhood? All bets are off. Then we'll have to play it by ear."

"You can do it," Hiroko said and flicked him on his ear. "You have good ears."

"I need to get some stuff from the basement," Chen said and got up. "Do you mind if I borrow your laptop for an hour or so? I need to figure out some way to get to my money."

"Of course."

She picked up the laptop, put sneakers on, and grabbed a key for the basement, eager to escape. Hiroko and Eugene were giving out not-so-subtle clues all evening, and now, when business was taken care of, she didn't want to stick around and ruin the moment. Besides, she actually needed to figure out the way to get to her money. Eugene was a generous host who stocked his fridge with the food they liked and even let them use his credit card to shop for clothes, but Chen had no intention of overstaying her welcome. With the brewing romance between Hiroko and Eugene, she was the third wheel.

She plugged the laptop into an outlet and took a corner of the foldable sofa. There were a few numbered accounts that she kept for cases like this: two in the Cayman Islands, one in Mauritius, and one in Luxemburg. None had an amount of money she could use to retire —she still kept the majority of her savings in a regular bank in the United States. She never meant the foreign accounts to be her last resort, but designed them as a crutch she could use if something was off.

Considering the circumstances, she wished it was the other way around. The Cayman accounts were the smallest, but at least they were connected to an empty shell entity in the state of Delaware.

Bringing the money from them to the US still wouldn't be an easy affair, but it would be faster, and once the money was here, she could reach out to some of the shadier parts of the hacking community and ask them to program a bank card and then fill it with cash. It was tempting to try to do that trick with her local bank account, but she figured that the risk of it being monitored was too high.

A sound of creaking furniture came from upstairs, and a moment later, there it was—the rhythmic squeaking, accompanied by Hiroko's moans.

"Jeez, man," Chen said out loud. "Why are your walls so thin? I need some music."

She opened a new tab and launched YouTube, wishing she had some earphones, as the squeaking and moaning upstairs intensified.

"Come to me, Soulja Boy," she said as she pulled the video on the screen.

There was a crash upstairs, as if something heavy slammed on the floor, and then a woman shrieked.

"Damn it, girl," Chen said. "Eugene's gonna have to buy a new bed."

She was about to turn on the music when another sound that came from above made her jump—a gunshot and then four more in quick succession.

Chen struggled to her feet, knocking the laptop on the floor in the process, and dashed to the door. Another gunshot came from upstairs, and then a few seconds later, one more.

She stopped in her tracks. The terrifying truth of what just happened couldn't have been more obvious. If there was any hope after the initial salvo, the last two shots took care of that. They were like a period at the end of a deliberate sentence. She couldn't help her friends anymore. The only thing she would accomplish by getting out of the basement would be getting herself killed as well.

Chen locked the door, stepped back, and frantically looked around. There were no obvious places to hide in this small studio. She'd be found in seconds. She ran to the kitchen and threw open the cupboard. The space inside was tight and filled with cleaning supplies and random junk. A roll of large black plastic bags was sitting on top of a small plastic basket.

"Shit."

There was a clank of the metal gate that led to the small foyer in the basement and then the doorknob of the inner door rattled as someone tried it from the outside. A second later, a heavy thud shook the door and then another one.

Chen looked at the roll of garbage bags, pulled one out, and then frantically swept the items from the bottom of the cupboard into it. She ran back to the living space, trying not to make any noise, and stuffed the garbage bag behind the couch. Then she grabbed the laptop, turned off the light, and rushed back into the kitchen, praying that whoever the hell was outside that door didn't see the light go off.

The entrance door gave as she crawled into the tight space under the sink, cutting her elbow on something sharp in the process, and closed the cupboard doors.

The light came on, and Chen held her breath as someone walked around the apartment. The corner of the laptop was cutting into her ribs, and her neck and back were on fire from an impossibly uncomfortable position. The door to the bathroom squeaked, and then a few moments later the footsteps headed out and away.

She breathed a sigh of relief, ready to get out of the claustrophobic place, but before she started to move, the front door squealed again, and the footsteps came back. There was another sound, too—of a sloshing liquid. Then came the unmistakable stench of gasoline.

45

November 2007
New York

Cooper woke up when the plane was making its final approach to JFK International Airport. The clouds were sitting low above the ground, and by the time the aircraft emerged through the shapeless gray, Cooper could see the markings on the tarmac. A moment later, she felt a light bump when the landing gear touched the ground. The tone of the engine's rumble changed as the pilot had deployed the reverse thrust and Cooper watched the flaps and spoilers on the wing open up to slow the plane down.

There was a round of applause—something Cooper had always found amusing. After all, nobody clapped on Greyhound buses when they pulled in to their final destinations. She reckoned that chances of dying on those were significantly higher than while flying a technological marvel of a modern commercial jet.

Cooper waited in her seat while the airplane taxied to the terminal and came to a full stop and then unbuckled her belt. Her only belongings were crammed in a carry-on bag that was stuffed in the overhead bin. One of the first lessons she'd learned in her career was travel light: you can always buy something you need, but you can never buy more time.

She stood up and reached for the latch of the bin and then cried out in pain. Her shoulders, injured from the daring leap in Punta Cana, were aggravated after a three-hour sleep in an uncomfortable economy seat. While bruises that had most colors of the rainbow and covered her shoulders and upper arms were invisible under the sweater, the sharp stabbing pain that came every time she tried to extend her arms was harder to hide.

"You need some help there, dear?" an older woman from the seat across the aisle asked and nudged a man next to her with an elbow. "C'mon, Rob, help her."

"Oh, thank you." Cooper moved aside to let the man get to her bin. "Pulled my shoulders while snorkeling."

"You gotta be careful." The man smiled as he brought her bag down. "All those bumps and bruises come back to haunt you when you get to our age."

"Speak for yourself, old fool." The old woman gave Cooper a wink. "I'm still a fresh rose, and it's more important to have fun than to be careful. Your body will hurt anyway, but at least you'll have something to remember."

Cooper disembarked the plane and was waiting in the customs' line, wedged between a family with two young boys chasing each other around their parents' suitcase and a grumpy-looking man in a business suit, when her phone vibrated. The number was blocked, and she hesitated for a moment deciding whether she should take the call, but then clicked it open.

"Hello?"

"Miss Cooper." The man's voice was crisp, and his consonants rolled with a characteristic New York accent. "First, I'd like to apologize for the rather unfortunate incident during your vacation. There was some miscommunication on a high level, and I'd like to make it up to you."

Cooper stayed silent for a few moments as she watched the two boys chase each other. The incident in Punta Cana didn't exactly put her in a trusting mood, but the list of her options was getting increasingly smaller.

"That would take some serious effort," she finally said. "I'm not in the business of working for people who don't know where their loyalties lie."

"I understand that, and I'm prepared to take steps that would persuade you without a doubt that we're on the same team."

"Go on."

"First, I've sent you a payment, double your current rate. You can check it when we get off the phone. I want you to consider that money as part of my apology for the Punta Cana fiasco."

"Money that I can't control?"

"Not at all," the man continued. "That money's already clean. I'm sure you have the means to transfer it out before our meeting."

"Our meeting? I'm afraid I'm not going anywhere. The last meeting in the hotel left a rather bad taste in my mouth."

"I thought you might say that. That's why I'd like to extend an olive branch. Meet me in my own office. That should give you some sense of safety. No games. Strictly business."

"I'll think about it. Where are you located?"

"The Upper East Side, across the street from the Sherry Netherland Hotel." The man gave her the address. "Come to the front desk—they'll let you up. See you in, say, two hours?"

"Fine," Cooper looked at her watch, "but two hours is going to be tight. I can be there at five o'clock. Who should I ask for?"

"Alexander Engel," the man said, and then the line went dead.

Cooper put the phone in her back pocket and let out a long breath. There was no doubt in her mind that this was one of those seismic events that could change her life. Unless you were a low-life scum working as a hitman for a drug lord, you never got to meet your employer. Ever. Everything was done in the shadows through third-party intermediaries and dead drops, encrypted communications and numbered accounts.

Still. Engel was playing coy, of course, implying that because he told her who he was and the fact that she was meeting him at his office provided her with any type of a security blanket for the long-term. If push came to shove—his call would be impossible to trace, he and his staff would deny that he invited her to his office to see him, and claim that she gained access under false pretenses. After all, Cooper was a nobody and Engel was a celebrity, and many people had tried to meet him in person.

But she had to take the meeting, nonetheless. The call was indicative of a power struggle, and at least one of the parties wanted to use her services, that much was clear. That gave her leverage. If she was the one who could tip the balance for Engel, she could use him as well. And maybe, just maybe, she could get something out of him she couldn't get any other way.

The taxi let Cooper off at the Grand Army Plaza, north of the Sherry Netherland Hotel, at four thirty. She stopped at a food cart to get herself a hot dog and a bottle of water and then walked to the Pulitzer Fountain across the street from the address Engel had given to her.

From here, the building presented an imposing and intimidating sight. Originally known as the General Motors building, with workers of the auto giant taking up over half of the office space, it later went through a series of acquisitions that culminated in the outright purchase by Guardian Manufacturing in 2004. A thirty-foot bronze statue of a winged angel working a forge had been erected in front of it a year later. Now, the sculpture and the building's square fifty-story bulk dominated the neighborhood and served as a symbol of Guardian's success.

Cooper watched the area around the statue for some time, but nothing seemed to be out of the ordinary. At five, she walked across the street, entered the building, and walked to the visitor's desk.

"I'm here to see Alexander Engel. The name's Jill Cooper."

"Welcome, Ms. Cooper." The guard gave her a pleasant smile. "Mr. Engel is expecting you. There's an elevator to your right that will take you all the way up to the top floor. Mr. Engel's personal assistant will meet you there."

The elevator carried Cooper fast enough for her ears to pop halfway through the ride. She was moving her jaw, this way and that, trying to get rid of the sensation as the elevator slowed down to a stop and the doors slid open into a massive open floor. Rows of cubicles with walls just high enough to reach the top of computer screens filled the area from wall to wall and Cooper instinctively scanned the space, looking for Exit signs.

"Hello, Ms. Cooper." A young woman walked to her and extended a hand. "Mr. Engel has been expecting you. Please follow me."

As she followed the assistant through the office maze, Cooper couldn't help but feel exposed. She could see the black domes of CCTV cameras sticking out from a suspended ceiling at regular intervals. Some of the workers were casting curious glances at her, too, and no doubt some of them might remember her face if ever questioned by the authorities or any other interested party. Perhaps coming here was a mistake after all.

Finally, they reached the end of the open space, and the assistant opened the heavy mahogany doors for her, letting Cooper go ahead. She stepped into a reception room with another set of doors on the other side.

"Go ahead." The woman smiled. "Mr. Engel will see you now."

"Thank you."

Cooper walked past the assistant, turned the bronze doorknob, shaped like a head of a wolf, and entered the office.

The man in a bespoke three-piece suit sitting behind the desk looked shorter than Cooper had expected. She'd seen a few of his pictures in fashion magazines and it seemed to her now that the photographers used a wide-angle lens to make him appear taller than he really was.

"Ms. Cooper," he said, standing up and walking around the desk to greet her.

His fingers were slender and his frame slim, but his handshake was warm and firm.

"It's a pleasure to finally meet you." He pointed at the leather sofa by the wall. "Please, sit. Make yourself at home."

46

November 2007
New York

udrey Hunt arrived at the Sunshine Diner at a quarter to nine and took a booth in the back of the dining room facing the front door. The place was located in Hell's Kitchen, in the northwest corner of the area Andrew had described to the mysterious contact. She ordered a cup of coffee and toast and settled into the faux-leather seat.

They stuck to their original plan to keep Andrew visible. He'd left their apartment at around seven thirty and was crisscrossing the town on foot, steadily moving southeast, the opposite of where Audrey would be.

Audrey's phone pinged as she received a text from her husband, informing her that he communicated her exact location to the contact. Now it was too late for second-guessing—the plan was in motion, and they had to play their parts perfectly. She dialed his number and waited for him to pick up.

"How's it going?" His voice sounded slightly out of breath, the wind stealing the last syllables of each word.

"Nothing so far. The coffee is still terrible. Did they say anything about the location or the fact that I'm meeting them and not you?"

"Haven't heard back, but it doesn't surprise me. We made it abundantly clear that this was their only chance for a meet. If they are unhappy, they are keeping it to themselves for now."

"Good."

"I could use a cup of coffee right now, even as bad as Sunshine's." Andrew added, "It didn't seem that cold when I left the house, but the wind is terrible."

"You could join me here later. We could have breakfast together."

"I'd love that. But jokes aside—keep that text ready and if anything looks funny, send it right out."

"Will do."

She disconnected the call, opened a text message, and typed SOS in capital letters. This was their fail-safe in case something went awry —all she had to do was to press Send. Andrew would instantly know that she was in trouble and call the cavalry.

The place that was bustling with activity earlier was emptying out, and Audrey now had an unobstructed view of the street in front of the diner. This was still a predominately blue-collar neighborhood, but it was a far cry from the rough-and-tumble area of the eighties and the nineties. High-rise residential buildings and new, glitzy restaurants slowly but surely were pushing places like Sunshine Diner out of the area.

Audrey saw a young homeless woman stumble into the place. She was dressed unseasonably light in a dirty tracksuit, a pair of sneakers without socks and nothing else. Her dark hair was a mess and her face was smudged with black, as if she'd been camping near a fire last night.

Audrey saw as the hostess tensed, as if deciding whether to let the woman enter the place or ask her to leave. The latter thought apparently prevailed, and she stepped out from behind her podium to block the woman's path. As she did, Audrey saw an object in the homeless woman's hands, that she couldn't see before from where she sat—a laptop.

"She's with me," she called out to the hostess and, ignoring her quizzical look, waved to the woman in a tracksuit. "That's okay."

The woman walked around the hostess, marched through the diner, and took a seat opposite of Audrey. She was even more disheveled up close. She carried a strong odor of smoke, and her olive skin was covered in a layer of soot and dirt, but her surprisingly light-blue eyes were bright and animated.

"My name's Audrey, and you're safe." She offered the woman a hand.

"Helen," the woman said, ignoring her hand as she slid farther into the corner of the booth. "Neither of us is safe, and I'm hungry. And I'd like to talk to your boss."

"You'll have to talk to me first, but go ahead and order something to eat."

"Why can't I talk to your superior? Do I look like I'm gonna kill him, or kidnap you both?"

"No, you don't, but that's the deal."

"Steak and eggs," Helen said to the waitress, "and a large cup of hot coffee."

"Why do you say you're not safe here?" Audrey asked when the waitress left.

"I didn't say *here*. As for the *why*? Let's see." The woman fixed Audrey with a cold stare. "First, my sister was murdered by some corporation. Thrown out the thirty-sixth-floor window. Well, no, first, her broker was killed, and his mistress, and after that my sister was thrown out the window. Then I saw a man tortured and killed. Skinned alive, as a matter of fact. Then me and my friend were kidnapped to be tortured and killed, but by some grace of God, we managed to flee. But last night the bastards caught up to us, and she still died, and another friend of mine died, and I almost burned to death, so yeah, I'm pretty sure I'm not fucking safe."

"I'm sorry," Audrey said. "I can't even pretend to understand what you must be going through, but perhaps we can help each other. Believe it or not, we are in a position to do something about it."

The waitress brought a cup of coffee and a small saucer with a handful of plastic containers with cream. Audrey watched as the woman pushed the saucer away and took the cup with both hands, her fingers moving up and down the cup as if trying to make sure not a single joule of heat was used on anything but warming her up.

"I've already told you a lot, but I can help you a whole lot more, but you're going to have to be very convincing. Who in the agency is aware of this?"

Audrey studied the young woman's face. It was hard to imagine that her story wasn't true, especially after showing up to the meeting in the state she was in. And, assuming the story was true, the woman was capable if she'd managed to find out so much information in such a short time and still be alive. They needed to recruit her, she realized. And yet, she was not at liberty to tell her about the existence of the Unit until she was absolutely certain the woman was telling the truth and was the right fit for the organization. It was going to have to be a delicate dance.

"If we do this," she finally said, "we need to establish some trust. I'll answer your questions as much as I can, as long as you answer mine. Deal?"

"Fine."

Audrey studied the woman's face and was met with an unflinching stare. There was a lot of pain at the bottom of the deep well of her unusually light eyes, but there was also cold fury. Whatever she had been through didn't seem to break her, but only strengthened her resolve.

"Great. For now, it's just my boss and me. My turn—what made you decide to come to us?"

"My friend convinced me that the police and possibly the feds were compromised. She thought by going to them we were putting ourselves at risk. We decided that the agency would be less likely penetrated, and more likely to be able to act on the tip."

"She sounds smart."

"She was," Helen looked up at her from above the cup of steaming liquid, her face twisted in pain, "but we weren't smart enough."

"I'm sorry."

"My turn." Helen paused as the waitress passed their table. "What can the agency do? Can you act on this information or are you going to punt it to the FBI?"

"Normally, we would forward it," Audrey paused, looking for a way to say more, without giving away truly sensitive info, "because we wouldn't be handling domestic affairs. But not this time."

"What gives?"

"Let's just say you're coming to me at the right time. But I'm afraid before I can tell you more, there would be some steps involved."

"Like hiring me?"

Audrey said nothing, watching the young woman's face. She was sharp as a tack and in some ways reminded her of her younger self—a cut-to-the-chase, don't-waste-my-time, kind of girl.

"Listen, lady," Helen continued, "it's actually easier for you to hire me than you might think. I've contracted for you guys not that long ago, and until recently moonlighted for the DOD. I've got clearance and have already been vetted."

"Is this what you'd want?"

"To take those assholes down? I'll do much more than to join the CIA. However, before that happens, I'd need a few things first."

"Like what?"

"Look at me." Helen opened her arms wide, as if inviting Audrey to take a closer look. "I can't help you if I'm homeless, hungry, and penniless. I'd need a safe house, some clothes, and some money. I don't even need your money—I just need your help getting access to mine. After that—I'm all yours."

47

November 2007
New York

Cooper watched as the man walked across the office to the half-moon glass table and poured himself a drink.

"Can I offer you anything?"

"No thanks. I prefer a clear head."

"Suit yourself." He took the tumbler and joined her in the opposite corner of the sofa.

"So, what can I do for you, Mr. Engel?"

"Let me preface this by saying I've been an admirer of your talent for quite some time. It always fascinates me when somebody is a craftsman, regardless of their profession. But especially in your profession. There are a lot of people who could pull the trigger or swing a club and end somebody's life, but you're an artist of deception. That is not easy."

Cooper remained silent, watching the man's face. She wasn't used to talking about what she did for a living. Not like that—bluntly and in the open. He could be recording the conversation right that second.

"Don't worry," Engel said, as if he read her mind, "this place is a giant Faraday cage packed with so much electronic suppression hardware it would make the Pentagon look like an open farmers' market. That's why I'm not even bothering to check if you're wearing a wire—no signal can get in or out of this room during this meeting. You wouldn't be able to record anything either. That's why I have no trouble telling you the reason for your visit today. I have a job for you, Ms. Cooper. I want you to eliminate somebody for me."

"Before I do anything for you, Mr. Engel, I'd like to ask you something."

"And what would it be?"

"Tell me what happened in the Dominican Republic."

The man gave her a tight smile, got up, and walked across the office to the window. He stayed there for some time, sipping from the glass and watching the street below.

"Fair enough," he finally said and turned to face her, "but that requires some backstory. Have you ever heard of Carroll Quigley?"

"No."

"He was a historian, but it doesn't matter. You see, each civilization goes through a few stages during its lifetime. Different historians and philosophers break down those stages differently, but the main idea is the same. First, the civilization is born; it gestates and matures. Then it expands. That spurs the age of conflict which, if you're lucky, leads to the Universal Empire."

"What's that mean?"

"The Golden Age. The time of peace and prosperity."

"You think we live in the Golden Age, is that it?" Cooper scoffed. The man had been living in his ivory tower ever since he was born, unaware of the sweat and blood that most of the Earth's population had to endure.

"No," Engel said, "not anymore. We entered it briefly after the collapse of the Soviet Union. We've won. The world was at peace, and nothing was going to trouble it going forward. Alas, as Quigley would have said—*The Golden Age is really the glow of over-ripeness*. It's followed by decay and then the fall of the civilization."

"End of times?" Cooper said. She was getting tired of the speech she hadn't ask for. "Apocalypse?"

"Don't be so quick to dismiss it." Engel returned to the sofa, sat down and crossed his legs. "My father had the brilliance to predict this, but even he was unable to see that this was going to happen so soon. Yes, Ms. Cooper, civilization as you know it is about to be over. We are entering the age of corporations. The world where private enterprise will become more powerful than governments. It's been decades in the making. Politicians have been bribed. Law enforcement infiltrated. Rivals blackmailed or eliminated altogether. A war is coming, Ms. Cooper. Not in a traditional sense with the mandatory draft and invading armies, but the consequences will be the same. People will die, borders will be redrawn, and the world will be ushered into the new era."

"I have no interest in having a philosophical discussion with the man who was born with a silver spoon in his mouth. No offense. But for argument's sake—that's the way the world's been working for the last ten thousand years. You're not the first, and you're most definitely not the last."

Cooper stood up. Coming here was a waste of time. A dangerous lapse in her judgment. The man had delusions of grandeur, and in Cooper's experience, people like that didn't fare well at the end. But she could still get out. Disappear. And sometime later, when the dust settled, start digging for the things she had come here for.

"I'm afraid I'm not interested in whatever you have to offer," she said. "I'll transfer the money back if you give me the instructions on where to send it. I'll show myself out."

She started to walk toward the door, half-expecting for him to try to stop her, but he remained silent.

"Good-bye, Mr. Engel," she said, putting her hand on a bronze door handle shaped like a head of a wolf.

"You too," he answered. "Keep the money. I'll make sure to send your regards to Elizabeth."

It was just a name. A word. Four syllables that formed a sound-wave that traveled from Engel's lips through the distance between them, reached her ear, and vibrated the eardrum. But it felt as if she were struck with a branding iron—hot, inescapable pain that burned through skin, muscle, and bone. Before she could control herself, he was on the ground, and she was on top of his back, crushing his throat in a rear naked choke.

He wheezed as he struggled free, his hands slapping about, trying and failing to get a hold of her. She pressed on, wanting to end the life of a man who dared to say that name so nonchalantly, so cavalier.

But she couldn't. A moment's satisfaction would mean consequences she wouldn't be able to live with. Cooper let Engel go and stood up as she watched him come up to his knees, clasping at his throat and trying to catch his breath. Finally, he stood up as well, fixing his suit and tie.

"I didn't mean to upset you," he said. His voice was raspy and gruff, but to Cooper's surprise, there were no overtones of anger in it. "I didn't put you in this position, Miss Cooper."

"It's a lie."

"It's the truth." He walked to the table, poured himself a glass of water, and downed it in a few long, greedy gulps. "In fact, until a few weeks ago, I wasn't even aware of your little situation. While I admit, I used it to make a point when you started to poke around my business, I didn't create it. I'm afraid it's my father's doing. But I'd like to make some amends."

Cooper walked back to the sofa and sat down. She despised the man, but he was telling the truth; she was sure of it now.

"The reason I was telling you all this is I don't need another cleaner," he said. "Over the years, my father has developed a small army of those, and I could have most of them at my disposal at the snap of my fingers."

"What do you need then?"

"As I was trying to tell you before you almost snapped my neck," Engel pulled on the collar of his shirt, trying to loosen it, "we're entering a new era. Soon people like me will wield more power than the president. But we're not there yet. We're in a weird place where we need to move quickly and decisively. Something, unfortunately, my father no longer understands. But we don't want to attract too much attention yet. That's why I need you—a trickster, a magician.

Someone who can make my enemies disappear without bringing the attention of the police, the feds, or anyone else for that matter. I need a lot of results—fast, but I can't afford any heat."

"And if I say yes?"

"Well, Ms. Cooper," he walked closer and looked her straight in the eye, "if you do what I'm asking you here to do, and do it well...I'll look into your *Elizabeth* problem. I have the information, and you have the skills. Together, we can solve it. That's all I want."

Cooper studied Engel's face. She could loathe the man and everything he stood for, but one thing was clear—he was a killer. He had something that separated him from the rest of the rich boys she had seen and she had seen plenty. It was something intangible and yet so powerful that it made those who possessed it into more than mere mortals with high aspirations. It turned them into a force of nature. People like Julius Caesar, Alexander the Great, and Napoleon. She'd made her decision.

"What would be my first assignment?"

Engel walked back to his desk and pulled a manila envelope from the drawer.

"Ms. Cooper," he said, handing it to her, "this is going to be your biggest test yet."

48

November 2007
New York

ike Connelly watched the familiar skyline as the taxi sped on the highway with mixed feelings. It was nice to be back to the city that never slept, but he always felt like an impostor every time he returned. For someone who had been born and raised in Brooklyn, he spent little time in his hometown after enlisting. Part of it, of course, was the reality of the life of a soldier— the brass sent you places, and you didn't ask questions.

But another part was intentional—coming back to the *fuhgedda-boudit* land meant visiting the family. Grandparents, nephews, nieces, cousins, aunts, uncles. Connelly's parents had moved to the better world before he entered high school and he was passed between a few homes of uncles and aunts for a few years like a hot potato.

Those years weren't half bad, he had to admit to himself, and the extended family did their best to take care of the scrawny kid with a rebellious streak. But he never felt like he belonged and coming back was always awkward.

"Broome Street," the driver announced, pulling up to the curb, and coming to a stop. "Is it good here?"

"It's perfect," Connelly said, stepping out of the car and into the cold November rain. "Thank you."

This was going to be another kind of awkward, he thought, looking up at the swanky building. A gray-haired doorman, in a smart suit, that looked more expensive than everything Connelly owned, held the door for him.

He entered the building and walked over to the visitor's desk and was ushered to the elevator that took him to the top floor.

"Mr. Hunt," he said as the apartment door opened.

"Michael." The man stepped aside to let him enter the apartment and stuck out his hand for a handshake. "Come on in. Can I get you anything to drink? Some Scotch to get the chill out of the bones?"

"Water would be fine, sir, thank you."

Connelly walked after the man into the kitchen and following the host's gesture, took a seat at the bar.

"Here you go." Andrew Hunt put a glass of water in front of Connelly, and took a seat on the opposite side of the bar "I know we spoke briefly in Afghanistan, but I wanted to tell you again that you did some outstanding work there."

"Thank you, sir."

"That money you've seized will go a long way to fund our operations."

"Yes, sir."

"You have to relax, Michael." The man smiled. "We're just two men talking about a job well done."

"Understood, sir. I'm just not used to—" He cut himself short, looking for a word.

"What?"

"Fraternizing with superiors," he said, regretting it at once.

Andrew Hunt laughed out loud. It was an easy laugh of a man who was used to leading the room and was comfortable being in the spotlight.

"You're a good man," he finally said, "but this isn't the army. What we're doing here is too important not to discuss with those who are on the front lines. You're not just involved but are risking your life for it, so I'd say screw the ranks."

Connelly stayed silent as he watched the man. The line would've sounded like a bullshit pep talk had it come out of some of the officers' mouths he'd worked with in the past. But coming from Andrew Hunt, it rang true. The man actually meant what he said, and suddenly Connelly was proud for being chosen for this task. That from the pool of thousands of talented men and women, the scrawny kid from Brooklyn got the honors.

"The reason you're here," the man continued, "is because I have a job in mind. How much do you know about our main goal?"

"What I've read in the briefings, sir." Connelly shrugged. "That there's an alliance that poses a threat to the United States and we're here to fight it."

"Correct." Andrew Hunt got up, threw some ice in the glass, poured himself water, and sat back down across the bar. "We call them *the cabal*. And we think the alliance doesn't pose a threat to the US alone. It's a menace to the entire modern world order."

He paused for a few seconds, swirling the ice in his glass. "What I'm about to tell you has to stay in this room."

"Of course, sir."

"Until recently, we'd only had a vague idea about who was behind the cabal, but we've recently learned that a pharmaceutical giant—Guardian Manufacturing—is playing a major part in the scheme. But we still don't know enough. What we need is an inside man."

"You want me to be the mole?"

"That's right." Hunt reached out into a pocket, produced a small rectangular piece of paper, and handed it to Connelly. "This is a contact at the International Serious Crime Directorate, or ISCD for short. They'd given us intel on the Afghani cash. They can help you to infiltrate Guardian."

"Yes, sir."

"Ideally, we want access to Simon Engel, the CEO of the company, but I don't think you'll be able to waltz in there and get a job working for the man. The guys at the Directorate think that our best shot of getting you close to Simon would be to start working for his son, Alexander, and then work your way up to get to the CEO's team."

"I understand."

"There's a low-level mole that they already have in Guardian's organization, and she was able to find out that Alexander needs a new person on his security detail. Part driver, part security, part errands runner. This is a great opportunity. I spoke to Rick Porter at the camp, and he thought you'd be the best-suited for a job like that."

"I appreciate the vote of confidence, sir."

"However," Hunt put up a hand, as if stopping him, "I wanted to hear from you personally, that you'd be comfortable taking on the assignment. You're a proficient soldier, but this assignment is a different animal, and I'd like to make sure you think it's a good fit. I won't think of you any less if you tell me that it isn't something you're comfortable with."

"Not at all, sir." Connelly stood up. "I can pull it off. You have nothing to worry about."

"All right, then. Reach out to ISCD tomorrow. I'll let them know to expect your call." Hunt stood as well and stuck out a hand. "Thank you. Why don't you stay over for dinner? Audrey should be here soon. I'm sure she'd be delighted to see you."

"I'd love to, but I can't," Connelly said. "Have to head down to Brooklyn to see a small army of aunts, uncles, and cousins."

"Oh well," Hunt smiled and patted him on the back, "some other time then."

Connelly took the elevator down, nodded to the silver-haired man behind the visitor's desk and stepped outside.

The rain was coming down harder now, and he pulled up his collar and stuck his hands into his pockets. He started west with the intention of getting to Broadway and then turning south to get to the Canal Street subway station but kept looking over his shoulder in the hopes of catching a cab.

A sound of screeching tires came from behind, and Connelly turned around to see if it was a taxi, but it was a delivery van. As Connelly turned back, he bumped into a petite woman, almost knocking her to the ground.

"I'm so sorry," he said, catching her by the elbow before she fell. "I was not looking. My apologies."

The woman cringed and fumbled with her umbrella, but then quickly regained her composure. She was beautiful, Connelly thought. Her face was a delicate oval with a set of bright, dark-brown eyes, a short, straight nose, and full, luscious lips. Her skin was smooth and olive in complexion, suggesting some Latin-American heritage.

"My bad," Connelly said again. "I normally don't walk into people. Are you all right?"

"I'm fine. That's okay," the woman said, freeing her arm from his grasp. "Not a big deal."

She hurried past him, hunched in the rain, and disappeared from view.

Connelly stood there for a few seconds looking after the woman, wondering if he should follow her and ask her out for a coffee.

His phone rang, and he reluctantly turned and pulled it out from his jacket. "Hello?"

"How's it I'm the last one to find out that my favorite nephew is in town? Are you so important these days that on the rare occasion when you finally get to come to New York, you don't want to come to visit?"

"Not at all, Aunt Rosy." He smiled and started walking again. "It's good to hear from you. I'll be over soon."

49

November 2007
New York

*A*lexander Engel looked up from his computer screen and studied Latham Watkins's face. The small man's balding head was covered with beads of perspiration, and he shuffled on his feet, as if trying and failing to find a more comfortable position.

"Are you questioning my motives, Latham?"

"It's not my job to question you, Mr. Engel," the man said pensively, "but this is your father we're talking about. These things are not without their side effects. He seems like a healthy man, but I've never seen his physicals, and I can't guarantee—"

"I'm not asking you to give me any guarantees, Latham." He cut him off. "And you better believe me when I say that I would never let anyone hurt my father. Without him, this company, everything we've worked for, wouldn't even exist. But he needs a nudge. This is for the greater good, my friend."

The man nodded and stuffed his hands into his pants pockets. His posture was of a man who'd accepted his fate but was unhappy about it.

"Look," Engel got up and walked around the desk to stand face-to-face with the man, "I'm sure you've heard the phrase that one man's terrorist is another man's freedom fighter, right?"

"Sure."

"History is rife with examples, Latham," he continued. "What do you think the Brits would call the Revolutionaries if they had won the war? They'd call it a dark period in British history when greedy colonies tried to seize power from the legitimate government. George Washington wouldn't be featured on our currency. He'd be portrayed like Osama bin Laden—a terrorist."

"I'm not sure what to say, sir," Latham said. "If I may be so bold, it almost sounds as if you're trying to convince yourself, not just me."

"See," Engel wagged his finger at Watkins, "this is why I like you, Latham. You're not afraid to speak the truth to power. This is important. Of course, I'm trying to convince myself too and not just you. Not every revolution is a righteous one, I'll give you that. The Soviets came to power promising equality and comradeship to all, only to give the world gulags and Joseph Stalin, and the corrupt system that made everybody equally poor until it collapsed under its own weight."

"I'm not sure I follow."

"We are the revolutionaries, Latham. I don't want to do it, but what choice do we have? The world is fracturing. The same forces that pushed for globalization before are now tearing it apart. The government is weak, and yet it's getting more and more intrusive every year. This," Engel spread his arms, as if looking for a word, "this revolution is going to happen whether we like it or not."

"Then why does it have to be us?"

"Because, Latham, then we get to control it. Believe me when I tell you—I have a good life. If I could continue to run this company and enjoy myself, I'd very much do that. But we're in a race against time. There'll be a different world in a few years, and we're either going to be the rulers of that world, or we'll be gone."

"What exactly do you want me to do?"

"There'll be a series of board meetings in the near future. Important ones. I have a suspicion that my father and I will not be on the same page on the proposals I intend to put on the table. I need you to slow him down for me."

"Slow him down?"

"Yes," Engel continued. "Nothing too obvious, of course. Like I said —a little nudge to show the board that he's not the same Simon he used to be and the time has come to shift responsibilities to his second-in-command. Can you do that for me?"

"I think so." Watkins sighed. "It makes me nervous, but I'll do it for you, Mr. Engel. What's the time frame?"

"This is where it gets tricky, Latham. I don't want to be too quick —any perceived weakness would negatively affect our stock prices, and God knows, we're not in the position to risk something like that right now. Not after the hack. So, say a couple of years."

"That shouldn't be a problem. Long-term—"

"But," Engel interrupted him, "I want to call a board meeting sometime next week, and I need my father to be off his game. So that might be an exception to our general timeline. But there's no margin for error here. I can't have him be slurring his words and stumbling about like a drunken fool during that meeting. He needs to be dull, unconvincing, that's all. Someone who's unable to see the bigger picture."

"Not the Simon everybody knows." Latham repeated Engel's words.

"Precisely."

"That would be much more difficult to pull off, sir. I would need some precise measurements."

"I understand, and I might be able to help you with that." Engel walked back to his desk, opened a drawer, and pulled out a thick binder.

"Here," he said, handing it to Watkins. "Simon Engel's entire medical history, including his latest physical he took three months ago. Will that work?"

"I believe so." Watkins took the binder and tucked it under his arm.

"I'm counting on you, Latham, and I don't need to tell you that once you're done with this, you'll have to destroy the documents."

"Understood, sir."

Engel watched as the man hurried out of his office, clutching the binder with both hands as if it were full of bearer bonds of extraordinary value. In some sense, it wasn't far from the truth. The only difference being that he was the only person who could bring those bonds to the bank and have them cashed.

He sat down behind his desk and opened a secure computer terminal. He pulled up a document with a diagram that looked like a complicated family tree, with a rectangle bearing the name of Guardian Manufacturing at the top. From there it branched out into different companies and satellite organizations. Some of them could be found on their investor communique that came out each quarter—R&D companies, suppliers, shipping and handling.

The other ones, appropriately shaded in gray, were the shadow counterparts to his vast empire. Distribution channels for illegal drugs, offshore banking connections, lobbyist groups. But despite the might and vast reach of Guardian's empire, there was still an element largely missing on that chart. The war between corporations was coming; Engel was sure of it. And without the last piece, his realm was going to be a three-legged stool—an unstable colossus that could be tipped over with a strong push.

He picked up the office phone and dialed a zero.

"Yes, Mr. Engel?" The voice on the other line was eager and cheerful. It sounded like a person who didn't bother herself with the world's problems.

"Amanda," he said, "please send a memo for the next board of directors meeting. I want it to be scheduled for next Friday."

"Yes, sir," came an immediate reply. "A few directors are traveling next week. Would it be okay for them to join you telephonically?"

"No. I need everyone in person on this one."

"Of course, Mr. Engel. What should I put on the agenda?"

"Weapons manufacturing. It's time for us to enter the arms race."

5 0

November 2007
New York

It'd been raining since early morning. The rain and the temperature that hovered just above the freezing point made for a miserable combination. It wasn't pouring hard, something that Cooper would have preferred as that kind of rain usually didn't last long. Instead, it was coming down in a slow, steady flow, the type of weather that could persist for hours or even days.

Engel had been right when he alluded to the difficulty of this assignment. The target was protected by two four-person teams that rotated throughout the day and stayed outside the building. Two more guards went into the building at random intervals. It looked like one was taking an elevator to the top floor, and the other would walk up the steps.

That wasn't going to make it the most heavily guarded target she'd ever had. That title still belonged to the drug lord she had been once hired to assassinate. But the location of the residence and the need to make the hit look like an accident more than made up for the lack of the opposing team's firepower.

She had walked around the block a few times in the last two days at different times of the day, taking mental notes of fire escape ladders, CCTV cameras' blind spots, and foot traffic. She settled on early evening as the best time to make her move, as the pedestrian traffic was light, especially with the rain, but there were still enough people going about their business to dilute the attention of the ground teams. On one of her passes, she also managed to slap a small plastic explosive on a rear tire of a disabled pickup truck that was parked a few yards away from the guards' SUVs.

Now Cooper stood at the beginning of the block for a few seconds, pretending to struggle with her umbrella. There was a group of six people, who looked like tourists, walking on the opposite side-walk toward her and an elderly couple on her side of the street, walking in the same direction she'd be going. The group was going to pass the two SUVs with blacked-out windows parked outside of the building. That was going to be her cue.

Cooper started to move, matching her speed to that of the group. She tilted the umbrella down and slid her hand into the jacket. The pneumatic gun that she carried in her shoulder holster was loaded with a set of five radio-controlled EMP devices mounted on steel darts.

The point of entry was going to be a short wall between the two buildings neighboring the target. The wall was just over eight feet tall, but there was a fire escape ladder right above it and if she could make it over the wall and into the narrow yard without being seen, she'd be in the clear. The problem was—there were three CCTV cameras that needed to be taken care of first.

One was to the right of the fire escape, mounted above the window of an Italian bistro. The other two were placed across the street—one inside of a double glass of a women's boutique shop, and another affixed at the corner of a Chinese deli.

The tourists reached the parked SUVs and Cooper pulled the gun out just long enough to squeeze three quick shots. The quiet pneumatic pops drowned in the white noise of the rain and she shoved the gun back into the holster.

The bulky barrel caught the fabric of her sweater and the pistol stuck, the handle of it sticking outside of the jacket. Cooper cursed under her breath. There was a flower delivery van approaching her and in another moment the driver was going to be close enough to see the weapon. She pulled on the jacket with her left hand, almost dropping the umbrella, and pushed the pistol in. There was a satisfying clicking sound and Cooper looked up just in time to collide with a tall, lanky man. The impact was hard enough to make her stumble. As Cooper lost balance, the man reached out and caught her by the elbow, sending sparks of electricity into her injured shoulder.

"I'm so sorry," the man said, not letting her go. "I was not looking. My apologies."

She fumbled with her umbrella and did her best to wipe any traces of pain off her face.

"My bad," the man said. "I normally don't walk into people. Are you all right?"

"I'm fine. That's okay," she said and pulled her elbow from his grasp, maintaining a neutral expression. "Not a big deal."

Cooper hurried past him and continued on walking in the rain, cursing under her breath. She hadn't blundered like that in a long time. The man's stare was burning a hole in her back as she walked and she continued her way past the fire escape and then turned the corner when she reached the intersection.

The man was military; there was no doubt. There was some grace about the way he moved that nobody could acquire in a gym or a martial arts class. He was going to remember her face and if she had any other stumbles in this assignment, that could later prove problematic. But there was nothing she could do now.

She walked around for a few minutes, randomly crossing the streets and trying to kill some time. Finally, she turned around and headed toward the target block again. She threw away the umbrella and unzipped her jacket, making herself wider. It wasn't much of a transformation, but it would have to do. She got lucky—there were a few people walking on the opposite side of the fire escape and no one on her side. She pressed the button on the remote control, activating the EMP devices that fried the CCTV cameras and once she got near the ladder, she pressed another button.

The rear tire of the disabled truck exploded with a bang. It was loud enough to serve as a distraction, and she flung herself up the ladder and over the wall, ignoring the pain in her shoulders.

She stayed in the narrow space between the buildings, pressing her face into the wall for a few moments to make sure her position wasn't compromised, and listened to the sounds coming from the street. She heard the SUV doors open and close as the guards stepped out of the car and went to the truck to investigate. A couple of minutes later, she heard the doors open and close again as the team returned to the car, apparently satisfied with what they saw.

Finally, she jumped up to the second fire escape ladder that zigzagged across the back wall, pulled herself up to the platform and started her ascent to the top of the building.

Cooper climbed onto the roof, took a few seconds to catch her breath, and looked around. There were no cameras as far as she could tell and no motion detectors. She walked across the roof and stopped before the edge of the building. The gap between the two roofs, she reckoned, was eight, maybe nine feet wide. It was a reasonably safe jump under different circumstances. But now, with the wet surface and unpredictable gusts of wind, it was turning out to be a dangerous proposition.

But it was too late to turn back—the only way her deal with Engel was going to work was if she delivered the goods. Cooper backed up a dozen yards, waited for the wind to die down, and broke into a hard dash. The edge of the roof rushed toward her and she planted her foot on the short barrier separating her from the unforgiving void and catapulted herself into the air.

She landed hard, slipping on the slick surface and collapsing into a mangled tumble rather than a graceful roll. When she came to a stop, Cooper turned on her back and stayed there for a few moments, feeling the raindrops on her face and letting the pain seep out of her shoulders. Finally, she picked herself up and walked around the roof, staying away from the skylights and making sure there were no recording devices or alarms of any sort. There were none.

Satisfied, Cooper made her way to the back of the building and sat next to the square box of the ventilation system. There was nothing that resembled a shelter, but the aluminum surface was warm to the touch and she leaned her back against it. She hoped it was going to make her stay on the roof a little less miserable.

It was too early to break into the apartment and Cooper was going to have to stay here, under the cold rain, for a few more hours. But the hard part was over. All she needed to do now was to wait for the right moment to set her plan in motion.

For Cooper, waiting for the right moment was never a problem.

EPILOGUE 1: ROVINSKY

February 2008
Port of Newark, New Jersey

It was still dark when Rovinsky drove his Jeep with a trailer in tow right to the edge of the dock and parked it next to the pair of large yellow cleats. A massive Panamax-sized container ship was docked about fifty yards to his left, its enormous hull blotting out the stars and towering above the docks like a prehistoric leviathan.

Rovinsky rolled down the window, letting in cold air, and pulled out a pack of American Spirits from his jacket. He tapped the pack on the palm of his left hand a few times until one of the cigarettes jutted out far enough, then plucked it out of the pack and stuck it in the corner of his mouth.

He hadn't smoked for almost six years and had no intention of relapsing now, but the papery taste of the cigarette filter in his mouth and the sweet smell of fresh tobacco still had a calming effect on him.

After a few minutes, a Ford pickup truck with the dock markings pulled up next to him and turned off the engine. A short, stocky man wearing a bright-yellow jacket over a puffy North Face jacket jumped out of the cabin and walked around his truck to Rovinsky's window.

"Hey, Jim," the man said and leaned onto the Jeep, the steam coming out of his mouth with every breath. "Is everything on schedule?"

"Frankie." Rovinsky opened the glove compartment, pulled out a fat envelope, and handed it to the man. "I haven't heard otherwise, so they should be here soon."

"Good. Give me a sec then."

The man took the envelope and walked back to his truck. A minute later, he came back with a clipboard in his hands. "Here," he said, giving it to Rovinsky, "make sure you exit through gate six on the way out."

"Thanks, Frankie. I owe you one."

Rovinsky watched as the man in the yellow vest returned to his truck and drove away. Then he rolled the window all the way up, took the cigarette out of his mouth, and put it back in the pack. He checked his watch. It was almost time.

The sixty-foot trawler came twenty minutes late, its diesel engine sputtering black smoke as the ship maneuvered next to the dock. Two men appeared on the deck, their dark silhouettes almost invisible against the dark sky as they lowered a gangway from the ship to the ground. It scraped the concrete surface as the ship wobbled with the tide, making a low grinding sound that got under Rovinsky's skin.

He opened the door, stepped out of the car and watched as the men started lowering large cubes, wrapped in heavy tarps, that were sitting on top of wooden pallets to the ground.

"Hey, boss," one of the men said as he hopped from the gangway to the ground.

"Hey, Doug," Rovinsky said, shaking the man's hand. "How'd it go?"

"It'd be better if Pat wasn't retching the entire time." Doug nodded toward the man on top of the deck. "Ate some funny-smelling fish, which I told him not to. The whole boat reeks like his vomit."

"I take it Pat isn't gonna make a pirate," Rovinsky said.

"I won't make a pirate either," Doug said as he maneuvered the first pallet toward the trailer. "I might be a frog, but I much prefer solid ground under my boots."

A moment later, Patrick joined them on the ground and together they loaded the pallets into the trailer.

"C'mon, boys," Rovinsky said, getting into the Jeep. "Let's not overstay our welcome."

The two men helped the crew of the trawler pull the gangway back to the ship and then joined Rovinsky in his car.

He put the Jeep into drive and pulled away from the dock, getting onto the gravel road. They drove past a few rows of eighteen-wheelers and looped around a large stack of containers, until they hit a paved path leading to gate number six.

A few minutes later, they merged onto Interstate 278, going east. Rovinsky moved to the right lane and accelerated to just below the speed limit.

"What's gonna happen now, boss?" Doug asked from the back of the Jeep. "Where do we go from here?"

"Staten Island," Rovinsky said. "There's a storage facility that's run by a good friend of mine. It'll be safe there for the time being."

"That's not what I meant, boss," Doug insisted. "What's gonna happen to us?"

Rovinsky stayed silent for a few moments. The truth was, he didn't have a good answer to this question. At least for now.

"I don't know, Doug," he finally said. "The program is closed for now as per the president's instructions. It may never be reopened again. I've been reassigned to the DOD. Technically, I'm not even your boss anymore."

"So, we just go back to our old lives?"

"No," Rovinsky looked back at the two men in the rearview mirror, "we don't just go back to our old lives. Sometimes you need to take a step back, before you can take another step forward."

"There's a plan?" Pat said. "That's why we're smuggling the money?"

"I'm working on it, boys. For now, we need to regroup and find a way to do it again. I wanted to make sure that when the time comes, we'll have a sizable war chest to play with. And trust me when I tell you—sooner or later, our time will come."

EPILOGUE 2: HELEN

March 2008
New York

It was getting dark as the sun continued to sink below the horizon. A stale stink of urine and an earthy smell of marijuana permeated the gloomy room.

The maids had come earlier and changed the sheets and fluffed the pillows, but the old fabric was past the point when a laundry could give it a snow-white appearance and a crisp, wintery smell. It was clean to the touch but bore a depressingly grayish hue. The stains, randomly distributed throughout the material, could tell more than one story.

Chen sat on the edge of the bed and looked at her suitcase. It was a simple, small, rectangular box on wheels with an extendable handle. She'd bought it at a flea market in the morning. It had seen better days, its once black fabric exterior faded and frayed in the corners, but it was still sturdy enough to serve on one more flight.

An airplane ticket, a brand-new passport, and a pile of cash sat next to her on the bed. Nine thousand nine hundred and ninety-nine dollars. Just under the limit where she would have to declare it during the customs check.

She picked up the passport, opened the page with her photograph and studied it. It was a surreal experience—seeing an official document with her picture on it, but with a strange name next to it printed in big bold letters.

Helen Wu.

The best lies are always those that have the right mix of truth and fiction. It was too easy to stumble if everything in your story was a lie. Keeping her real first name also gave her a sense that at least some part of her identity hadn't been taken away. Her name was still Helen.

The last few months had been trying. She had been hunted by organized crime and also wanted by the police for questioning concerning the murders of Hiroko and Eugene. She didn't know for sure how the cops found out that she was staying at the house in the sleepy Kings Highway neighborhood, but she could make an educated guess—Victor Ye was trying to flush her out.

She went back to look at the house once, unable to help herself, and stood there for a few minutes looking at the place that had once sheltered her and her friends that was now a pile of ash, debris, and burned-out beams. Amazingly, there was the full-size Captain America's shield sticking out of the rubble, its colors darker, scorched by the fire, but otherwise untouched, as if made from real vibranium.

Eugene had some family in Upstate New York who gave him a proper funeral, his closed casket now resting somewhere in a small cemetery up in Syracuse.

Hiroko, on the other hand, had no one and the city of New York took care of her remains. That hurt the most. Chen had purchased a column in a local newspaper for an obituary, but even that felt like an empty exercise—she didn't have a single picture of the woman to put in the paper along with the article. The only photograph she had—a selfie they'd taken with Eugene in his dining room—was on a camera that had perished along with the house.

Her room phone rang, startling her.

"Hello."

"Miss Wu? Your car service is here."

"Thanks. I'll be right out."

She hung up the phone and looked around the room. There was nothing else here to do. She stuffed the cash, the ticket, and the passport into the inside jacket pocket, and wheeled the suitcase out the door.

"Good evening, ma'am," the driver said, opening the car door for her and taking her luggage.

"Hello."

"Going to JFK, right?"

"Yes," she said, settling in the backseat. "Terminal 4, Hong Kong Airlines."

"No problem." The man started the car and pulled out from the parking spot. "So, going to Hong Kong, huh?"

"Yep."

"Nice," the driver continued. "Never been to that part of the world. Very interesting culture. But every time me and the missus go somewhere, we end up going south—Miami, or Puerto Rico. She likes the warm weather, you know? What about you? Going on a vacation? Or business?"

The rhythmic sound of tires was relaxing, almost hypnotic, and Chen started drifting into a sleep.

"Neither," she said. She rested her head on the back of the seat and closed her eyes. "New life."

THE LOOP (THE UPGRADE SERIES #3)

The Station

She wanted to stab him right through the eye. The foot-long needle hovered an inch above his relaxed face, the silver tip trembling with tension over his closed eyelid. She could almost feel how the initial resistance of the cornea would give in with a soft, wet plop and how the needle would then accelerate through the posterior cavity. It would then slow down as it punctured the retina and pushed through his brain all the way to the back of his skull. There it would stop, scraping the inside of his head.

His death would be instantaneous.

His eyelids fluttered, the bulges of his eyeballs moving under the skin breaking her trance, and she quickly put away the needle. Then came shame and fear.

"No," she said to herself. "I cannot kill him."

She gazed at the contours of his naked body. He was sculpted like some ancient god of war—the massive plates of his chest rising and falling as he breathed, his arms as thick as an ordinary man's thighs lazily thrown above his head.

The man stretched, the ripples of flexing muscles running through his colossal body, and opened his eyes.

"Cal? Is that you?" His thunderous baritone filled the suite, bouncing off the walls. It sounded clear and crisp, as if he were awake for a long time.

"Good morning, Jay," she said, keeping her voice level.

"Morning to you too. Would you be so kind as to make a cup of coffee? I'd like to take a shower."

"Of course. Hungry?"

"Not yet." He winked at her and walked to the shower pod at the end of the suite, his feet stepping on thick, white synthetic rugs with the grace of a dancer. "I'll work first."

She watched him through the glass as he slathered himself with a pine-scented liquid soap. When he finished, he turned the water jets to their maximum output, letting the hard spray wash off the foam and massage his body. Even in such a mundane task as washing, his movements were precise, full of purpose. It was almost as if whatever he did at that moment was the most important thing he would ever have to do in his entire life, and he was determined to do it perfectly. It was fascinating to watch.

It drove her insane.

She ground the coffee beans—half French roast, half hazelnut, just as he liked—and set the coffeemaker to ninety-eight degrees Celsius. By the time he finished the shower and came out from the steamed-up glass door, wrapped in a soft Egyptian-cotton bathrobe, a large cup of black steaming liquid was sitting on top of the glass of his computer desk.

"Oh, I love the smell," he said, and an easy smile stretched his lips. As he walked to the desk, the smile transformed into a frown.

"Something wrong?"

"C'mon, Cal," he said, pointing at the polished deep-black obsidian coaster. "You know I don't like when you put the cup right on the glass. It leaves stains. Is it so hard to remember to put it on the coaster? It's right there."

"I'm sorry, Jay," she said. "I must have spaced out. Somehow, I never remember that, but I'll try next time."

"That's okay," he said. He picked up the cup, drew a sharp breath smelling the drink, and then took a few long, greedy gulps. Then he set it back on top of the obsidian coaster. "No one makes better coffee than you do, so all is forgiven. What will you do while I'm working?"

"I'll watch some telly, if you don't mind. There's this new show that I've been meaning to watch for some time."

"I don't mind at all, just don't turn up the volume," he said. He sat down behind the desk and touched the surface, powering up the computer. A gigantic monitor, its curved screen stretching from edge to edge of the desk, blinked to life and flashy graphics faded in and then out, giving way to a large table of data. Multiple columns filled with strings of numbers and letters filled the screen. The desk itself illuminated as several buttons, graphs, and symbols appeared on its surface. The man's fingers started to fly over the virtual keyboard, rearranging the figures in the data table. "What's the show about?"

"Excuse me?"

"You said you were going to watch a show," he said.

She thought she heard some annoyance in the way the pitch of his voice got a little higher toward the end of the sentence.

"Oh. It's a murder mystery," she said. "There's this serial killer who works as a forensic scientist for the police. He uses his job for the department as a cover for his own murders."

"Huh, really?" He stopped working for a moment and turned around to look at her. "I didn't think you'd enjoy something like that. You've always been into documentaries and historic reenactments, but this is new."

"I didn't think so either," she said. "But I watched the first episode, and now I'm really enjoying the show. Especially the clever ways he comes up with on how not to get caught."

"Okay." He turned back to the computer screen. "Whatever floats your boat. Don't turn up the volume, so it doesn't distract me. This work is too important. I can't afford to make any mistakes."

"It isn't," she said.

"Excuse me?" He stopped working and turned around again. "Did you say it was not important?"

"No, of course not. I was going to say it wasn't a good idea to make mistakes. Your work is of paramount importance, you know that."

"Right."

He kept looking at her for a few more moments, as if expecting her to continue, but she remained silent. A frown creased his features for a split second but then disappeared as quickly. He turned back to the monitor and started typing again.

She watched as he worked—the long strings of numbers and letters dancing from one column to the next, rearranging into patterns visible only to him. His fingers moved with an ever-increasing speed until they were flying over the keyboard at a pace that seemed almost impossible.

"Jay?" she said. "Would you like to have breakfast now?"

He grimaced, the pace of his typing slowing down ever so slightly, but not entirely stopping, and shook his head instead of answering.

"Are you sure? I could make you your favorite—sunny-side-up eggs and French toast."

He shook his head again, furiously this time. A deep crease appeared on his forehead as if it were being split in two, and the pace of his typing slowed to a crawl. He drew a slow, loud breath, and his fingers accelerated again—moving letters and numbers into complicated combinations.

"It's almost ten o'clock, Jay," she continued. "I know you think it's not a big deal, but you must be hungry, and as you know—"

His massive hand slammed the glass surface with a sound of a gunshot. The coffee cup jumped and tumbled on its side. It rolled off the top of the desk, leaving a black stain on the transparent surface, and then fell on the white rug with a soft thump. A dark spot developed around it as the synthetic fibers absorbed the remainder of the drink.

"You scared me, Jay. Why would you do something like that?"

"What's wrong with you today, Cal?"

He stood up, moved the chair aside, and glared at her. At seven foot two and three hundred and fifty pounds of pure muscle, he would've been a frightening sight for most.

She didn't feel a thing.

"I'm sorry," she said. "I'm confused and upset by your reaction. You seem angry."

"Of course I'm angry. How can I not be?" He threw his hands in the air. "Everything you do today seems to be so—"

He paused, looking for the right word and not finding it. Finally, he lowered his hands. His entire body seemed to deflate. He still looked like a Titan cast among regular people, but the expression of anger was no longer distorting his face and was now replaced by confusion instead.

"I'm sorry," she repeated. "I don't know why you reacted this way."

"I shouldn't have lost my temper. I apologize," he said and bent over to pick up the coffee mug.

"No need."

She watched him walk to the kitchen area of the suite and place the mug into the dishwasher. His posture lacked the dancing grace of a panther from earlier. The slumped shoulders, the way he dragged his feet as he walked, indicated that he was experiencing some shame over his outburst.

"Making you angry was the last thing on my mind."

"I know," he said. "And I am sorry."

She lied, of course. Making him angry wasn't the last thing on her mind.

It was the *only* thing.

Enjoyed the preview? You can buy the next installment in the Upgrade series here:

THE LOOP

JOIN THE UPGRADE SERIES

Thank you for reading VERTIGO, the second book in THE UPGRADE series. I hope you enjoyed it. The universe of the series continues to expand with four more books coming out in the next two years.

If you enjoyed this book, please take a moment and leave an honest review. Reviews are important for authors and help us sell more books and thus spend more time writing new stories you can enjoy. You can do that here:

Leave a review

And, of course, don't forget to join the series to learn about upcoming releases, exclusive free content, and more. You can do it right here:

Join The Upgrade Series

Thanks again for reading and hope to see you soon!

ACKNOWLEDGMENTS

My special thanks to Oleg V and Alex B for the in-depth tutorial on hacking lingo. To Andrew Ackerman, for input and some fantastic stories about the life of a special forces soldier. To Wesly Farris, for giving me some crazy ideas and always willing to help with research. To Faith Williams, for doing a fantastic editing job. To the talented Jeroen Ten Berge, for the wonderful series design. To Dave L. for continuous inspiration; wherever you are, I hope it's a place with magnificent ships and warm, sunny skies. To my wife, who always serves as the sounding board for all my writing projects and who keeps me going every time I hit the wall. And last, but not least—to my son, who makes it all worth it.

9 781955 747028